CW00735382

BEAUMONT HOLIDAY

~~The Beaumonts~~

Books 10 & 11

Angie Daniels

Caramel Kisses
Publishing

ISBN-13: 978-1-941342-53-4

Copyright © 2021 by Angie Daniels

All rights reserved. Except for use in any review, the reproduction or utilization of this work in whole or in part in any form by any electronic, mechanical or other means, now know or hereafter invented, including xerography, photocopying and recording, or in any information storage or retrieval system, is forbidden without the written permission of the author.

This is a work of fiction. Names, characters, places and incidents are either the product of the author's imagination or are used fictitiously, and any resemblance to actual persons, living or dead, business establishments, events or locales is entirely coincidental.

For questions and comments about the book please contact angie@angiedaniels.com.

Caramel Kisses
Publishing
Caramel Kisses Ink
www.caramelkissesink.com

DEDICATION

To my readers... thank you for giving me the best job in the world!

Stilettos & Mistletoes

~~The Beaumonts~~

Angie Daniels

Caramel Kisses
Publishing

CHAPTER 1

Shrill laughter ricocheted across the showroom floor, drowning out the musical spirit of Christmas streaming through the PA system. Everyone was happy, smiling, and having a good time. Earlier, her father had given out the yearly Christmas bonuses. That alone gave their employees a reason to smile.

While glancing around at all the friendly faces, Sage Beaumont sauntered toward a fifteen-foot Christmas tree decorated in white and red blinking lights and hand-crafted ornaments, where her youngest brother, Remy, was standing. The closer she got; the more challenging Sage found it to swallow. Her sudden anxiety had nothing to do with her brother's towering presence but instead resulted from the dominating masculine presence who stood beside him.

Cser Grant.

With his tall stance, he had to be around six-five. At five-eight, Sage loved the way she had to tilt her head every time she spoke to him.

For months, she had hoped he'd come, had seen the invitation, and even made sure her father's administrative assistant had received an RSVP confirming his attendance. Yet, Sage didn't allow herself to believe it until she'd seen it for herself.

Cser was back in Richmond.

As she moved closer, admiring his handsome profile, a shaft of heat coursed through her body.

Cser had a squared jaw and a smooth peanut-butter-brown complexion with deep dimples at each cheek. And then there was his body that was military bred. Yummy! She'd always had a weakness for a man in uniform, although, at the moment, Cser was wearing pleated black slacks that in no shape or form hid his long legs and large, powerful thighs. Broad shoulders in a crisp white shirt beneath a black V-neck sweater showcased the massive arms crossed against his muscular chest. His gorgeous physique had been the subject of her dreams and now the reason for her nipples beading beneath her dress.

As she drew closer, Cser lifted his head, and instantly, Sage felt a jolt, and her breath hitched.

She found herself staring into the most arresting chocolate brown eyes. Dark and so intense, they'd always stolen her breath away. The closer she drew near, the stronger the desire to throw herself into Cser's arms and kiss him beneath the nearest mistletoe.

He winked at her but resumed his conversation with Remy as if she wasn't walking his way. But the look in his eyes was enough to send goosebumps cascading down between her inner thighs. Was that sparkle interest? She wondered. Of course, it was, she told herself. There was no way he couldn't have noticed her in the thigh-high black stiletto boots, black leggings, and the red sweater dress that hung off her bare shoulders. On her head was a Santa hat. Large hoop earrings hung from her lobes while bangles at her wrist clattered like jingle bells. She looked sexy. The outfit was hot. So why wasn't he looking, *dammit?*

Sage drew a shaky sigh. She had been in love with Cser for too many years to give up now. She'd adored him, but so far, she had been unsuccessful at getting him to see her as more than Remy's sister. For once, she wanted him to notice her, dammit!

Captain Cser Grant was home on leave after six months on deployment. And while he was still on United States soil, she planned on getting him to see her as a desirable woman. *This is it.* This was her last chance, and she was not going to fail. Otherwise, all those years of wanting and waiting would have been for nothing.

"Mom's looking for you," Sage announced as she moved to stand beside her brother. Cser fixed his dark chocolate eyes were on her face and nodded in acknowledgment as she approached.

At least her heart had slowed down slightly.

Remy rolled his eyes and asked in a low, throaty voice. "What did I do now?"

"It probably has something to do with the show you had on the air last night. Sedona's giving Mom an earful," she teased

Her brother was the co-host of the nationally syndicated radio program, *He vs. She,* with thousands of listeners across the country. Last night's topic had been the side chick and the eighty-twenty rule. Female listeners had been outraged at Remy supporting a man needing a little variety to hold his marriage together; the station's phone lines blew up with calls from angry women.

Remy laughed. "What? I was just being honest!"

Sage shook her head, disappointed but not at all surprised. "You are ridiculous."

"I heard you've been starting trouble," Cser chimed in as he sipped a glass of eggnog. He had a sexy deep voice that seemed created solely to swoon a woman.

"Dude, yo, you've missed a lot since you deployed. You know how women are bugging." Remy was looking to his best friend for his support.

"That's why someone flattened your tires last month," Sage muttered with a disgusted snort. Her response caused Cser to chuckle most adorably.

"It was probably Desiree." Remy scowled as he took a sip of the brown liquor in his glass.

Sage sucked her teeth. "I wish you'd just find someone to make you happy and shut it down. All these women you be parading around is getting ridiculous!"

"What are you talking about?" he screeched. "I came alone."

"I'm not talking about today," she retorted with a wave of her manicured hand.

Cser cleared his throat. "Sage does have a point. Rance and Reese are married. Sedona is engaged. It's about time you settle down." Sage could tell by the smirk on Cser's sensuous lips he was teasing.

"Settle down?" Remy's eyes grew wide. "You're one to talk!"

Cser tossed up his hand. "I'm not the one on the radio giving relationship advice."

Sage shook her head, and the bell at the end of her Santa hat jingled. "Cser, I think my brother is beginning to look like a hypocrite to his listeners. That can't be good for ratings."

"Hmmm?" Remy's brow rose. "What are you talking about?"

"You know … do what I say, not as I do. You preach relationships, but I can't remember the last time you've had one that lasted more than a month," she added with a saucy grin.

Her comment caused Cser to chuckle heartily and Remy to wave his hand dismissively.

"Yeah, whatever!" Her younger brother, by nine months, was a piece of work.

Remy was known as Dr. Feel. He loved the ladies as long as the situation "feels" sound, but the second a woman tried to put on the chains, he was off to the next. Sage loved him. And at twenty-six years old, he was so handsome she could see why the women were falling at his feet. Tall and toasted brown, Remy took after their mother with his Samoan features. A broad nose, high cheekbones, and as usual, he had his long wavy shoulder-length hair pulled back with a leather strap.

"Y'all tripping! I'm not ready for wifey."

Sage chuckled, and then as she sobered, she couldn't resist the opportunity to ask Cser, "And what about you? You found your soulmate yet?"

Her breath stalled when Cser shifted his gaze that strolled across her face. Instantly, she noticed the five o'clock shadow grazing his jaw.

"You could say that," he replied, eyes darkening wickedly.

Sage felt sick. Had he found someone else? That had been her worst fear, and the response caused her stomach to tighten in knots.

For as long as she could remember, she'd been doing everything short of shouting out, "Hey! Look over here at me," to get Cser's attention. Those words crushed all her years of hoping and waiting. Who was it? She wondered, and was the relationship serious? One thing for sure: that girl wasn't her. Had someone stolen his heart on the last deployment? She had no idea, but she was going to find out.

"Gigi! Come here."

She turned to spot her older sister, Sedona, signaling her from across the floor.

"I want you to meet someone," she mouthed and pointed to a tall, slender man standing beside her.

With a nod, Sage looked from Remy to Cser and smiled. "I'll catch up with you later." Turning, she sauntered off, feeling the unsettling heat of despair burning at her chest.

Cser had to catch himself from asking her not to leave.

He didn't want Sage talking to some square-looking dude who was now smiling all in her face. He wanted her over here, standing beside him. But if he had commented, it wouldn't have taken Remy long to figure out his best friend had feelings for his sister. Deep-rooted feelings for the feisty woman with gorgeous lips and a whole lot of mouth. He chuckled inward at the thought. It was rare for Sage to hold her tongue. She didn't believe in filters or watching what slipped from her throat in the heat of the moment, and he didn't want her any other way. Well ... maybe naked and lying on her back beneath him. But now, that wasn't even an option. Nevertheless, that didn't stop him from wanting her.

While standing beside her, the sweet scent of her body had filtered under his nose, and everything stood to attention. Hard and aroused, no mistletoe was required for the long sensual kiss he had in mind. He was dying to know if she tasted as sweet as she looked. Cser loved the fire in her and could think of several ways he could ignite the heat if he'd had half a chance. He wanted her now like he had wanted her last year and the year before that. Maybe now, even more than ever. Only two reasons were stopping him from claiming her as his—his career and friendship with Remy.

Dammit. He was a black operative with an elite military group. His deployments were frequent. Much too often for lasting relationships, and he preferred it that way. The last thing he needed was someone at home worried and waiting for him. He just couldn't see the point of putting a woman through that, which was why he preferred short-term, no commitments that only lasted as long as the moment. It was also one of the reasons why he refused to get involved with Sage. He knew she was interested in him. It was in her body language and the way she looked at him with desire burning in her amber-colored eyes.

He groaned inward and dragged a hand down along his face and knew without a doubt if she weren't a Beaumont, they would have already been lovers. Licking, sucking, and fucking for fourteen mind-boggling days and nights. And when his leave ended, he would head back to join his team in Afghanistan. No hard feelings. No false promises.

But he couldn't do that to her. Sage wasn't a one-night stand kind of girl.

And he couldn't risk Remy finding out.

They had an unwritten rule about messing with ex-girlfriends and his sisters.

Stay the hell away from them.

And he honored that rule the whole time with Remy's older sister Sedona, who was tall, statuesque, and equally beautiful. But there was just no comparison. When Sage walked into a room, everyone took notice. She was all woman: fierce, beautiful, and alive with a voluptuous body guaranteed to *slay* a man. And then there was that sexy walk of hers that kept Cser hard and wrestling with his libido whenever she sauntered within ten feet.

Yes, he wanted Sage; he wanted her bad.

As Remy continued to talk—mostly about himself—Cser took in Sage's long legs in a dangerous-looking pair of thigh-high come-fuck-me boots. When he'd first caught her gliding toward the Christmas tree with skill and ease in those stilettoes, he'd been ready to ask her when and where. Instead, he had silenced the emotions that brewed in his chest.

Half-heartedly, Cser continued to listen as Remy told him about a beauty he'd recently met at the mall while his eyes strayed from taking in Sage's generous smile and high cheekbones. Beneath the festive headgear, the dark beauty had shaved her head low and tinted it burgundy. The last time he'd seen her, her hair dangled past her chin on one side and her shoulder on the other. Now the style resembled Kanye West's ex-girlfriend, Amber Rose. It was a sexy new look, and he liked it on her. But then there wasn't much about Sage he didn't like, which was why he'd had such an increasingly hard time getting her out of his head.

The last six months in Afghanistan, he'd been able to put thoughts of Sage aside long enough to focus on the mission. But the second he'd returned home and spotted her sauntering across the restaurant Remy had reserved for his homecoming party last weekend, the need to possess Sage had started all over again.

What could he do? He was like a bit of kitten around her. She had a way of dominating the air he breathed. Sage was a strong, independent woman, just the way he liked them. Only she was in a class all of her own. He admired her decision to pursue a career as an auto mechanic before earning a double major in mechanical engineering and business management. Being around them as long as he had, Cser knew her choice of occupation was a sore spot in the family, especially with her mother. She was dubbed Dr. Fix-It because she believed she was just as capable as anyone else. Sage ran circles around her brothers when it came to working under the hood of a car. The beauty was a beast in the auto body shop. Sage managed to even help him out of a few jams when he'd had car trouble back in the day.

As he finished his eggnog, Cser remembered Remy saying

something about her working on an MBA at Virginia Commonwealth University. He wasn't sure how she did it, juggling a whole load of responsibilities. Nevertheless, he'd have to remember to congratulate her on all her efforts and hard work.

Sage managed both Beaumont Collision Centers and served as the general manager of two dealerships: Mercedes Benz, where they were holding the Christmas party, and Hyundai. Beauty and brains—what more could a man want?

Cser scowled. Why couldn't she have been born someone else? Unfortunately, that wasn't the case. She was Remy's sister, and they could not—and would not—ever be anything more than just friends.

So, if he knew that, then why couldn't he stop thinking about her?

For years, he'd been able to deny his attraction to her. But now, ever since he'd returned five days ago, he felt an overwhelming urge to stop pretending. Sage had him wrapped in a web with no escape, and now he wanted more, even though that was impossible. He couldn't date Remy's sister. He shouldn't even be thinking—let alone dreaming— about her. He could not deny that just being around her made him feel whole again. Sage made him forget all the sadness and death he had seen. She made him feel as if anything was possible. And yet, they could never be. He couldn't risk his career or his friendship. He just had to remain focused on the mission. He'd just have to find a way to ignore her. No matter how difficult it had become.

"I better go find my mother," Remy said, pulling Cser away from his thoughts, then finished his drink in one gulp.

Before he could get away from him, Cser asked, "Who is that?"

Remy followed the direction of his eyes. "Oh, that's a

colleague of Sedona's. He's some kinda motivational speaker she's been talking about touring with."

Sage was laughing at whatever the guy was saying with a slender hand planted at her waist. While Cser watched, jealousy began to brew its ugly head again.

"Look, there's my mom." Remy tilted his head in the direction of Bettye Beaumont, a beautifully distinguished woman, walking over to join her daughters. He lowered his glass to a table and sighed. "Might as well get this over with. Bruh, come with me. I may need back up." He was joking, of course, but Cser was happy for the excuse to head over to where they had gathered beside a beautiful Mercedes.

Their father had removed most of the cars from the showroom floor, allowing plenty of space for mingling and dancing. But this vehicle—Richard Beaumont had left at the center of the room as a conversation piece. As Cser walked past it for the second time, he let out a low whistle. The car cost more than he earned in a year, even before taxes.

Cser's temper flared when he spotted the guy stroking Sage's arm. He had to fight the urge to rush over and push him hard in the chest.

While Remy pulled his mother aside, Cser moved toward Sage. A warm smile greeted him.

"Sedona."

"Cser, welcome back." Sedona's eyes widened, then she pulled him into a warm, comforting hug. As she released him, her wild spiral curls bounced with motion. "I'm so sorry I couldn't make your party."

He grinned down at her smooth, light brown face and replied, "No problem. I hear you and Keith are engaged?"

Sedona blushed, and he could tell she was not only proud but in love, the way she was waving the large diamond on her fingers. For the beautiful, kind-hearted woman, it was well-deserved.

After earning a double major in women's studies and psychology, the beauty, who stood at five-ten in bare feet, spent years as a psychologist before deciding to become a life coach. She spent most of her time doing motivational speaking engagements and coaching professional fortune-five-hundred corporations. Before Cser had deployed, Sedona mentioned her real passion was coaching people who wanted a more satisfying personal life.

Cser let out another whistle. "Nice ring! I guess that means you're doing something right," he added with a wink.

"I'll never tell," she grinned broadly, warmed by his appreciative response. "Keith's somewhere around here. I'm sure he'd love to see you."

"Make sure you send him my way," he replied, but by then, his attention had zeroed in on Sage and her admirer. "Hey, who's your friend?"

"Cser, this is Benjamin, a friend of Sedona." Sage moved beside the guy and hooked her arm through his. "We were just talking about him working with T.D. Jakes on a ministry project."

Ministry? Cser suddenly felt bad about wanting to punch a man of the church. "It's a pleasure to meet you, Benjamin." He shook the extended hand.

"Ben is a fascinating man," Sage purred, and Cser noticed the way the guy was staring down at her cleavage. There was nothing holy or Christian about the thoughts he was sure were going through that guy's head.

Someone turned up the volume, and the music changed to Donny Hathaway's "This Christmas." When Cser noticed several moving to the left to dance on the empty showroom floor, he lowered his glass and said to Sage, "Dance with me."

"But I—"

He was already dragging her—away from Benjamin—and onto the floor.

"That was rude," Sage snorted.

Cser smiled softly and pulled her tightly into his arms. "You think he'll forgive me?"

"I won't."

His smile widened. "That's too bad."

Sage shot him an annoyed look as she brought her hands to his shoulders. "I was going to ask Benjamin to dance."

"I know. I saw it in your eyes before your lips had a chance to move." He met her annoyed gaze. "If you're interested in him, then I apologize for being rude."

"I'm interested in you. You're just too blind to notice," she answered without preamble.

"Oh, I noticed," Cser replied and managed a straight face that failed to reveal what he was feeling.

Damn him! His confession didn't make her feel any better. It was one thing to think he hadn't noticed her. But it was another to know he had and still wasn't interested.

"I think I'll go dance with Benjamin now." She tried to turn in his arms, but Cser tightened his hold.

"No, you're going to finish dancing with me." Her whole body tensed as his fingers caressed the area right above her ass.

Lifting her eyes to his, Sage got the satisfaction of seeing a hint of jealousy flicker in those dark depths. "What does it matter?" she taunted. "He asked me to dinner tomorrow night, and I accepted. Besides, you already have a soulmate, remember?"

There was a fire now blazing in his eyes, and his arms

around her waist gripped her possessively. "My soul belongs to the military."

She gave him a curious look. "So, there's no woman in your life?"

Cser shook his head. "You are the closest I've been to a woman in months." His voice was husky and slightly amused.

"Then come home with me tonight and show me just how close to a woman you'd like to be," she cooed.

He threw an annoyed glance at her. "You're starting something."

"I'm sure if I ask Benjamin, he won't say no." Leaning in close, she whispered, "I wonder how long it would take for him to find my spot."

He growled like a caged animal against her ear. "Stop it. If I told your brother how you—"

"But you won't." She cut him off and drew back, so their eyes locked. "We both know you won't."

Cser said nothing. The lethal expression on his face spoke volumes.

She gave him a curious look. "Wait a minute ... is that what this is all about? You're pretending you're not attracted to me because you're worried about my brothers?" She started laughing joyfully. "You let me worry about them." She tried to assure him then leaned in closer, pressing her body against his.

When he finally spoke, his voice was calm and measured. "Who says I'm interested in you?"

"Me and *that* down there," she said, rubbing her body along the thickness of his erection.

Cser jerked back, putting a little space between them, and scowled. "I don't have time for this, and even if I did, it wouldn't be with Remy's sister. We've been boys for way too long," he said gruffly.

Sage laughed at his response. She finally had her answer, and there was no denying his attraction. The revelation had her heart soaring. She was one step closer to getting what she wanted. She hoped.

"Why are you making this difficult?" he whispered in a sharp tone.

"Because I can. I know you want the same thing I want, which is why I can't understand why you deny how you feel."

His expression was impenetrable as he gazed down at her. "I don't allow myself to feel much and for obvious reasons. Women are a distraction I don't need. That way, I stay focused on the mission."

Sage gave a rude snort. "Even our Commander-in-Chief needs someone to warm his bed at night."

"I can find a woman to warm my bed when I'm home, and you're not *that* kind of woman. You deserve more. Much more than I can give you at this point in my career." The husky timbre of his voice poured heat into her ear.

"Who are you to tell me what I want? Maybe all I'm looking for is a fling."

Cser stiffened. "I'm not risking my friendship with Remy for a fling."

Seeing the adamant refusal in his eyes, she let it go. He must have noticed the disappointment because Cser leaned in and whispered, "I'm not good for you, Sage. I don't want to hurt you."

Her temper flared. "You can't hurt me unless I let you," she said with a hint of defiance.

She was lying, of course. Cser had the power to hurt her a great deal. Hell, he was already hurting. She wanted to be more than just his friend. They could be good together. Why couldn't he see that?

Cser said softly near her ear, "Your brothers are watching

us."

She turned and looked over toward her right, and sure enough, Remy and Rush were staring her way. "Let them look." This was one of those days she hated having five overprotective brothers.

Gazes locked, Cser's eyes darkened as she stared at him, and she felt her body heat. He was gorgeous, and he looked at her like she was the most important thing in the world. If only she could get him to see that despite every excuse he'd given, she could be that woman. His woman.

The music had slowed even more, and they were now slow dancing to some Christmas song she'd never heard of but was a love song. Wrapping her arms around his neck, Sage leaned in close. Cser's body tensed, and there was a slight hesitation before she felt him relax again, drawing her closer into the circle of his arms. Perfect fit. She rested her head against his chest, and she never wanted the moment to end. Being here— with him holding her—made everything feel right in her life. No other man made her body come alive as he did. No other man made her heart thump so hard and loud. They were meant to be together. With relentless determination, she planned on letting Cser know how interested she was in him every opportunity she got.

The song ended, and reluctantly she raised her head and stepped away. It was probably one of the hardest things she had ever done. "Thanks for the dance." She turned and sauntered away. As soon as she turned her back, the smile slipped from her lips. Cser was not going to make this easy for her, but one thing about her, she'd never been a quitter.

CHAPTER 2

"You're very intelligent."

Thank you," she replied, batting her eyelashes at Benjamin like some smitten teenager.

"I would love to get together for lunch next week and talk to you some more."

She found the tall, slender man charming. He was attractive without being handsome, but she didn't have the heart to tell Benjamin that would probably never happen. Especially not with Remy, Rush, and Rance staring down her throat. Sage drew a sigh. Dr. Benjamin Bartley seemed too sensitive to handle the interrogation of the male members of the Force MDs—Rush, Roman, Remy, Reese, and Rance. Half African-American, half Samoan, and all doctors...each in their unique way. They were all her brothers and a force to be reckoned with. Growing up, they had always looked out for one another. If you messed with one, you had to deal with all of them. Even after all those years, her brothers were still overprotective when it came to her and Sedona. Now that her older sister was engaged, that left Sage to deal with them every time she decided to date. Luckily for Benjamin, she wasn't interested in him. Hell, she wasn't interested in anyone but one man.

Sage dared to look over at Cser, who talked to her sister just a few feet away. As soon as he lifted his head, their eyes locked, and her breath stopped. What was going on in his head? She wondered.

"If lunch doesn't work, how about dinner?"

"Dinner?" she repeated, drawing her attention away from Cser and back to Benjamin. She had lied to Cser about the two of them having a dinner date tomorrow night, but this was an opportunity to make that true even though her heart wasn't in it.

"Sure, why not." She heard herself say. Benjamin was a nice enough guy. Who's to say Cser would ever recognize her?

Speaking of Cser.... she caught him now standing near the Christmas tree again. His penetrating gaze raking her body left her feeling hot in all the right places.

C'mere, she mumbled inward. *C'mere and show me what you're thinking.*

Sage wanted nothing more than for Cser to move toward her with steady, powerful strides and claim her as his. Unfortunately, he didn't come her way. Instead, he just stood there, looking pissed off that Benjamin was dominating so much of her time and personal space.

Good for him.

She went around mingling with employees and friends. Over the next hour, she kept herself busy not to focus on Cser, even though she was keenly aware of those yummy brown eyes that followed her, keeping her body humming at attention.

Sage moved toward Sedona, who was standing by her handsome fiancé, Keith.

He was a tall glass of water and a breath of fresh air for her sister after the death of her last fiancé, Derrick Webb. Keith, retired Navy, had come into her life and taught Sedona how to love again.

They were laughing at Remy, who—as usual—was acting a fool when Rance, Rush, and Roman came over to join their group. While everyone exchanged greetings, Sage admired her brothers.

Although Rance, a.k.a. Dr. Dribble, was the tallest at seven-two and a professional NBA player, they were all tall. Roman, a few inches shorter, played football in high school before pursuing a career in dentistry. Her eyes shifted to the shortest of the bunch at six-three. After their father suffered a heart attack, he stepped away from the day-to-day operations and handed over the reins to Rush, now the CEO of the Beaumont Automotive Group. He had a doctoral degree in organizational management, and since taking over, had expanded the group by adding five new locations.

Sage scowled at the reminder; she'd been salty ever since. She believed she was more capable than anyone else and even ran circles around her brothers when it came to working on vehicles. She was determined to be ready for more responsibility through sweat and hard work and deserved to be next to Rush in the driver's seat.

The only Beaumont missing was Reese. He and his wife, Dominique, would be flying in the day before Christmas. The couple lived in Hawaii, where she was the human resources manager for the Beaumont Waikiki Hotel. Reese had once been one of the top thoracic surgeons in the country until a car accident damaged the nerves in his hand and ended his career. But over the last two years, he seemed satisfied with being an instructor at a teaching hospital in Waikiki.

Life was almost perfect, and Sage didn't want for anything except for part-ownership of the Beaumont Automotive Group and the love of the man standing only a few feet away.

Cser grabbed a beer and brought the bottle to his lips. Anger brewed at the surface. For the last hour, he had been watching her drinking and drawing attention from other men. Mostly from Dr. Benjamin what's-his-name. He had no right, and yet, he didn't like it. Every time Cser saw him reach out and touch Sage, he felt the burning rage to break every last finger in that man's hand.

Mine. All mine.

As much as he knew it wasn't so, in his mind, she belonged to him.

"Why are you over here all by yourself?"

He looked up to see Rance's wife, Debra, standing in front of him and smiled. He had met the owner of the Sheraton Beach bakery *DebbieCakes* at the couple's wedding and took an instant liking to her.

Cser held up the glass bottle. "I'm drinking a beer."

Amusement slashed across her pretty face. "I've been watching you. So, forgive me if I'm being nosy, but I saw you staring at Sage. Is there something going on between you two?"

Dammit. He was busted. If Debra saw him, there was no telling how many others had witnessed the same. He swallowed hard, meeting the woman's keenly intuitive greenish-brown gaze. "She's like a sister to me. I'm just keeping my eye on that guy standing beside her."

Debra gave him a look that said she believed only half of what he'd just said. "She doesn't need another brother. She's got too many of them as it is."

That was one fact he couldn't argue.

"What she needs is a man with a spine." A knowing smile curved her lips as Cser chanced another glance in her direction.

"No, what she needs is someone who knows how to say no to her." Everyone knew Sage was spoiled and used to getting whatever she wanted. Like all of the Beaumont grandchildren, their grandfather had left them each a sizable trust fund. Money was no object, although they all lived so simple.

Sage lived in a gorgeous condo in downtown Richmond with city views to die for and a mortgage payment he couldn't begin to fathom with his income. He was happy in the three-bedroom farmhouse he owned on three acres of land in Chesterfield County. His deployments had allowed him several entitlements, and he'd saved almost all monies earned while overseas. Every year he maxed out in his retirement plan because he believed in preparing for the future. Someday soon, he planned to retire the uniform and land a position with the federal government, but for now, his life was fine the way it was.

Almost.

He'd admit the nights were lonely, especially now that he was spending them dreaming about Sage. And after holding her soft curves in his arms, he was going to have an even harder time sleeping tonight.

"She's my best friend's sister," Cser said as if that should be settled. Instead, Debra looked confused.

"What's that got to do with anything?" She winked at him before his eyes traveled back across the room, and he noticed Sage had another drink in her hand. That made her third. He had known her long enough to know she was a lightweight. Two wine coolers, and she was laughing and acting silly. And what she had in her hand looked much more potent.

A woman came over and handed Debra a little boy with his toasted brown complexion and fine wavy hair.

"This here is my one-year-old son, Tyrese," she said adoringly.

Cser smiled and stroked the little boy's cheek with affection. "He looks like Rance."

"Yes, he does." She nodded in agreement.

Family. A familiar ache began to tighten at his chest. Instantly, he reached into his pocket for a pack of antacids, diagnosing it as indigestion.

Cser was trying to make Tyrese laugh when he caught Sage slipping into her coat and saying her goodbyes.

Goodbye?

Benjamin was right beside her, shaking hands with her father.

Cser clenched his jaw. "Will you excuse me?"

"Of course." Debra's mouth twitched humorously.

He lowered the beer onto the counter with a heavy thump, then stalked over and intercepted her escape to the door.

"Going somewhere?"

She glanced up at him with eyes that hinted at intoxication. "As a matter of fact, yes. I've been drinking, so Benjamin offered to take me home."

Yeah, I just bet he was. Cser was sure that Benjamin would find a way to wiggle an invite to her condo during the ride. Anger threaded through his body, but he controlled it with years of practice.

"I was just on my way out. I can take you home." He signaled with his hand for her to follow.

"No, I—"

"I insist." Cser was practically growling as he stared at Benjamin long and hard until he finally dropped his head and retreated. Once he was gone, Cser retrieved his coat and then took Sage by the arm and escorted her out into the parking lot. A chill blanketed the city, and he was anxious to climb into his vehicle and turn on the seat warmers.

She pointed. "My car's over there."

"We can take mine."

Sage's CLS550 would be just fine sitting out in the parking lot of the dealership. Unlike his Silverado.

Cser pointed over to the side of the building and fell into step beside her. Sage was quiet and not saying much, so he assumed she was pouting. *Too bad.* He was doing what he thought was best for both of them.

Walking around the truck, he opened the door for her, and she climbed in without saying a word. Cser wasted no time getting in on the other side.

Within minutes he was racing down I-95 toward her downtown condominium.

"Why are you so quiet?"

Sage turned her head and glared at him. "I'm trying to figure out what it is you want from me, or better yet, if you want me at all. I'm there at the party, having a good time with a handsome man—who offers me a ride home—and you decide to cock block."

Cser pushed out a deep, heavy sigh. "I know how men think and getting you home safe was not what Benjamin had planned."

She shrugged. "So what? We are both consenting adults."

His fingers tightened around the steering wheel as he grumbled, "Don't go there."

"Why not?" She taunted and swung around on the seat. "You don't want me, so I gotta get some TLC from someone."

That was one visual he did not want in his head. "You're grown. You can do what you want but not on my watch."

"Who asked you to watch out for me? My family was there, including four of my brothers. What the hell do I need you watching over me for?" she spat angrily.

"Look, I'm just trying to make sure you get home safely." Annoyed, he focused on the road, but that only pissed her off.

"I'm tired of you pretending you aren't interested in me when it's clear you're attracted to me. I felt it when you were holding me in your arms. I see it in your eyes." She began a tirade. "You want to keep behaving as if I don't exist, then dammit, you go ahead. But don't expect me to stop living just because you have."

Cser flinched, and there was a long, intense silence. Her words hit him hard. Was that how she saw him, walking dead around the living? He had to admit he had become very standoffish and reserved over the last few years. He rarely allowed anyone to get close, which was why his friendship with the Beaumonts meant so much. But his job made it difficult for him to have lasting relationships. And the few women he had risked his heart to had stabbed him in the back. He needed to stay focused, and he just wasn't in the mood to be mind-fucked at this stage of his life. There was too much at stake for that.

"I told you before; I'm not getting involved with my best friend's sister, no matter how I feel about you."

Her nostrils flared. "Then stay the hell out of my personal life!"

Stunned by the force of her anger, Cser took his eyes off the road briefly to look at her. "What the hell is wrong with you?"

"You! You're what's wrong with me." Sage yanked the cap from her head, crossed her arms, and stared out the window the rest of the ride.

As he maneuvered his truck down the off-ramp, Cser decided maybe she was right. He did need to butt out if he wasn't interested in having more. It was only fair, but the selfish part still wanted her all to himself and refused to share.

He pulled in front of her condominium and left the engine idling as he climbed out, walked around, and wrenched open the door. Sage stepped out, swinging her purse onto her shoulder, then headed toward her unit. "I can walk by myself," she called over her shoulder.

Cser viciously swore as he followed her, mesmerized at the way she moved in those boots. "Too bad. Remy would kick my ass if he knew I didn't walk you to the door."

"Remy this ..., Remy that. Why does everything always have to be about Remy?" She reached into her pocket for a key and angrily stuck it into the door before she swirled around and barked, "What's wrong ... you afraid to think for yourself?"

"I'm a grown man," he snarled back at her.

"Oh yeah? Then show me!"

Cser wasn't sure if it was to shut her up or because of how sexy she looked, blowing off steam that possessed him to reach out and deliberately pull her lush curves against his. Eyes wide with surprise, Sage's lips parted just as he dragged her head down and pressed his lips against hers, giving her a kiss, he'd tasted in his dreams for months. The pressure of her mouth practically ripped the air from his lungs.

The moment their lips collided, tension escaped his body. He had denied himself for far too long. He slipped inside and mated her eager tongue. Sage had skills and enough confidence to make him feel half-crazed thinking about all of the others she may have kissed before him. Her mouth was sweet and inviting, and the soft moans slipping from her throat were music to his ears. The more he kissed her, the more he wanted. His hands were sliding up and down her body, caressing, squeezing, and teasing her to arousing limits. Dammit, he wanted more. Much more.

He growled against her lips. "You think I don't want to show you..." he began, then drew back, staring into her eyes. "I would like nothing more than to suck on your breasts, then fuck the shit out of you. Do you think I don't want that? If that's what you think, then you don't know me."

Sage had a stunned expression on her face when he planted his mouth to hers again. At first, he thought he had frightened her, and she was going to push him away, but instead, her arms came around his neck, drawing him nearer. Cser took his time stroking and mating, making sure he gave as good as he got. Kissing her was like making love. It required a great deal of time and patience. Not meant to be rushed. Her lips were delicious, and he quickly got so caught up in it, he had no desire for it to end. Neither did she. Sage was clinging to him, holding him in place.

When he felt her body arching towards his, Cser realized he couldn't think. Not with her succulent lips pressed against his. Not with the mounds of her soft breasts against his chest, her pussy gyrating his thigh.

His hands were now locked at her waist, refusing to let her go.

"Damn you, Sage. Is this what you wanted?" he taunted against her lips, grinding his erection against her. "Tell me! Is this what you'd been waiting for?" He needed to hear her say it. He wanted her so badly, his loins ached. "I can feel it in the way your body's responding to my touch."

"Yes!" she gasped in agreement. "I want you so bad."

This was maddening, so annoying. Cser abruptly drew back and whispered, "We better stop."

"Stop? You know you don't want to stop," she replied with confidence. "Why do you keep denying yourself?"

She was right, Cser thought as he arched against her body. Being here with her felt right in so many ways that it scared him enough to know if he didn't stop, there would be no returning from the mistake he was seconds away from making.

"Please, make love to me," she cooed. "There's no one else I want to be my first but you."

He stilled. "What did you just say?"

Shyly, Sage looked down at his chest before meeting his

gaze again with eyes that were so innocent. "I want you to be my first."

His voice came out on a ragged sigh of disbelief. "*You're a virgin?*"

The desire in her eyes scorched his flesh, and for a moment, she stared at him. "I've been saving myself for you."

No fucking way! The way she flirted and teased; how comfortable she was with her sexuality.... "How the hell is that even possible?"

Sage shrugged. "I wasn't ready. Sure, I flirt, act wild, and outta control, but that's just a front. My family knows the truth."

And then, suddenly, it all made sense. No wonder her brothers were so overprotective. They were watching every man who was within one hundred feet with hawk eyes. They knew their sister had been saving herself for the right man.

And that man was not him.

"Get inside."

"Come inside with me," she coaxed, her sweet breath fanning his face. "We can talk about it."

"I don't do virgins." Reaching over, he pushed the door open. "Get in the house," he snarled and gave her a light push.

Reluctantly, Sage glared before she turned and headed inside. "Fine! Keep lying to yourself," she hissed and slammed the door behind her.

Sage stormed across the foyer and up to her bedroom, mumbling a string of obscenities.

What is wrong with him? She had offered Cser her virginity on a silver platter, and yet he refused.

Stupid jerk!

Anyone could see he wanted her. Hell, Remy would see it if

he wasn't so stuck on himself. There was no denying; they were good together. She always hoped they would be, and now she knew they were meant to be together. If only Cser weren't so dumb, he would see it as well. She dropped her purse and keys onto her nightstand and blew out a long, frustrated breath. So, what if she was a virgin? If anything, Cser should have felt privileged to know she had been saving herself for him.

Stupid jerk!

While Sage unzipped her boots, she felt slightly intoxicated, but that didn't stop her mind from revisiting their kiss, simmering some of her anger. Cser had been gentle, and his lips had felt so soft, caressing hers. The memory caused a shiver to race down her spine. Goodness, the man had skills, but she had expected as much. Cser alluded to confidence, and it showed in the way he touched and kissed. All those years she had spent wondering what his mouth would taste like, and now she knew. There was no guesswork or imagining the feel of his gorgeous lips because now she had hands-on—or better yet—lips-on experience. And it was far better than anything she had ever dreamed.

"And he makes me so damn mad," she screamed. Being around him drove her insane. She wanted him to be her first. Why was that hard for him to accept?

While she removed her clothes, she remembered the first time Remy had brought him to their house. She had just come in from volleyball practice, and instantly Cser grabbed her attention. He was tall, dark, and handsome in jeans and a high school football jersey with bedroom eyes that tore at her soul. Cser grew up in the foster care system, and as far as she knew, he didn't have any family. After high school, he graduated from Virginia State University and was immediately commissioned in the army. The military had become his life, traveling to different countries, volunteering for missions.

She had spent twelve years hoping he would eventually notice her and finally stop looking at her as a sister and pen-pal. Taking the reins, Sage started with subtle hints that went unnoticed before she decided to start being a little more obvious. It still didn't make a difference. There had always been someone else—Tiffany, Rachel, and Chanel. Between him and Remy, she'd lost count, and she couldn't remember him ever having a serious relationship with a woman. The few he'd had were all short-lived, more like one-night stands. Part of her knew she was stupid to expect anything lasting with Cser. Not with his track record. So, she convinced herself that one night could be enough. Just enough to let her know what it feels like to be a woman and for Cser to see just how great they could be together. She was confident it would make all the difference.

Why did you tell him you were a virgin?

Her confession had lost all the progress she had made. If only she had kept her virginity to herself, she might have been able to convince him to come inside.

As she dragged the leggings down over her hips, Sage frowned at the thought. She could have been one of those women who did not tell a man until it was too late, but she didn't want it to be that way between them. She wanted Cser to know what she was giving him was special and had been meant only for him.

As she removed her undergarments, Sage told herself today had been a minor setback. It was time for a bit of refinement, she thought as she moved into the ensuite and turned on the shower. While under the water spray, Sage planned a course of action that she was certain Cser would notice. If all failed, she would finally leave him alone, but Sage felt confident that wasn't going to happen. Failure was not an option she could accept. She would have to show Cser what he'd been missing.

Cser stripped to his boxers and went to the refrigerator for a beer before plopping down in front of the television. Clicking on the cable, he quickly turned to ESPN to catch highlights of the game he had missed tonight. The Washington Football Team was his team but being able to see Sage had been worth missing it.

Fuck!

Why couldn't things be different? He asked himself for the umpteenth time. If Sage had been any other woman, he would be in her bed with her legs spread, plunging deep inside of her until the wee hours of the morning. After he was done, he would have kissed her goodbye and been on his way. But he couldn't treat her like all of the others because Sage was special. He didn't do emotional attachments, and he didn't do virgins. Robbing her of that would be like asking for an ass whipping he was sure to get once her brothers found out.

And yet, he couldn't stop thinking about her.

Maybe it was because it had been over six long months since he'd last been with a woman, and his dick was throbbing for something more than hand action. The problem was he didn't screw while deployed. Not in close quarters. Besides, even if housing were different, he wouldn't have risked it. He was always on alert and didn't believe in allowing his mind to dwell on sexual pleasure while on deployment. Being in the desert was a time to think with the head not swinging between his legs.

It was always about the mission.

But when he was home. It was all about titties and ass, and

in Richmond and the surrounding areas, he'd planned to self-indulge with whoever was ready, willing, and able.

So, if any woman would do, why can't I get one particular woman out of my head?

While he attempted to watch the sports highlights, all that kept running through his mind was that delicious mouth of hers, sucking his dick.

Fuck! Fuck! Fuck!

Cser dragged a frustrated hand across his close-cropped hair. He was starting to think he was losing his mind. Maybe his recent madness resulted from a close call with an IED a few weeks ago. Ever since, he'd been thinking about where he was and wanted to be. Nothing worse than living the rest of his life with regret and shoulda, woulda, coulda. Maybe it was time for him to learn to lighten up a little and quit walking dead among the living. But *this* here, *this* attraction he had for Sage, he knew it would only end up being wrong. Sage was a good girl and deserved someone better than him.

And yet she saved herself for you.

What the hell made him so damn special that she wanted him? he scowled. She was beautiful, intelligent, sexy, and a virgin. What was the likelihood of that at twenty-seven? And yet, it only magnified his positive image of her. Sage was one of a kind, and any man who won over her heart would be one lucky sonofabitch.

She's a virgin.

Cser groaned as he shifted on the chair uncomfortably. It was going to be a long night. He was going to have to find sex quick, fast, and in a hurry. Otherwise, the next time Sage propositioned him, saying no might be next to impossible.

CHAPTER 3

"Sage, you have a phone call."

She slid the creeper out from underneath the Hyundai Sante Fe to gaze up at her assistant. "I need to finish this oil leak. Can you take a message?"

"It's your father."

Sage stalled and took a long, deep breath. Clara knew the few people who were allowed to interrupt her when she was in the garage. One of them was her father, Richard Beaumont. For a moment, she'd thought it may have been Benjamin calling to invite her out to dinner again. He was a nice guy, but there was no chemistry between them, so once was enough.

She slid out further, then reached for a rag and wiped off her hands before taking the phone from her assistant's outstretched hand. As soon as she placed it to her ear, Clara exited the body shop.

"Hello?"

"Hey, princess."

Sage's lips curled at the endearment. Her father had been calling her his princess long before she was old enough to remember. "Hey, Pop. How was your doctor's appointment this morning?" she asked, remembering that her mother had mentioned he'd had a six-month check-up with his cardiologist.

"Everything is fine. A clean bill of health. I need to continue to get my morning workout in, eat right, and I will be around a long time to rain havoc on your life."

She leaned back against the vehicle and sighed with relief. "That's good to hear."

He cleared his throat and quietly continued, "Well, the reason for my call is I just received the quarterly sales reports for the dealerships."

"And?" Sage held her breath.

"And all of your stores are up more than twenty percent."

"Yaay!" She leaped into the air excitedly.

"You have been our top performer, and I must say, I am *really* proud of you."

"Yes, dear, we're very proud." Her mother abruptly came onto the line.

"Thank you, Mama," Sage said into the phone.

There was a tsk sound. "I just wish you would stop getting all greasy and focus on the business end. You're so good at that."

Sage rubbed her temple wearily. "Because I love getting my hands dirty," she said defensively.

"Yes." Bettye Beaumont pushed out a deep, heavy sigh. "That's the problem. I bet there's grease under your nails right now."

Self-consciously, Sage looked down at her hands. So what? She loved working on cars. Where was the harm in that?

Her mother grunted her mild disapproval. "A man wants a woman who is feminine, not a grease monkey,"

"*A grease monkey?* Really Mom?"

"I'm just saying. You're a beautiful young lady. I just wish you'd show more of that," came her gruff comment.

"Mama, I don't know if you noticed, but I dress up well," Sage conceded. One thing about her she had never had a problem picking up a man. Well, maybe one in particular, but she was confident that was just a matter of time.

In the background, she could hear her father asking for the phone back. *Thank you for the small favors.*

Before hanging up, her mother added, "Gigi, I'll see you at the bridal shop in Short Pump on Friday. Maybe seeing Donie in her wedding gown might help you get some ideas about what it will take to snag yourself a man."

Sage rolled her eyes and had to bite her tongue to keep from snapping off with a comment that was sure to start another argument. She loved the way she was, and she wasn't going to change for anyone. If a man wanted her, then he would have to accept her for who she was.

"Princess don't pay your mother any mind. You know she only wants the best for all her children," she heard her father say, trying to salvage the moment.

"I know, Dad. I wish she understood the dealership, and the cars are what make me happy."

"She understands more than you know. It's taking me a while to accept you are a female version of myself with that same fire and determination. I'm truly proud of you. You have proven you can run circles around me. With that said, I think you'll find something extra in your Christmas stocking this season."

She giggled because the stockings had always been something special between them. Her father used to fill hers with miniature cars. "I can't wait."

They talked a few moments longer, then she ended the call and was smiling ear to ear. She had outperformed Rush. Sage giggled again. She would give anything to see his face when her father called to tell him. *A woman's place is in the kitchen.* Ha! She'd shown all of them. She knew how to look sexy, even covered in dirt and grime.

Sage decided to take a break and headed out the body shop into the showroom, where her sales team worked hard.

Every new member, she'd personally spent time teaching the tricks of the trade. And it had paid off.

She climbed the stairs to her office on the left side of the dealership. Clara was ending a phone call.

"Schedule a staff meeting for five today," Sage instructed her.

"Okay," she replied with a questionable look.

Smiling, she added, "I've some good news I want to share with the entire team."

Her blue eyes lit up. "I'll get the conference room ready."

Nodding gleefully, Sage stepped into her lavish office, which boasted expensive hardwood furnishings that included a large desk and a floor-to-ceiling bookcase covered with accolades: awards and newspaper clippings about her and the automotive group.

She walked across the taupe Berber carpet, covering the floor to stand in front of a large glass picture window that looked out onto the showroom floor. This was her world. She was proud of everything she had done so far—education, hard work, and determination. Other than a specific army officer who was determined to deny his feelings, nothing was stopping her from having it all.

Turning away from the window, Sage moved over and took a seat on the leather chair. She was a tad bit too grimy to lounge across her chocolate sofa.

It had been two days since the Christmas party, and yet she hadn't been able to stop thinking about Cser or the kiss they'd shared. Being in his arms with his lips over hers had been everything she had imagined it would be and more. The problem was that it only added to her madness. Now more than ever, she wanted Cser in her life. It didn't matter how much she tried to understand his reasoning; it made no sense to her. He wanted her; that much was obvious. But he'd rather keep Remy as a friend than take a chance on loving her. Where was the sense in that?

She reached down for the water bottle at her desk and took a long thirsty sip. It wasn't that she hadn't had sex opportunities. And it damn sure wasn't because she wasn't attractive. Even with grease under her nails, there had always been some guy sniffing behind her. No, what she had always wanted was someone special. Most of the guys she had met were assholes. They would wine and dine her, and just when she got to the point that she started to think that maybe it was time to give up on Cser and give someone else a chance, they always seemed to show their true colors. After that, no one compared to Cser, and she finally concluded that he had ruined her for all other men. And that was why she had decided it was time to go for it. Put herself out there, making it impossible for him to resist. A wave of determination passed through her. She loved a challenge, and that's precisely what Cser had become.

As she brought the bottle to her lips, a mischievous smile curled her mouth. Cser was not going to have any idea what had hit him.

Cser could sense something was about to go down.

It was that familiar burning at his chest that developed over years of military combat training. It was also that keen sense of awareness that managed to keep him alive.

He often performed critical missions, but this one was different. Failure was not an option.

Beside him, his partner lay on the cold ground, scanning the woods for any activity. Their eyes met, and Cser signaled with his hand for them to move forward. Crouched down low on the ground, he and his team advanced several feet, paused, and listened, but there was nothing but the whistling of the bitterly cold wind. At the moment, the only thing he was confident of was that snow was in the air.

Suddenly, he heard a distance gun exploding and a battle raging between forces. But the area he was patrolling was still quiet. To his right, two more of his men leaned against trees armed and ready.

Just then, there was the sound of branches breaking, followed by a male voice that carried through the air.

Quietly, they inched closer. Cser looked both ways, then held up his free hand as he counted down three..., two..., one..., "Go!"

They jumped through the brush, guns drawn, going right and left, and ambushed their targets, catching them by surprise. Everything went like clockwork. The team swooped in, guns popping off several rounds. They had barely neutralized the group when shots blasted from the woods behind them.

"Oh shit!" His partner cried, and then his team started running. They had barely gone a few hundred feet when Cser felt a sting at his side.

"Dammit! I've been hit!"

Not ready to accept defeat, he swirled around with his finger on the trigger letting off a fury of shots hitting his target in the chest and arms, then watched as he dropped to his knees. His triumph was short-lived when he caught quick movement to his right. Before he could aim, another team member let off a round, knocking the opponent to his feet.

"Fuck!" Cser said and realized he'd been holding his breath.

He turned around to find Remy standing behind him. "Good looking out." He gave him a thumbs up.

Remy winked. "You know I got your back."

By then, it was a full-blown paintball assault.

Rance came rushing over, followed by Rush, who had been hit multiple times.

"Ain't this some shit," he muttered, and there was a collective peal of laughter.

Cser grinned, weapon raised. "C'mon, let's end this."

Within minutes paintballs colored the air from every direction until the other team finally had no choice but to accept defeat. For the third year in a row, Cser's team was triumphant.

They were walking back to the locker room. The wind had picked up, and snow flurries were dancing around in the air when Remy joked, "Dude, I hope you do better than that in the desert."

The others laughed.

Cser glanced down at the paint that had plummeted his side. "A wound this small would have barely slowed me down. Now that one you got at the center of your chest ..., I would have been taking you home for Ms. Bettye to identify."

"Oh, hell no! What would the ladies do without me?" Remy retorted with a cocky grin.

Rush scowled. "Maybe then the rest of the men in this city might have a chance."

As they showered, the raucousness continued. Cser laughed and thought about the brothers. They were his family, the only one he'd ever had. They understood when he was home; he needed time to digress and temporarily forget about the mission before he was back at it again. What they'd just simulated hadn't even come close to what he'd done and seen in combat.

With a towel around his waist, Cser headed back to the locker room. Remy was sitting on the bench texting on his phone. "What you got planned for tonight?"

Cser shrugged. "Nothing. Why?"

A slow smile curled his mouth as he explained, "I met this chick, but she's asking me to bring someone for her friend."

As he turned the combination lock, he asked with curiosity, "What does she look like?"

Remy used both hands to draw an hourglass. "Sexy as hell."

Images of Sage filled his brain that Cser forced himself to shove away.

"Yeah, sure. Count me in."

CHAPTER 4

This was not what she had in mind.

Sage pressed her foot on the gas again, hoping she would get some traction, but ended up with the same result.

She was stuck in a snowbank.

When she had first decided to confront Remy, there had only been snow flurries dancing around in the sky, but by the time she had left the dealership and headed out, the snow had already started to accumulate. Cars were skidding around on the road. Visibility was at a minimum. Any other woman would have had sense enough to go home and not even dare drive out in this mess. Oh no! Not her. She was a speed demon, a know-it-all. If anyone could drive a vehicle, it was her. She had even taken one of the four-wheel drives that a customer used as a trade-in because her Mercedes was a piece of crap in the snow, but even the F-150 wasn't good enough.

Since when did Richmond have blizzards?

Sage reached down for her cell phone and tried to make another call to triple-A, but there still wasn't a signal. Even each of the text messages she tried to send to her brothers bounced back undeliverable.

"Unfucking believable," she muttered.

As she stared out the window at the snow collecting on the glass, Sage reached down and turned on her windshield wipers. It was a waste of time because more snow accumulated and ice-coated her wipers as fast as they cleared.

So much for being aggressive and going for what I want.

Now she was stuck in a ditch. No sensible person would dream of driving down this winding back road. Sage punched the steering wheel as if it would do more than just allow her to let off steam and didn't know if she should laugh or cry to the extent, she had been willing to go to get Cser's attention. Was she that desperate or just hopelessly in love? She decided to go with the latter. Cser was leaving in a week, and she was determined to show him how she felt before he shipped off again. If anything, she would have given him something to think about until he returned in the spring.

"Maybe I should have waited until spring," she muttered under her breath. At least then, she wouldn't be risking her health and welfare out in a storm that was sure to be marked as one of the worst the city had seen in years.

A flicker of light caught her eye. Sage glanced down at the dashboard, then started swearing under her breath. "Great. Just great!" She was low on gas and now likely to freeze to death long before someone came to her rescue.

Leaning back on the seat, she momentarily closed her eyes. *Think, Sage. Think.* She had been to Cser's house once before, an old farmhouse in the middle of nowhere. She and Remy headed to a college basketball game between rivals Virginia State University and Virginia Union. They had dropped by briefly to pick up some stupid jersey that was supposed to bring good luck. Sage was sure she had already passed the fork in the road, which meant his house couldn't be more than half a mile up the road on a good day. And this definitely wouldn't count as one of those.

Sage scowled. She couldn't just continue to sit there and freeze to death. She was running out of fuel, her phone didn't work, and the snow was just going to get worse. At least if she got out, she could walk to the nearest house and call for help.

Only, she didn't remember seeing any other homes on the way out to the farmhouse.

Damn him.

What man wanted to live out in the middle of Chesterfield County down a winding back road all by himself? But then again, Cser had never been like any of the other men she had met in her life.

She considered leaving her purse but thought better of it. It was Prada, and she wasn't about to part with it. Instead, she shrugged out of her coat and was glad she had decided to wear her heavy wool coat instead of the leather jacket. Sage swung the strap over her shoulder, slid back into her coat and zipped it up tight, then lowered the cap over her ears. Thank goodness she had remembered her leather fur-lined gloves because she was good for forgetting.

"Here goes nothing," she muttered, then climbed out. Using the flashlight on her phone, she lit the path in front of her. The wind was beating down on her face, so she kept her head low and a hand out in front of her as she tried to block the impact of the wind. Snow was coming down hard, and visibility wasn't as easy as she had thought it would be. Neither was walking. She had barely made it a few feet, and the snow that was at her calves seeped through her UGG boots and denim jeans.

"Oh, God!"

What in the world had she been thinking? Snow swirled around her, blinding her, mixing with tears. Sage moved a few steps further before deciding she had been better off taking her chances in the truck. However, when she tried to turn around, she tripped over something and fell on her ass. The phone slipped from her fingers and disappeared under the snow. She tried, searched, but was unsuccessful at finding it, and got up from the ground after she couldn't.

"Dammit!" The wind was sending the snow at her so fast; it

was sticking to her eyelashes and stinging her cheeks. No matter what direction she managed to look, she couldn't find the truck. What have I done to deserve this? she wondered. It was dark, cold, and the air was stinging. Panic filled her lungs. She had to either find shelter or assistance fast—no point in just standing there because she was sure to turn into an icicle.

Turning, Sage started in the direction she was almost sure she had been heading before. The entire time she chanted to herself it was better to keep moving because the further she traveled, the better chance she had of finding smoke snaking out of someone's chimney ahead. But the snow was so slippery she kept sliding and fell twice more and was so wet her teeth began to chatter.

Damn you, Cser. The lengths she had gone to get him to notice her had suddenly topped the list as extreme, she told herself. Why hadn't she waited for a better opportunity than this? Ugh!

She could barely walk. Her body was hurting. Sage was cold and suddenly craving the hamburger she had left untouched at lunchtime. Now was not the time to be thinking about food, although if she happened to be stuck out here all night, it sure would have been nice to have had a burger sticking to her stomach.

A few feet ahead, which felt more like she had walked an entire mile, with her last blast of energy, she moved over to a tree and stood behind it, trying to block out the snow long enough to catch her breath. It was so blinding she had to wipe her eyes once or twice because she swore, she saw someone coming toward her. Blinking snowdrops from her eyes, Sage was sure that was a man headed her way. Was it an angel coming to rescue her? Sure enough, he was moving toward her, looking large-and-in–charge in a thick Eskimo coat with a fur-trimmed hood. She couldn't make out his face, and at the moment, it didn't matter just as long as he was there to help.

She heard a deep voice over the howling of the wind. "Give me your hand!"

Sage extended her arm, and he guided her away from the tree. As soon as she was close enough, she stared up at him through the falling snow. She couldn't see his eyes, and yet she knew.

"Cser?"

"Sage, walk behind me. I'm going to try and block the wind so that I can get you inside."

It was him! He had come to rescue her.

She moved behind him. with shivering hands, she held onto his coat while Cser guided her through the snow and up the driveway to the house. She had been closer than she had imagined, yet with limited visibility, she might have never found it. As soon as they reached the porch, Cser helped her up the stairs and into the house. Once inside, she collapsed on the sofa.

"Oh my God! Thank you," Sage gasped. She was so happy there were tears in her eyes.

"What the hell were you doing out there?" He removed his gloves and coat.

"I came to see you," Sage replied, teeth chattering.

With disbelief, Cser searched her face.

She shrugged out of her wet coat.

"You're soaked!" he barked.

She was dripping wet. "I fell a couple of times," she admitted with a grim, shaky laugh.

Cser skewed her with a glare and looked ready to strangle her. "Come move over near the fire." He retook her hand and led her over to sit in front of a crackling fire.

"T-Thanks. T-This feels wonderful."

He slid her a sideways glance. "What are you doing out in

this weather?'

"I told you. I wanted to see you."

"Couldn't it have waited?" He searched her face.

"No," she said with a defiant tilt of her chin. "I-I tried talking to you the other night, and t-things didn't go well, sooo, since you wouldn't listen, I figure if I came out here, you w-wouldn't have any other choice but to listen to what I had to say," she shuddered, teeth chattering.

"And you decided to have this conversation in the middle of a snowstorm." But he was at least smiling now.

"Well, I wasn't expecting the w-weather to do all this." She emphasized with a sweep of her hand. "This just s-sort of happened. By the time I realized the weather was nasty, I was already in the ditch."

Cser mumbled something under his breath that she couldn't make out. Reaching down, he gently pulled her boots off. Inside, her socks were soaked.

Sage looked at him curiously. "How did you know I was out there?"

He gave her a fleeting glance before yanking the socks from her feet. "I was upstairs and saw a flashlight. I went to investigate."

She swallowed and drew her knees up to her chest. "I'm so glad you did."

Reaching up, he ran the pad of his thumb across the tip of her nose. "So am I."

They stared at each other, and she licked her lips as he lowered his head, and for a moment, she thought he was getting ready to swoop in for an affectionate kiss. Unfortunately, before his lips could reach her, a chill snaked up her spine, causing her to shiver.

"You're shivering," Cser growled with renewed fury.

"I'm wet. That's what happens when you f-fall and lose your

phone in the snow."

He shook his head. "Don't you know everything is shut down? Businesses, schools, you name it. The governor has declared Virginia a state of emergency." Rising, he grabbed a Washington Redskin's throw from the sofa and tossed it over to her.

"Thanks, but I rarely watch the news," she replied and, with a shrug, wrapped the blanket around her wet body.

His keen eyes zeroed in as he said, "You need to change that. Everyone should be aware of what's going on in the world."

She used to watch the news all the time, but then there would be reports of local murders and police brutality, and even worse, a fallen member of the armed forces. She couldn't bear to listen to the details, afraid it might have been Cser.

He disappeared into the kitchen, grabbed two bottles of Dasani water, and handed one to Sage. She smiled. "Thanks, I was thirsty."

"I figured as much." He lowered onto the rug, twisted the cap from the bottle, and took a long thirsty drink. She was doing the same when she caught those big brown eyes observing her.

Reaching over, he yanked the cap from her head and threw it over near the fire. Cser was now staring at her hair. "What?" she said and self-consciously brushed her fingers across her fade.

"I like your hair that way. It's funky."

"Funky?" she sputtered with laughter. "I guess you could call it that. I got tired of the ponytail and trying to figure out a low-maintenance way to wear it. This here is easy, wash and wear."

He stroked her head, and her breathing sped up. "I like it. Not every woman can wear her hair shaved that low, but it looks terrific on you. It has that Amber Rose kinda look, just burgundy."

She smiled. "That's exactly the look I was going for."

"Only you're far prettier than she is," he added and winked.

She shivered at the raw sexuality in his voice.

Sage was the first to break eye contact; her gaze swept around the room and found it warm and inviting. The front area had a massive television and a very comfortable-looking over-stuffed black leather sofa. She took another swallow, then asked, "How did you end up in this house?"

Cser gave her a lazy smile. "It used to belong to my grandmother."

"*Grandmother*?" That gave her pause. "I thought you didn't have any family, and that's why you were in foster care."

Frowning, he replied, "I didn't have any *parents*. I never knew my father. My mother left me in the hospital and disappeared." He shrugged. "I had a grandmother who just wasn't in a position to take care of me, but that didn't stop her from bringing me to her house to visit two or three times a month." He beamed at the memories. "I used to love coming here."

"Was she one of those who baked cookies and read bedtime stories?" Her question caused Cser to explode with a peal of laughter.

"Not Laverne. Weekends were for gambling and fried chicken platters."

Her eyes widened. "You're kidding?"

Grinning, he stretched his legs out in front of him. "Nope. I spent the weekends selling dinners, popping caps off of beers, and making sure there were plenty of coins in the jukebox."

"This was a party house." She grinned wryly.

"Yep, pretty much. As well as a rooming house." Cser winked. "Do you now understand why I never officially lived with her?"

His charm was infectious. Sage grinned at him. "Loud and clear."

"Laverne drove around in a fancy Cadillac. Every year she bought a new fur coat, but she had no way of explaining how she earned her money."

Sage giggled and leaned back against the sofa, completely fascinated by the story. She had always loved history, and this story was one tale she could have heard again and again.

"This house was known as Mooney's and started during prohibition when alcohol was illegal. Grandma once told me her father refused to be a sharecropper. Instead, he made and sold moonshine. With the money he earned, he bought this house." His mouth curled into a smile of satisfaction.

"Interesting. When I heard you had moved out in the country, I thought maybe you just preferred to be secluded, but nothing like this."

"I do," he confirmed low and husky. "This is more space than I'd ever use, but the house has fond memories. When Laverne told me she would leave it to me, I thought she was joking until a lawyer showed up at her funeral with the deed. She passed away while I was serving in Iraq. One of her friends sent a Red Cross message over there to me. I've been living here ever since."

"Who watches the house when you're away?"

"Remy. But I have a cleaning lady. She knows I'm here for a holiday, so she'll be back after I'm gone."

The smile slipped slightly from Sage's lips. She wasn't ready yet to think about Cser leaving to return to the Middle East. She was just getting used to him being back at home. How do army wives do it? She wondered.

Sedona was once engaged to a seaman who died during an explosion onboard the ship. Sage had been there when

Sedona received the devastating news and watched as it had taken years for her sister to get over his death.

"I-I love hearing you talk about your grandmother," Sage said, teeth chattering again.

"That's enough for one evening." Cser sprung to his feet. "Come, let me show you upstairs so you can get out those wet clothes."

Sage sighed and rolled her eyes heavenward. "But I don't want to! Not yet."

"Later." Cser didn't even wait for her to stand. Instead, he lifted her over his shoulder and carried her up the flight of stairs to the landing above.

"I'm wet, not crippled," she grumbled when he lowered her to her feet.

He reached over and smacked her on the ass.

"Ow!" she winced.

"Be glad it wasn't my belt after the stunt you just pulled."

The idea of him spanking her caused her stomach to quiver.

With an arm draped across her shoulders, Cser led her down the narrow hallway. "You can use this bathroom. I have one at the other end."

Meaning she didn't have to worry about him walking in on her or having the pleasure of barging in on him.

"You can sleep in this room tonight." He pushed open a closed door. "There should be some clean t-shirts of mine in the closet." Sage stepped into the small room with faded wood flooring and dim lighting. There wasn't much in furnishings other than a full-sized bed covered in a handmade quilted bedspread and white lace curtains on the windows. On an oak end table was a small lamp with a ruffled lampshade. What kind of house was this for a bachelor? It was so old and cozy— like going to grandma's house.

"Towels are across the hall. You'll probably find a toothbrush and soap in the closet."

Probably? She wondered about the comment, but she yawned and found she was too tired to push. She stood there shivering, eyelids drooping. Goodness, the snow had worn her out.

"You need a shower and some rest. Go ahead and get out of those wet clothes. I'll toss them in the washing machine for you."

Her eyes widened. "Is that your sneaky way of seeing me naked?"

Cser frowned. "I plan on waiting out in the hall. You can throw your clothes out the door."

"Why waste time?" Sage said, and without preamble, she lifted the sweater up and over her head and tossed the wet fabric onto the floor. She noticed the way his appreciative eyes took in the sight of her in a black lace bra before his eyes shifted back toward the window.

"You're a piece of work," he muttered.

"So, I've been told." When she reached down for the zipper of her jeans, Cser quickly cleared his throat and left the room.

"I'll be downstairs."

She exploded with laughter.

After he was gone, she finished getting undressed, then disappeared and shut the door behind her. A few minutes later, she stood underneath the spray of hot water.

She still couldn't believe Cser had spotted her out in the storm and had come to her rescue. Talk about being someone's hero! He had looked like a member of an Alaskan search and rescue team coming out of nowhere with his large hand extended. Now she was in his house, taking a shower.

So, what's next?

Sage was still thinking about that when she made it back

to the bedroom wrapped in a large white bath towel. She reached for an old Lakers championship t-shirt that had seen better days but was at least clean. By the time she had slipped it over her head, she was eager to slide under the covers.

Moments later, Cser reappeared his arms behind his back. "Feel better?"

"Worn out." She could barely keep her eyes open and decided there was no point in fighting it.

"I figured as much." He reached down and scooped her clothes off the floor. "Get some rest. I'll come back and check on you later."

"Okay."

Cser smiled and held her gaze for what seemed an eternity before he walked over and lowered to press his lips to her forehead. Her stomach quivered. It wasn't the deep seductive kiss she'd received a few days ago, but she was so tired, it would just have to do for now.

Finally, he drew back and left the room. Sage rolled over onto her stomach and closed her eyes. She needed to wiggle her way into that man's heart, and that would require a clear head and some much-needed sleep. After that, she would put her plan into action.

Cser was seated on the sofa watching the ten o'clock news. He should have known the moment Sage confessed her feelings, a storm was brewing.

And what the hell of a storm it was.

He squeezed his eyes shut. Sage was going to be trouble. Rejecting her advances wasn't going to be enough. The stubborn woman had traveled out in lousy weather determined to get his attention.

She had his attention all right, in more ways than he cared to admit. Dammit. Just knowing she was lying upstairs in bed in nothing, but his t-shirt had him battling a hard-on for the last two hours. All he could think about now were those long legs of hers wrapped around his waist. He winced at the pressure of his zipper against his pride and joy. How the hell was he supposed to sleep across the hall from her, knowing she'd rather have him sharing her bed?

He took a long drink and released a heavy breath. She tempted him on so many levels that he wasn't sure how to deal with a woman like her. He wanted her, and her feeling the same way made it one of the most challenging decisions he'd ever have to make. Therefore, he'd rather not allow that temptation to have an opportunity to manifest.

One thing for sure, he needed her gone fast. The longer she was there, the larger his problem grew. But according to the weather reports, that wasn't going to happen anytime soon. Road closures. Dozens of accidents. Fifteen-inch accumulation forecasted. She wasn't going anywhere.

Of all the women in the world, he'd gotten snowed in with Sage. Where was the irony in that?

One thing he knew about Sage, she wasn't going to give up. He knew how relentless she could be when she set her mind to something. She had never been one to allow a man to control her actions, and that was not going to change. If he had any hope of resisting her, he would have to keep his distance and stay the hell away from her.

Cser sucked in a long breath as he stared at the television screen. He wasn't scared of her. He was more afraid of what he might do when the situation presented himself.

At the end of the day, he was still a man.

CHAPTER 5

Sage woke to stare out the window at the snow still falling heavily outside. Snowflakes were sticking to the window glass. How long had she been asleep? she wondered. Rolling over toward the nightstand to check the time, she remembered her cell phone was somewhere outside in the snow. The Android case wasn't waterproof, so the phone was now useless even if they did find it.

Thank goodness for the cloud.

As she lay there, a smile curled her lips with pleasant memories of Cser rescuing her from the snowstorm. Her hero! One more reason to love him. Goodness, she *did* have it bad.

Lying still, she listened for any sign of him stirring about in the house, but there was none. She decided he had probably already gone to bed. Sage blew out a long breath then rolled over onto her side. Was he ever going to make a move on his own? Probably not. Cser was a man of honor and integrity. Nope, she was going to have to continue her pursuit and take control of a perfect opportunity. Cser was willing to continue to deny his feelings for her for the sake of honor and friendship. *Screw friendship.* If Remy had a problem with her and Cser, then she would deal with him. She was tired of her brothers standing in the way of her happiness. First, there had been Rush with his determination to control the Beaumont Automotive Group and Remy's threats to Cser if he ever thought about getting close to her. If the weather outside was as bad as she suspected, she and Cser were stuck together until roads were cleared.

During that time, anything could happen.

Hearing the sound of running water, Sage smiled with delight and knew Cser was taking a shower.

It's now or never.

Sage slipped out of bed and padded across the hall. There were two other bedrooms: one looked preserved for his grandmother's return. As soon as she stepped into the other, it was apparent Cser was using the room. Male clothes hung over an oversized chair; his smell was all over the space. Cser had made the queen-sized bed with hospital corners, and along the wall, his shoes were neatly lined.

She walked across the cool wooden floor and took a seat on the edge of his bed. There was no time left to rethink her decision. Taking a deep breath, she lifted the t-shirt over her head and tossed it across the room. While she waited, she found herself resting her head on his pillow, engulfed in that familiar masculine scent.

"What the hell are you doing in here?"

The sound of his voice startled her. She hadn't heard the water stop or his bare feet padding down the hallway.

Sage swallowed and ignored the rage she saw blazing in his eyes. "I came to see you."

There was a long pregnant pause with his eyes on her naked body. No matter how much he tried not to look, there was no way he could avoid what was lying in front of him, sprawled out on his bed.

While she allowed him to get his fill, Sage did some looking of her own. She drooled at the gorgeous sight standing in the doorway with a bath towel wrapped loosely around his waist. Goodness, she was drooling! She had seen naked men before but never anyone with a body like his—hard and peanut-butter brown. The hair on his chest, narrowing to a silky line down his abdomen, disappeared underneath the towel. Droplets of water glistened and drew her gaze to a broad chest packed with muscles and perfect pectorals and forearms that made her throat go dry. She stared with fascination and awe. The man could grace the cover of *Military Man* magazine if there were such a thing.

"Get out of here," Cser commanded in a low chilling voice. He didn't move as if he didn't trust himself to come any closer.

"No. I'm not going anywhere."

"Sage, get out!" he barked. "Go put some clothes on."

Defiantly she shook her head. "I'm tired of you pretending you don't want to be with me when I know you do."

Cser dragged a shaky hand down his face, and every muscle of his torso seemed to flex with the movement. "Nothing good could ever come of us."

She gave a nervous laugh. "How do you know unless you give us a chance?" She shifted on the bed, sitting upright, and realized she had parted her thighs when she heard a slow intake of air. Cser's eyes dropped to the area between her legs.

"Sage, you have no idea what you're doing," he said, only his tone had dropped to a warning.

"I know exactly what I'm doing. I've waited for this moment for more than a decade, and I'm tired of waiting for you to notice me."

He cocked one eyebrow. "Notice you? How the hell could I miss you? he replied with exasperation.

"Then make love to me," she said with a nervous smirk.

His gaze raked up and down her body, and she saw the appreciation. "I don't have time for this foolishness. As soon as they clear the roads, I'm taking you home!"

She rose from the bed, her breasts bouncing with motion. "Fine, we can worry about that tomorrow. But tonight, is about you and me."

He didn't respond.

"Look at me, Cser," Sage said as if he could have missed her. The dark intensity in his eyes said he couldn't stop staring. "I know you want to. Look at what I'm offering you," she added with a sweep of her hands.

"I don't do virgins. And I don't do my best friend's virgin sister."

She sauntered toward him, swaying her hips, and noticed the surprise gleaming in his eyes.

"There's only one man I want," she cooed. "It has always been you. I'm not asking you to marry me. I'm just asking you to show me what it's like to be made love to by a man." She moved closer, her large breasts swinging with each step. Before she could reach him, Cser stuck out a hand, halting her advance.

"Sage, get the hell out my room, get dressed, and then we can talk. I don't have the patience for virgins tonight."

Her cheeks burned with rage. "I'm a grown-ass woman!"

"Who's behaving like a child," he scolded.

"I'm not a child!" she retorted. "I'm a woman with wants and needs. You know you want me, so why are you denying yourself?" She saw his eyes travel downward, taking in her firm stomach and tiny waist. "I know you want me, so take me. Please." She sounded almost as if she was pleading, but at that moment, she didn't care anymore. This might be her only chance, and she was going to seize the moment. If she came up empty-handed, at least she could walk away and know that she had given it one last chance.

Cser studied her. "Virgins need someone gentle and patient. I'm not that man. I love to fuck. Long, hard and rough. You think you can handle that?"

Desire coursed through her body, tightening her nipples. "I

want whatever you have to offer. All that matters is that I'm with you."

She moved forward and was relieved he didn't try to stop her from reaching out to touch his chest with the palm of her hand. He stiffened at the contact, and then she felt his body begin to relax. "I don't want you to be anything other than yourself," she whispered. "You don't scare me. I know you enough to know that you would never do anything intentionally to hurt me."

Lust blazed in his eyes. She started painting figure eights across his chest and then allowed her fingers to glide downward. While gazing up at him, she saw the hunger burning in his brown eyes. He wanted her. Cser wanted this. He could deny it all night long, but the truth was right there in front of him. "I'm tired of being a twenty-seven-year-old virgin, but if you don't want me ... I guess I'll just have to ask someone else to be my first."

"You wouldn't dare," he growled.

"Try me," she challenged.

She leaned forward until her mouth hovered within inches of his.

"Quit fighting it and kiss me."

"You think you're in charge?" he said, and his lips quirked.

"Always," she whispered, then brushed her mouth against his, drawing back, then touching his again. Finding minimal resistance, she pushed his lips apart and slipped her tongue inside. Cser sucked in a breath.

"Damn you," he swore and then circled her beneath his large arms and drew her closer.

Sage released a sigh of relief as he took control of the kiss that quickly became so intense it took her breath away. His mouth was warm and delicious. His lips were firm, and when he parted them, the warmth of his breath brushed over her. His tongue tasted her in long fluid strokes, and she forgot everything.

Cser brought his arms around to settle at her hips. She closed her eyes, enjoyed the moment, and felt his erection stir, nudging at her center before he jerked away.

"Look at me," he ordered.

His dark eyes looked serious and intense when they met hers.

"You better be sure about this because there's no undoing it," he emphasized by cupping her breast and squeezing, drawing a low gasp from her. There was no denying the glimmer of want blazing in his eyes. Everything she was feeling and wanting, she could see mirrored in his.

"I want you. That's all I've ever wanted. Now quit stalling and make love to me," she said again.

Cser led her backward until she tumbled over onto the bed. Slowly he unfastened the towel and allowed it to fall onto the floor at his feet. Her eyes immediately looked down at the clear indication of how badly he wanted her, pulsing against his inner thigh. At the size of his penis, there was only a second of panic before she pushed it away. He would never hurt her. That much, she was sure.

She looked up into his eyes, his pupils dilated with desire and exhaled as Cser moved onto the bed and lowered his rock-hard body over hers. It was finally happening. After all the years of lusting after him, it was finally happening!

Cser pushed her legs apart with his muscular thigh, then settled on top of her again. His mouth lowered, and again the kiss was hot and intense—first, her lips, then over to her cheek before moving to nuzzle her neck. Cser dipped lower and murmured something under his breath before biting down on her nipple, causing Sage to cry out ecstasy.

"This is what you wanted," he reminded her between nips

with his teeth. "This is the reason you came out in a blizzard." She whimpered and moaned as the moment of pain turned into pleasure. His wet tongue laved her flesh before he closed his lips and suckled her stiff nipple soothingly. He lavished one and then the other until she was squirming uncontrollably. Heat flowed through her body, arousing her in ways she wasn't used to feeling.

That went on for long moments before Sage felt his penis nudging against her damp folds. Even as her breath hitched, her body arched toward him. Cser released her long enough to lean over to the nightstand, reach inside, and she spotted the black foil packet in his hand.

"Let me do it," she insisted and took it from him. The surprised look on his face caused her lips to curl into a satisfied smile before she ripped it open with her teeth and removed the condom. Sliding up slightly on the bed, Sage reached down and slowly rolled it over his length. He was thick and hot under her hand as she stroked him.

"You sure you haven't done this before?" he managed to ask between gritted teeth.

"I guess you'll find out soon enough," she murmured and was pleased to see her touch affected him. His cock was gorgeous. Nothing like the ones she had seen in the movies or the magazines. It was thick, long, and strong, exactly what she expected from him.

"Slide down and spread your legs for me," he said in a voice that, even though soft, could command her to follow him to the ends of the earth if he'd asked her. "Open for me," he demanded, his voice husky and deep, sending delicious thrills down her spine.

Taking a deep breath, she did as he instructed and laid flat on her back, and then suddenly, she feared the unknown. Cser settled between her legs, probing at her opening with the tip of his penis until she felt the head sliding along her folds. His eyes were almost black now and heavy-lidded. He rubbed up and down, probing and teasing until she felt her body relax and her body was ready. Little by little, he pushed forward, preparing her to become one with him.

"This is going to hurt a little," Cser warned, and then before she could draw another breath, he plunged inside. Sage jerked and drew a sharp intake of breath at the burning sensation. Cser paused, drawing soft small kisses to her lips and throat before he started winding his hips slowly. As her body began to relax again, she started rocking her hips until he was deep inside of her.

Lifting his head, Cser looked down at her. "You good?" he asked and touched his mouth to hers.

Sage nodded and wiggled her hips. "I thought you didn't do gentle?" she teased even though tears pooled her eyes at his gentleness.

"You're right. I did say that."

Eyes locked, Cser drew back then thrust inside, causing her to arch off the bed. Then he pumped his hips, again and again, moving in a rhythm that had her melting beneath him.

"Don't stop," she gasped.

"I have no intentions," he muttered, and he caught her bottom lip between his teeth. "I told you once we started, there was no undoing."

"Oh, I remember," Sage whispered and brought her legs up around his waist. The pain had turned into pleasure like nothing she'd ever experienced before. The fire began to build within her, and she began rocking wildly against him. She was breathing as she had just run a race. Cser started to move at an uncontrollable speed, then he lifted onto one arm and brought his other hand between them to stroke her overly sensitized clit.

"Oh, God! Yes!" she cried out as he rode her harder.

"You like me fucking you?"

"Yes!" she cried out.

"That's it, bae. Come for me."

She lifted her hips, meeting the pumps of his powerful cock, the glorious sound of him penetrating her filled the room. Hard and fast, then slow and so intense he had her squirming wildly on the bed. "Now! Come now."

Sage screamed with her release, and when he plunged deeper, her eyes rolled closed. She could barely breathe at the overwhelming explosion that roared through her body.

He lowered his mouth to hers, kissing her long and hard until the last wave passed through her blood. Lifting her hips off the bed, Cser sunk even deeper.

Sage marveled at the sound of his moans, knowing it was because he was inside of her that was drawing those emotions. Cser pumped his hips until her legs were quivering. She felt his body tighten and his dick jerk before Cser released a loud howl that was music to her ears. For the longest time, they lay there breathing heavily. They were perfect for each other. If only he could see that. Cser was still deep inside of her, raining kisses down along her jaw and neck. She loved the way he felt on top of her as well as being inside her body.

Finally, he rolled over and drew her close in his arms. "You okay? I didn't hurt you, did I?"

"No, not at all." She had heard the stories about girls losing their virginity and nothing compared to what she had just experienced. Already she was ready for Cser to make love to her again.

Once their breathing resumed to normal, he rose and walked into the bathroom. She smiled at the sight of his perfect ass. He was sexy.

Cser returned with a washcloth in his hand. "Open your

legs."

Sage complied and laid there shyly as he cleaned her. The towel was warm and soothing, his strokes arousing.

He leaned in. "You need anything? Some water, maybe?"

His kindness had tears prickling at the backs of her eyes. "No, I'm good. Just tired."

With a nod, Cser disappeared and came back shortly, climbed back in bed, and pulled the covers up over their naked bodies.

She tilted her head, brushing his lips with hers, allowing the shyness that wasn't a part of her to fade away. She was a confident black woman who had always been comfortable in her skin. She was not about to change now. "I'm new to this, but what do people normally talk about after sex?"

Smiling, Cser pressed his lips softly to hers. "Nothing usually. Sleep."

"Sleep sounds good," Sage replied softly. "We can talk tomorrow."

"C'mere," he said gruffly and patted his chest.

Eagerly, she slid over and laid her head on him, loving the way Cser wrapped his arms around her, holding her as if she was the most important person in the world to him.

Tonight, she would sleep and enjoy the moment. She had plenty of time to worry about their future tomorrow.

CHAPTER 6

With a coffee mug in his hand, Cser walked across the galley-style kitchen and gazed out the window. Outside, snow covered the lawn. So far, fifteen inches of it had fallen upon the city in a record-breaking snowstorm, according to the morning news. He had planned to go out and shovel the driveway, but at the rate it was still coming down, it would be a waste of time. Instead, he was stuck inside, where it was nice and cozy with Sage.

His loins stirred to life as he thought about what had happened the night before. Lord knows, he'd tried to resist, but once he spotted her lush body lying across his bed, there was no way he could continue to deny what was destined to happen. Sage had been an erotic creature sauntering naked across his room, with her breasts jiggling, her eyes warm and inviting, begging him to take her.

And he had.

Cser took a sip of the espresso blend as he remembered her soft, hungry moans filling his ears and the way her eyes had gone all soft with pleasure as he sank inside her tight virgin pussy. She had felt so snug and warm his brain had almost shut down. He cursed under his breath as he was reminded, he hadn't been as gentle and he should have been, especially for her first time. But he'd warned her. Cser knew he wouldn't have been able to control the urge to be nestled deep inside of her. The moment he had, he felt like a crazy man knowing he was the first man to have ever made love to her.

And now, he felt an overwhelming urge to be the only one. Possessiveness filled his chest as he thought about the gift she had given him that she couldn't give anyone else. Now what? He didn't do commitments. He didn't need people caring or worried about him. He wasn't looking for a relationship, or was he? Cser blew out a long breath; he wasn't sure what he wanted anymore. It had been hard enough trying to stay away from her, but now that he knew what it felt like to become one with her, he wasn't so sure.

Now, what, burned at a depth of his brain. He knew the answer. As much as he tried to deny it, he knew. Now that he'd had her, there was no way he was going to be able to stop. And if he were honest with himself, he would admit he didn't want to. There was something about Sage that stirred him deep inside, woke him up as if he'd been in a deep sleep.

I was walking dead among the living.

She had been right again. It was time to accept the inevitable because there was no going back. In no way could he change what had happened between them. And he wanted more.

While Cser sipped from the mug, he decided he was no longer against the idea of them being friends with benefits. He didn't want Sage sexing anyone else. Just the thought sent jealousy possessive and red-hot storming through him. But if he put claims on her, it would be just sex. Or would it? Would he be able to guard his heart and keep the relationship strictly about sexual pleasures?

He pushed the thought aside. They were friends, and there was no reason why they couldn't maintain their current relationship, just with a few revisions. How hard could it be? They trusted each other, and sex was fantastic, so why not continue enjoying each other some more without putting any label on what they had other than friends? Cser groaned as he thought about the possibilities. He was semi-hard just thinking about introducing her to foreplay.

"Hey."

Whipping around, he drew in a long breath. He thought he'd never seen Sage look so beautiful, or maybe he was finally looking at her through a new pair of eyes. He loved the fuller curve at the bottom of her lip and how her large brown eyes became glossy every time she smiled. She was drowning in his white t-shirt, yet she managed to make the outfit look both adorable and sexy on her. Her feet were bare, her toes had French tips, and her legs were smooth, toasted brown, and miles long.

"Good morning, babe."

A smile turned her lips as she moved forward. Cser noticed her nipples and the outlines of her large, lush breasts through the thin material. The sight caused his mouth to salivate with memories of ravishing them last night with his hand, tongue, and mouth.

Leaning down, he kissed her briefly as he tried to keep his emotions intact, then turned away and pointed toward the coffee pot. "Would you like a cup?" Cser asked, trying to take his mind off her breasts.

"Yes, that would be great." She walked over to the small table, pulled out a chair, and plopped down on it.

Cser focused on pouring her a mug so he wouldn't think about making love to her again. Friends with benefits was a great idea, but something different was developing between them, which was dangerous for him.

"Here ya go." He lowered the mug in front of her and carried over the sugar and creamer before taking a seat.

"Thank you." She gave him a dreamy smile as she doctored up her mug.

He sipped and pressed his spine against the back of his

seat. Sage stirred her coffee, then leaned back, and again he saw her soft mounds through the thin t-shirt. His stomach clenched with vivid sexual images of her nipple in his mouth.

"It snowed all night."

Her eyes flicked toward the window. "I figured as much. It's a little chilly in here."

He did not attempt to disguise the direction of his eyes. "That might be because you don't have any clothes on."

She glanced at him over the rim of her mug. Those wicked looks made his groin tighten. "I'm not complaining," she said flirtatiously.

Neither was he.

Smothering a wide yawn, she said softly, "I guess this means I'm stuck here for at least another day."

He winked. "Yep, it looks that way."

"What are we possibly going to do with all that time on our hands?" she asked with a false Southern drawl that caused him to chuckle.

She was baiting him and doing a good job so far. He wanted to strip her naked, lift her onto the table before sliding down his pajama pants, and seated himself deep inside her. However, if he gave in to his sexual urges, it would feel as if they were building a relationship, and that wasn't the case, even though it might seem like he wanted to do just that.

"I've got some bills to pay online and plenty of other things to do."

With a sultry gaze, she brought the mug to her lips. "You know what they say about all work and no play."

"What do you suggest?" he asked as he, too, took a sip.

Sage's brow lifted, and he knew she was considering a few ideas. "You have a Christmas tree in your living room with no decorations."

"That's because your mother insisted Remy bring one

over."

Sage wagged her head knowingly. "That sounds like my mom," she said and arched a curious brow. "Do you have any decorations?"

"Yep," came his sheepish response. "She sent over a box as well."

Her eyes lit up and got all glossy again. "Well, then it sounds like we've got work to do. That is, after breakfast. What do you have to eat in this place?"

"Cheerios," he announced.

Sage laughed. "Then Cheerios it is."

She had to remind herself that this man hadn't offered her any more than he had last night. But it wasn't easy. Cser stood in front of the refrigerator looking like a temptation in a blue t-shirt and flannel pajama bottoms that hung low on his hips as he retrieved the box of cereal from on top. Who would have known being snowed in together would give her what she had been hoping? Thank you, Lawd! She'd shout it at the top of the mountain if she could. She had finally gotten what she wanted, even though in her heart, she knew it would never be enough. But for now, while stranded at his home, she was going to enjoy the moment.

Cser swung around, shaking the box. "There's still half a box and plenty of milk. I eat cereal at least twice a day."

She laughed. "Sounds like my house."

"You still don't cook?" he asked, with his dark eyes smoldering in a way that rattled her to the core.

"Uh-uh, I don't have time for that."

Cser's sensual mouth twisted in a lazy grin. "I guess not since you're too busy trying to take over the world."

Playfully, Sage stuck out her tongue. "Nope. Just the Beaumont Automotive Group. I don't understand my dad. I'm the best he's got."

He nodded. "I agree. You got mad skills."

She smiled. "Thank you. That makes me feel good."

Cser walked over to the cabinet and removed two bowls as he said, "I think your brothers notice a lot more about you than you think."

"I can't tell," she replied with a rude snort.

"Of course not. You're their younger sister. They don't want you to know they're watching."

With a smile, she thought about what he said as she looked around the room. The kitchen was nice and looked recently renovated with stainless steel appliances, granite countertops, and a small butcher-block island. Cser had a point. Maybe her brothers were watching her professional career. After all, they made her personal life their business, so why not her job.

When Cser returned to the table, Sage noticed the troubled look that had fallen across his face. "What's wrong?" she asked quizzically.

"We've gotta talk."

Oh boy. Here we go. There was no way she would let him say, 'thanks for the ride, but I don't know if we can do that again. "No, Cser, there's no need," she blurted, breaking the awkward silence. "I wanted last night to happen. Thank you. But I'm not asking for anything more." She lied.

He frowned, and Sage was surprised to hear him say, "What if I want more?"

Her heart started pounding. "What?"

Cser gave a slow smile. "What about friends with benefits?"

She felt as though she'd been showered with cold water. For a second, she'd thought he was going to say something else. She should have known better. "Sure, why not? Friends with benefits. I can handle that." When it came to him, she was willing to take whatever she could get to have him in her life. Was that pathetic or what?

Cser looked so serious. "I don't want to lose that. I can no longer call you my sister, but I don't want to lose my friend by complicating things."

In other words, don't get clingy. *Got it.* She understood loud and clear. Although deep in her heart, she knew if she ever saw him with another woman, it would crush her and end whatever this was he wanted to label as friendship. When the day came that Cser chose another woman, their relationship would end. She hated it, but there could be no other way.

While reaching for the box of cereal, Sage forced a lighthearted tone. "No problem. I'm not looking for forever either. But you have to promise me one thing."

He hesitated before saying, "Okay, what?"

"You won't tell Remy," Sage said in a rush.

"Whoa! I can't—"

"No, you have to," she interrupted. "I don't want him ruining this. He'll make more of it than it really is, and he definitely won't understand."

Nodding, Cser blew out a breath. "I can't argue that."

"Then you agree?"

"Okay," he agreed, low and husky.

It would be their little secret.

After breakfast, Sage headed into the bathroom for a shower. Cser had washed her clothes, and she was anxious to put them back on so they could begin decorating the tree. Christmas had always been a special time for her, and decorating the house was one of her favorites. Even as adults, she and her siblings still went to her parents the day after Thanksgiving to help decorate their family home.

As soon as she stepped inside the shower, she drew out a long breath and exhaled. She felt more alive than she had in months. Maybe rest and good company were just what she had needed to alleviate some of the day-to-day stress. Or maybe Cser just had that kind of effect on her.

Reaching for her washcloth, Sage lathered it with soap then slid it across all the areas of her body Cser had paid close attention. She was sore but in a good way.

While Sage allowed the spray of the water to run down her face, she sighed, frustrated with herself and the direction of their relationship. She was spending way too much time thinking about him.

Friends with benefits.

If that's the way he wanted it, then so be it. However, she was going to make sure she was a friend like no other. As she lathered the cloth, Sage gave a rude snort. She wanted more, but if Cser thought she would start acting clingy, he better think again. She had way too much going for her to beg a man to be with her. If they were going to be together, it would be up to Cser to decide. In the meantime, she would continue to put something on his mind while they had fun and enjoyed the ride.

Hearing movement, she opened her eyes to find Cser stepping into the shower. "What are you doing?"

"What does it look like I'm doing? Saving water," he replied with a teasing smile.

Her eyes lowered along the contours of his sculptured body until they landed on his magnificent penis. He was hard and demanding her attention. Oh, she noticed. "Saving water, huh? That sounds like a wonderful idea," she purred.

He shut the door and stepped close until her nipples

brushed his chest. Instantly, Sage felt herself arching toward him.

Dipping his head, Cser feathered his lips across hers, and she tasted the fresh minty taste of mouthwash before his lips were at her breasts, sucking and licking. "You have the most amazing breasts."

At the intensity of his touch, she leaned in closer to his lips. "I'm glad you like them."

His hands came up to hold the curves of her hips before sliding around to squeeze her ass. The entire time his lips continued to nip and tease. This was heaven or at least something considerably close. His tongue swirled around her, licking and suckling some more.

"Delicious," Cser moaned and latched on hungrily to the other nipple before slowing down to tease her again.

"It's my turn. I wanna taste," Sage crooned close to his ear. Her hand slid between them. She fingered his erection, loving the way Cser flinched on contact.

"You keep playing with him; I'm gonna have to put him somewhere," he warned as he released her breast.

"That's the plan unless you object to me giving you a little TLC?" she asked, although she could feel him surging beneath her fingers.

He hissed. "Hell yeah! I have no problems with that."

"I'm so glad you agree. So, tell me, Captain Grant, how you like it?" she asked as her fingers squeezed, then loosened and tightened again.

Cser tensed with pleasure. "Anyway, you're willing to give it to me."

"I was thinking of first taking it slow," Sage explained as she fisted him with her fingers, then slid up high to the base before sliding down to the end. The entire time her thumb was caressing the head.

"Oh yeah ... that's what I like," he moaned as he settled one hand on her hair, caressing, encouraging her.

"I could also do this fast," she said and started stroking him at a frantic rhythm.

"Sheesh! Do whatever you want." She was aware of his accelerated breathing. "Just as long as you don't stop."

"That's one thing you do not have to worry about."

Sage closed her fist around him, then moved up and down, around and around.

She could hear gurgling sounds coming from Cser's throat. He had one hand braced on the shower wall. The other, he placed on her shoulder. His hips were rocking back and forth, matching her rhythm. Sage grinned, loving the power she had over him. She was inexperienced, and yet she could make Cser lose control; foreplay felt so natural.

Sage lowered onto her knees and did what she'd always wanted to do. Cser watched as she swirled around the tip using her tongue.

A string of curse words escaped his mouth, and that was all the encouragement she needed. Sage took him between her lips before drawing back and doing it all over again.

"How the hell did you learn to do that?" Cser sputtered between breaths. "Never mind. I don't want to know."

Sage giggled around his length then began deep throating him again. She would never tell, but she had spent years practicing with a cucumber. It was an experiment she and one of her college roommates had done when Sage thought she was finally going to get with this guy she'd liked. But he'd showed his true colors just in time for her to make the decision. She wasn't giving it up until either Cser gave in to his feelings or she fell in love with someone else. Falling in love was hard to do when your heart already belonged to someone else.

Sage massaged his balls and tightened her fingers around

his girth, then concentrated as she just sucked the head while her hand did all of the work.

By that time, Cser was sputtering and rocking his hips. "Take me deeper into your mouth," he urged, pushing softly at her head, and she drew in more of his length. "Now suck," he growled. "That's it, bae, suck me ... just like that."

His voice hitched, and the ridged feel of him beneath her fingers were signs that he was close. Sure enough, the moment she began to massage his balls again, Cser gripped her so close she could barely draw a breath. She felt the spasms of his erection and then the taste of his release inside her mouth. Cser loosened his hold, and she bobbed her head, pleasuring him until the last drop.

"What am I going to do with you?" Cser groaned.

Sage had a few ideas, but she had a feeling he wasn't quite ready to hear her answer yet.

CHAPTER 7

They set up the tree in the living room near the fireplace, then looked inside the box of ornaments that Mrs. Beaumont had insisted Remy bring over to the house. The sweet woman had planned to have the tree already decorated before Cser's return from Afghanistan, but since he had started his leave early, he had put a halt to that idea.

Cser could care less about a tree, but he knew it meant a lot to Sage. She came from a large family who celebrated Christmas with all of the bells and whistles, and he did not want to disappoint.

Most years, he didn't even bother decorating the windows with lights, let alone buying a tree, unless he was dating someone seriously. He scowled at the memory. That had been a long time ago. With him deploying all the time, women just didn't stick around. And after a while, he'd decided it had all been for the best.

After strung the tree with blinking lights, Cser attached the hooks to the glass balls while Sage determined ornament placement. Rocking back on his heels, he watched in fascination as she took her time deciding where to hang each of the white and blue balls, felt snowflakes, and the ceramic snowmen. It took over an hour, but it was worth every moment to see the childlike smile on her face.

"You ready?" he asked.

Sage nodded eagerly.

Cser stuck the plug into the wall outlet and grinned at the

festive sight. Even in the middle of the day, the tree lights managed to brighten up the room.

"It looks great!"

Cser had to agree. "You did a fabulous job."

"I did, didn't I?" She was beaming like a little girl on Christmas morning.

"It's going to look even better after dark." He was already thinking of the night ahead with another fire crackling and mugs of hot chocolate with marshmallows.

Where the hell did that come from?

A frown suddenly marred her beautiful face. "I wish I had my camera so I could take pictures."

Cser reached inside the back pocket of his jeans and removed his cell phone. "You're more than welcome to use my phone."

As she contemplated, he watched Sage nibble on her bottom lip while deep in thought and had to resist the urge to draw her close for another delicious kiss. He remembered the way she'd taken him in her mouth. The way she had sucked him with little instruction. Had she done that to another man? Cser's chest stung with jealousy. He did not want to share her, but he had no right to expect that of her.

"I could, but the fun is in posting on social media and sharing with my friends. In this case, I can't do that. Otherwise, everyone will know."

He knew how much she loved sharing, especially during the holidays. Cser remembered all of the photographs she had mailed to him over the years while deployed, capturing candid moments. It always made him feel good knowing even when he was far away, there was someone who cared.

A chilly realization snaked his spine.

She'd always cared.

One problem with getting involved was that he didn't want

anyone to care about him or his welfare, yet someone already did.

What freaked him out was he wanted her to care. He wanted her thinking about him, sending him letters and care packages overseas that as soon as he saw her personalized purple stationery, his heart somersaulted. She was important to him, more than he cared to admit. He didn't want to care about anyone and, yet he wanted her to care about him.

Damn, was he really that selfish?

"Earth to Cser," he heard Sage say, breaking into his reverie.

He blinked and focused on her curious expression. "Sorry. I was thinking about something." He slung his arm over her shoulders, loving the feel of her soft and curvy, beside him.

"Did you have Christmas trees growing up?" she asked while they watched the lights blinking.

"Nope, not really, which is why this one is super special." He pressed a kiss to her temple.

With his cell phone, Cser took a few pictures. The tree, Sage, and then the two of them together. He wrapped his arm around her waist, and Sage rested her head on his chest as he extended his arms out as far as he could to capture the shot.

"This is one of those days when I wished I had my selfie stick," she said, laughing as they squeezed in tight to take photos at awkward angles.

"What are you, Kim Kardashian?" he teased, then snapped several shots of them making funny faces. The last was with her pressing her warm lips to his cheek, heating his loins to scorching levels.

"Oooh! Let's take a few of the snow," Sage suggested. She had him so caught up in the excitement. He headed over toward the large picture window where he snapped shots of the tires on his vehicle buried underneath the snow.

"This has been fun," she began. "But I can think of something that would top the charts this Christmas holiday."

"What's that?" he asked as he lowered the phone. Her eyes were beaming with excitement.

"Let's make a snowman!"

"Sage."

She stuck the twig into the face of the snowman, then turned to look over at Cser. The second their eyes locked, her lower jaw dropped. He was holding a handful of snow.

"What are you planning to do with that?"

She found out soon enough when he tossed the snowball at her head. She screamed while icy snow ran down her cheek and slipped inside her coat.

"Oh, you are in trouble now!" Quickly, she scooped up a handful of snow and ran after him. Cser was fast, but Sage got close enough to hit him smack in the back of his head. After that, it was a full-fledged snowball fight. Snow was tossed in every direction, and she was having the time of her life. Cser dodged behind his snow-covered truck while Sage gathered enough in her glove-covered hands to pack a fastball. When he looked up, she pelleted him square in the face.

"Gotcha!" she screamed.

Shock widened his eyes before he started after her. Rushing away, Sage stopped to scoop up more snow. Two snowballs hit her in the back and the other at the center of her head.

He wanted to play, and then the fight was on.

She went after Cser and successfully tagged him with a ball to the side of his head. Before he could recover, she hit him with another.

Sage laughed aloud. "You forget I have five brothers! Donie and I learned big time how to defend ourselves against those rascals."

He made a dash toward her with a big block he'd scooped off the hood of his truck. In a panic, she took off, running across the lawn.

"Don't you dare!" she screamed, but Cser had no mercy. He closed in on her, then landed the pile over her head. The icy mess was all over her hat and running down her cheeks and coat.

Laughing, Sage launched a series of balls in his direction, but the decorated officer quickly closed in on her again. She turned, and with a snowball, she held her hands up in surrender. "I give up." She conceded and batted her eyelashes.

"About time." He laughed and dropped the snow from his hand. As soon as he lowered his arm, Sage hit him smack in the face and exploded with laughter. His eyes widened with shock.

"Oh, so you wanna play dirty."

Cser rushed, grabbed her in his arms, and knocked them both to the ground. Still laughing, Sage rolled onto her back and stared up at the sky. The day couldn't have been any more perfect.

Cser made lunch, which ended up being peanut butter and jelly sandwiches, and afterward, they played a round of Scrabble that Sage ended up winning.

They curled on the sofa and watched the new Jason Bourne movie. She had forgotten how much they loved the same films and especially the sci-fi channel.

As she leaned beside him on the sofa and breathed in his masculine scent, heat spiraled at her gut. She was amazed at the way her body always responded to his presence.

Closing her eyes, she savored the moment, lying back against his powerful body. He kissed her temple, and then Cser dragged her on top of him.

"I need to kiss you," he said huskily.

She opened her mouth to say something flirtatious and sassy when his lips captured hers. The taste was exquisite, soft, and devilishly talented as his tongue moved with precise expertise inside her mouth.

Desire burned deep in her stomach as the insatiable kiss continued. Cser nibbled at her mouth, cheeks, and neck before returning to her lips again. Gently, his hands stroked her back and shoulders, then dipped to squeeze her ass.

"You're addictive," Cser murmured. His words made her heart soar, but Sage knew better than to read more into his comment than was meant to be.

Rising, he stood from the sofa, cradled her in his arms, and carried her up to his bedroom. Once there, Cser lowered Sage slowly to her feet. She slipped the sweater over her head and unclasped her bra while his eyes shifted down to her breasts, his breathing irregular.

Instinctively, Sage raised her arms to cross them, but Cser caught her wrists in his hands.

"I never took you as shy," he said gently.

"I'm not shy. I'm cold," she lied with a snort. "Can we hurry this up and get naked under the covers?" Her response caused him to chuckle.

"Not yet. I'm not done looking at you." His eyes perused her length. "Do you have any idea how beautiful you are?"

"I do now," she replied and smiled.

With feelings of empowerment, she slid the jeans down over her hips, followed by her panties that she kicked away while doing a little striptease. The entire time his eyes were feasting on her.

"You like?" she cooed.

"*Like* is an understatement."

She grinned and was pleased to see the lustful expression in his eyes.

For the longest time, Cser hesitated, staring down at her large breasts, trying to conceal his hunger. "Oh yeah, I like everything I see."

"Well ... then why don't you join me?"

Sage leaped onto the bed and slipped beneath the covers. Grinning, Cser stripped away his clothes then joined her, rolling beside her.

After one quick sensual kiss, he lowered his head, drew one nipple in between his lips, and Sage gasped on contact. She forgot about the world waiting for her or the people who were probably looking for her. All that mattered was what was happening right at that exact moment. She loved the way it felt to be loved by a man in such an intimate way. Cser made her feel wild, wicked and with each stroke, her breathing became increasingly unsteady.

"You want me to stop?" his voice was husky.

Sage shook her head, mutely, her body, a ball of fire, heated by desire. "Don't you even think about it," she whispered.

With a smirk, he lowered his mouth to her breasts again and tortured her with his confident assault. She squirmed beneath him. Cser suckled one; his fingers tortured the other before sliding down to explore her apex. She barely had time to catch her breath before he followed the downward path with his tongue and pushed her thighs apart.

"Cser!" she cried out in astonishment when she felt his mouth licking and stroking her intimately.

"I intend to kiss every part of your body."

"Cser, please ..." she cried out at the sensational feel of his lips. She never knew it could feel like this. Nor had she known, being intimate with him could be so intense.

He used his mouth until she exploded, cried out his name, and her legs quivered. Before her breathing slowed, he lifted his head and covered her body with his. She couldn't believe what she'd just let him do.

Staring into his eyes, she saw something unsaid that mirrored the confusion she had once felt. Now she wasn't embarrassed or confused. She knew what she was doing, and there was no one she'd rather be doing it with. She hoped in time he'd come to the same realization—you can't fight the inevitable.

"You're mine," Cser growled softly; his chocolate eyes stared at her as he used his fingers where his lips had explored. "By the time I'm done with you, there won't be one area I haven't touched." Her pussy was throbbing, ready for what only he could give.

"Baby," she moaned and stared at him. Her body was totally outside of her control.

"I need to be inside you," he purred huskily. Taking her hand, he guided Sage towards his length, encouraging her to touch him. Her fingers stroked him gently, and she barely had enough time to savor the feel of him before Cser was positioning himself between her legs. She stared up at him with slow breaths as she waited for him to be inside of her again. The tension between them had built to such a mind-boggling level she was more than ready for what was next.

"I'll try and take it slow, but I'm so turned on I can't guarantee how long this is going to last," he growled softly. Words were unnecessary; her body wanted—correction—she needed him. Hard and fast. Going slow would be much too unbearable.

Cser pushed forward, and Sage's toes curled at the impact

of his penetration, stretching her farther than she'd remembered. Pausing, he lifted his head and stared down at her, his eyes aroused with passion. Reaching down, he lifted her hips off the bed and thrust forward until he was deeply seated.

She released a long breath, and then he was moving. Her body quickly responded as if they had been making love together for years. All thoughts evaporated from her mind, and the only thing she focused on was rocking her hips to meet the rhythm of Cser's strokes. The sensation built fast, and she felt herself spiraling to new levels.

"Cser!" Sage cried and continued moving with him in a frantic attempt for the release that hinted at being seconds away.

His thrusts were hard and fast, and he sent them both soaring toward ecstasy until finally, she felt her body tense and then explode. The orgasm was so hard and intense, she screamed and raked her nails along his back and shoulders. Cser continued his powerful thrusts until his body stilled. A loud hiss slipped from his lips and heated her ear as he spilled inside.

Long after, he held her safely in his arms. Sage nuzzled close as she sighed with pleasure, loving the feel of his powerful body beside hers. This was how she had always dreamed it could be between them. Too bad it was only temporary.

CHAPTER 8

Sage woke up to the sunshine beaming through the window the following day and Cser already out of bed. That man was up before the cows, she thought, grinning to herself. After years in the military, he was used to waking up early and heading to the gym before reporting to the unit. While in Afghanistan, his day had begun even earlier.

Shifting on the bed, she moaned at the soreness between her legs, but in no way was she complaining. Cser had made love to her most of the night in slow, deep thrusts. His stamina was out of this world. By the time she'd finally drifted off to sleep, Sage had been both mentally and physically exhausted but sexually satisfied. She giggled. Who knew sex could be so good between them? Sex required chemistry, and Cser was the only man with who she'd ever felt a connection.

After an insatiable night, she lay wrapped in his big strong arms. Each moment together fueled her deepening love for him.

Rolling over onto her back, Sage groaned. How could she not love him? Cser was caring, compassionate, funny, and so damned gorgeous. With a single touch, he had her melting and her nerves in a tailspin.

Hearing the television, Sage disappeared into the shower. Afterward, she slipped into a red t-shirt she'd found slung over the arm of a chair in the bedroom. She made it down the stairs, greeted by the smell of coffee. Cser was lounging on the sofa, watching the morning news.

"Hey."

"Good morning, beautiful." A look of intense male satisfaction was on his handsome face as Cser patted the space beside him on the sofa. Sage flopped beside him, and he planted a kiss on her cheek. "Looks like they've started to clear the main roads."

"Oh, good. I probably need to call my family," she replied half-heartedly. She was in no rush. She wished the snow would start falling again. Another twelve inches would be nice. Cser had made it clear he wasn't looking for a commitment, but that didn't change the way she felt. The more time she had him all to herself, the better chance she had of eventually winning over his heart.

"You want some coffee?" he asked, looking at her through wickedly thick eyelashes.

Sage grinned. "Yes, please."

Before standing, he leaned in for another delicious kiss. His tongue explored with skills so intimate, she was whimpering with disappointment when he finally drew away.

Cser winked. "I also have Pop-Tarts."

"A man after my own heart," she replied while she watched him walk into the kitchen. "Can I use your computer today? I would like to get an email out to my staff," she called into the other room.

"Sure, of course," she heard him say.

Smiling, she settled on the sofa, curling her feet beneath her. *I could get so used to this.*

Cser returned, carrying a cup of coffee. "I stuck your Pop-Tarts in the toaster."

"Just the way I like them." Sage took the mug from him and took a cautious sip. It was hot and doctored just the way she liked it.

His dark eyes, lazily amused, slid down her long legs. "Let me go get that laptop for you."

"Cser?"

"Yeah?" He swung around.

"I'm curious about something," she began, drawing a leg up against her chest. "Have you ever thought about finding your mother?"

Humor slid over his face. "You can't find someone who isn't lost."

Her brow bunched. "What?"

Cser gave a humorless smile. "My mother, who prefers to be called Denise, isn't lost. She just not interested in being my mother."

"You mean you know where your mother is?" Sage whispered; her eyes fixed on his face.

"No, but it wouldn't be hard to find her." Something flickered in those dark eyes before he looked away and concentrated on the television. "She was always around." Cser lowered onto the arm of the sofa as he explained. "A lot of those weekends I spent here, she would pop up and walk right past me as if she didn't even know I existed. And then there were the days when she would kiss my cheek and give me a dollar. She never wanted to be a mother, and she never was." He shrugged. "After a while, I got used to it and accepted that was just the way she was."

"Wow!" Sage didn't even know how to respond to that. She studied his face for some element of emotion. There was none. Instead, she noticed the heavy stubble along his jaw.

"I think she did me a favor."

Her eyes whipped up to meet his. "Why would you say that?"

Cser winced and rubbed a hand across his jaw. "I think I would have been more fucked up in the head with her than I was growing up living with strangers." With that said, he leaned over the sofa and kissed her swiftly before rising to his feet. "I'll be back." As he left and went up to the bedroom, Sage stared after him.

She didn't care what he said, his relationship with his mother bothered him. As she waited for him to return, she decided that maybe Denise was the reason why it was so hard for him to commit. Fear of heartbreak, again.

The doorbell rang.

"Can you get that?" Cser called from upstairs.

Sage rose from the sofa and padded over to the door, and without giving it any thought, swung it open. Her heart plummeted as soon as she spied the man standing on the porch.

It was Remy.

"Sage?" He looked confused before his eyes took in her standing there in nothing but a t-shirt. Her legs and feet were bare. "What the hell is going on here? We've been calling all over the place looking for you!" Lowering the hood from his head, he brushed past her and stepped into the house before she could even find the words to speak.

Cser emerged from upstairs so abruptly; she couldn't even prepare him for Remy's unexpected visit.

"Hopefully, the internet is working. I haven't been able to get a signal all morning." The moment Cser spotted him, his handsome face paled, and the smile fell from his lips. "Remy, what are you doing?"

"Are you fucking sleeping with my sister?"

Cser didn't answer fast enough because a hard fist landed at his left jaw. He stumbled back, recovered, and lunged forward, but Sage jumped between them.

"No, stop!" she exclaimed.

Cser caressed his jaw. "Bruh, I'll give you that one because

I'm sure this comes as a shock to you. But if you try that shit again, I swear your sister will not be able to stop me from coming after you." She saw the lethal look in Cser's eyes and knew he meant every word.

Ignoring his comment, Remy spat, "I'm still waiting for an answer. Are you screwing my sister?" When he made another menacing step forward, Sage pushed against his chest.

"Stop it! Stop it!"

She wasn't aware she was screaming until she saw Remy's shocked expression. "What are you doing here with him?" he asked in an eerie calm voice that was lethal.

"That's none of your business." Sage blustered.

He blinked. "You're my sister, so anything to do with you is my business."

Some of the anger and surprise had left Cser's eyes as he said, "Look, Remy, I didn't want you to find out this way."

"Find out what? You're sleeping with my sister!" he barked.

"It's not like that," Cser replied in a low voice.

Sage chimed in. "He's right. It's not. We're both grown. This was a mutual decision that— "

Remy lifted a hand to silence her. "Do you hear yourself?"

"Of course. Cser didn't make me do anything I didn't want to do." She looked adoringly up at Cser, who held out his arms. She took a step toward him, and he cradled her to his body.

"Remy, I care about Sage."

Her brother looked coldly from one to the other with rage. "I told you not my sisters, and I meant that."

His eyes shifted to Sage. "When he breaks your heart, don't come running to me," he warned her.

"Why are you even here?" she retorted with a slender hand at her waist.

Remy was glaring at Cser as he spoke. "I came to tell you the main roads were clear."

The tense silence of the room was so thick.

Sage pressed her hand to Remy's forearm, pushing him toward the door. "Let me walk you out," she said, putting an end to the tension.

Remy turned and, without saying another word, bolted out the front door. It wasn't until he departed that she drew a normal breath. They had just dodged an explosion. Quickly, Sage went to retrieve her coat from the hall closet. As she hurried back into the living room, she found Cser still standing in the same place.

"I don't need you fighting my battles for me. Let me go talk to him," he insisted.

She shook her head. "Hell no! You need to let him cool off first," she explained as she slid her arms into her coat and ignored the stubborn set to his jaw. With those two hotheads, the next eruption she might not be able to contain. "Let me go talk to him before he leaves." She pressed a reassuring hand to his arm, then slipped her feet inside her boots that were by the front door.

Sage stepped outside. Snow flurries were drifting in the air. The worst of it was over. At least, she hoped. And she wasn't referring to the weather.

Pulling her collar up over her ears, she made her way across the snow-covered yard. Remy had his Range Rover running at the end of the driveway. She climbed in, glad it was warm inside, and shut the door. Neither of them spoke right away. She stole glances at the stony profile, his tense body language telling her he was still angry.

"Why him?"

"I love him," she confessed. "I've loved him since I was fifteen."

Remy turned on the seat at her confession and looked at her, eyes wide with disbelief. "He's like a brother to me."

Sage closed her eyes and let out a long breath. "Maybe to you, but I don't see him that way. I see a man I want to spend the rest of my life with."

His voice sounded rough. "You should have told me. As a matter of fact, Cser should have said something to me."

"How could he when he has a hard enough time being honest with himself?" She blew out a long breath before continuing. "Cser's been trying to deny his feelings for me because he didn't want to jeopardize your friendship."

"Too late for that." A solitary muscle ticked at his jaw. Remy had this pained look on his face as he'd just lost his best friend. It didn't have to be that way.

"I'm the one who persuaded him," Sage insisted.

"You?" he said inquisitively.

She nodded with a playful grin. "I don't know if you've noticed, but I'm simply irresistible."

"You're reaching," he warned.

"Oh, please! Get over yourself." Leaning over, she snatched the knit cap from his head. "This isn't about you." Sage combed her fingers through his hair the way she loved to do. "I've been playing Suzy badass for years, pretending I was somebody I wasn't, but with Cser, I'm not like that. I get to be myself."

Remy finally blew out a long breath. "How does he feel about you?"

That was a good question. One that she hoped to have an answer to soon. "He cares about me," she said, repeating what Cser had confessed in his living room. It was a start. Now, if only she could get him to fall in love with her.

"Is that going to be enough for you?" Remy asked as if he'd read her thoughts.

He wanted her to say something, she sensed it in his voice, but she couldn't do it. If she allowed herself to think about their time that would soon end, she would cry. "Would it be enough for you?"

"Whoa!" Remy drew back. "You know I don't do relationships."

"Well, you should! It's a wonderful feeling." Better than anything she had ever imagined.

He shifted his eyebrow. "No thanks. And quit changing the subject. We're talking about you and Cser. And you better believe I'm telling the rest of the force, and we're gonna have a family vote."

His comment irritated her. Remy sounded so much like a spoiled brat when he couldn't get his way. "You can vote all you want. I know who my heart belongs to."

He'd fucked up.

The last thing he wanted was for Remy to show up and find his sister with him. He should have known. Once the phones were down, his best friend was going to be concerned. Dammit, he scolded. Now he was going to have to find a way to fix it. But no matter what the outcome, he had no regrets about him and Sage.

Now that she had shared her body and his bed inside his house, there was no way they could go back, and he wasn't sure if he wanted to.

There was no denying the intimacy they'd shared had unlocked something inside of him that he'd kept buried all those years—fear of rejections. Fear of loving someone and leaving, and yes, the one emotion he'd never hoped to admit, insecurity. It came with giving your all and trusting somebody. Sage had changed all that. Now he could think of nothing more than being with her, but deep in his heart, he knew he could never give her what she deserved—commitment. His career was dark and dangerous; lives are lost all the time. Families were torn apart. He just couldn't do that to her.

Cser heard the sound of hurried feet running onto the front porch, and then Sage burst into the house, breathing heavily with that amazing grin on her face.

"Is he gone?"

She nodded, and he felt a hint of disappointment. He had been hoping to talk to him now and get the animosity out the way.

"Yeah, he's pissed, but he'll get over it. Just give him some time." She shrugged out of her coat and slid her feet from the boots.

"C'mere." Cser reached for her hand, fell back onto the sofa, and took her down onto his lap. Her beautiful, amber-colored eyes stared at him trustingly. "That was not at all how I wanted him to find out."

Sage nodded. "I know that, and neither did I. But there's nothing we can do about that now." Her eyes widened with alarm. "Look at your jaw! Does it hurt?" She touched it gingerly.

"Not as much as my pride. Nothing worse than getting sucker-punched in front of your girl."

Light rose to her eyes. "So, I'm your girl now?" Sage asked and grinned.

His eyes searched hers. "You gave me the greatest gift a man could ever get for Christmas."

"Christmas isn't until Sunday." She smothered a laugh.

"Well, then call it the best *early* Christmas gift."

She had a playful smile on her lips. "I can't seem to recall what it was I gave you."

His brow rose. "Do I need to refresh your memory?"

When her eyes sparkled with mischief, Cser scooped Sage into his arms and smothered her with a long sensual kiss.

Hours later, they lay on the floor in front of the fireplace wrapped in a large wool blanket, the military issued.

"I was thinking that maybe for New Year, we could go to Sheraton Beach."

Damn, dread filled him.

"My cousin Jabarie and his wife Brenna are having a big party." Cser assumed Sage mistook the look on his face as confusion because she added, "You met them at Rance's wedding."

"The one with all the kids?"

She laughed. "Yep, that's them, and guess what? They have baby number six on the way. Brenna announced it during Thanksgiving." Sage shook her head. "I don't know how they do it, but Jabarie wants another boy, so they keep trying."

As he studied her, Cser couldn't help but wonder if she'd ever wanted children of her own. But he had another issue that was much more pressing at the moment.

"Anyway, I would like to invite you to go with me. It will be fun," she concluded with a dreamy expression.

The time to tell her was way past due. And already, he had the feeling she wasn't going to take it well.

"I won't be here." His gut tightened at the thought of leaving her.

Sage's eyes widened as she looked up at him. "What. Why not?"

"Because I have to get back."

She sat upright. "Get back? I thought you were on leave until after the first of the year?"

As he shook his head, Sage watched, her brow bunching with confusion.

He cleared his throat. "I was, but I received a call the

morning of the snowstorm. I have to get back early."

"What?" The alarm on her face said it all. "Why didn't you tell me?"

Reaching up, he tried to caress her cheek, but Sage shrugged him away.

"I was planning to tell you," he explained.

Sage stiffened and slid over so she could look directly at him. "When were you gonna do that?"

Cser ran a hand across his head as he said, "I was going to tell you before you went home."

Sage went utterly still. "Unbelievable. After all, we've shared that's how you're going to treat me?"

"I wasn't trying to keep it from you. I just didn't know how to tell you."

"Easy … just open your mouth," she retorted with sarcasm. She struggled not to lose her temper, but it wasn't easy—not when emotions were involved.

"Sage, nothing about the last few days has been anything like I had planned. I figured I'd be here a few days and then ship back out." He shrugged. "Then you showed up." He saw the hurt on her face and continued, "If I'd had any idea this was going to happen between us, I would have declined and finished my leave. But now it's too late." What he wasn't saying was after the night of the Christmas party, he had pulled his leave, deciding it was best to get the hell away from her before he did something he would regret. In the end, he'd ended up hurting her anyway.

Her eyes turned frosty as she said, "I don't have a problem with you leaving. I already knew your time here would be brief; I just had no idea how short. Apparently, you felt I didn't matter enough for you to tell me."

"Babe, you matter. More than you'll ever know. But I don't need someone back home waiting for me to return. I see that happen to too many in my unit, and I can't do that to you," he said sincerely.

There was an unidentifiable emotion in her eyes. "So then, what has this time together been about?"

"Great sex," he replied jokingly, but when he saw the pained look, it made him take a warning, and he wished he could take it back. "Sage, you know I care about you."

"Sure, you do." She bristled at his tone and rolled over. "Because of me, you were able to come home and pass the time with a romp in the sack." There was pain in her voice.

"It's not like that. Not with us."

Sage ignored his response. "When are you leaving?"

Cser was almost too afraid to tell her. "The day after Christmas."

Three days.

He reached for her, but Sage twisted out of his reach and stood. "I'd like to go home. I'll send someone for my truck once the side roads clear."

"Sage, stay," he urged. "I want— "

"No, I need to get back to reality," she countered, interrupting him. "I had enough of playing make-believe for one week. And to think I thought we possibly had a future together." Sage gave a rude snort.

Standing, Cser took her hand. "Bae, listen to me." Reluctantly, she met his eyes. "I can't promise you a future when I can't guarantee I'll even make it back home. I can't put you through that."

"That's not your decision!" she emphasized with a hard punch to his chest. "I want more, and if you can't offer me that, then there's nothing else to be said."

His silence was all the answer she needed.

Turning on her heels, Sage departed to the bedroom to get dressed.

Cser tossed his keys into the dish on the coffee table and reached for the remote, hoping there was a game on television. He didn't care what NFL team was playing tonight as long as the game was good enough to take his mind off Sage.

She was pissed. He got that. And that was all the more reason why he hadn't wanted to get involved in the first place because getting involved meant he risked the chance of losing her from his life forever, and he couldn't bear that.

He tossed his coat onto the floor near the door, too lazy to hang it up, then flopped onto the sofa. While he flipped through channels, he remembered the hurt look on her face as he drove her home. Remy had been right. Most of the main roads had been cleared, but the side streets had yet to be addressed. Getting to her condo had taken quite a bit of maneuvering. If she hadn't been so pissed off at him, he would have turned around and brought her back home with him. But he knew that would have been a mistake. She wanted more than he could ever give her, yet he tried to protect her from being hurt any more than she already was. Giving her mixed signals was not the way to go.

A smile curled his lips at finding the game already in the second quarter; he needed something to dominate his mind. Steelers were losing to the Giants, and somehow, he managed to push thoughts of Sage out of his mind until the commercial break.

Reaching inside his pocket, Cser removed his cell phone and couldn't resist tapping the photo app. While he waited for the game to resume, he stared at the photographs they had taken together in front of the Christmas tree. Her wide-set eyes were full of expression; there were those parted lips he loved to kiss, and her buzz cut on a perfectly round head. Every photo captured an image of a beautiful woman who had become far too important and caused an instant erection. Even now, the tree lights were blinking and reminded him of the fun they'd had the day before, the hours they'd spent making love and then talking while holding her in his arms. All had been ruined. He couldn't blame it all on Remy. The real problems hadn't arisen until Sage realized he was leaving sooner with no plans for the future. The culprit was him.

With a deep sigh, Cser put the phone away. He knew what she wanted. A commitment. A promise that they were going to move their lives in a direction together. But he had made up his mind after his military career, and one too many heartbreaks, relationships were off the table. And to stay clear of women who not only made him want more than a one-night stand but especially those who made him want to love. Sage was one of those women. But somehow, she'd slipped past his defensive wall. In a matter of a few days, she had him wanting to make promises of a future together that he was afraid he wouldn't be able to keep.

The game resumed, and Cser tried to refocus his mind, which wasn't easy. Instead, he kept checking his phone, hoping she would have called, but then he remembered her phone was buried somewhere in his yard. By the halftime show, he'd convinced himself Sage leaving had been for the best. He knew he'd hurt her but letting go would be easier now than later. If he'd led her on, the pain would have been far worse.

CHAPTER 9

"Oh, Donie! You look beautiful!"
Tears clouded Sedona's eyes as she stepped out of the dressing room. Sage watched in awe as her big sister moved onto the raised platform in a vintage-style Oscar De La Renta ballroom gown. It was breathtaking, white and strapless with beaded lace appliqués, a tulle skirt, and a chapel train. "You gotta buy that one!" she insisted.

Sedona stood in front of the wall of mirrors and nodded in agreement. "Oh my God! *This* is it, Gigi."

Sitting on a chair with her stomach growling, Sage shouted, "Hallelujah!"

Her sister frowned, then started laughing. "It only took three hours."

Sage gave a rude snort. "Really? As hungry as I am, I thought it had been a lot longer."

"Very funny," Sedona mumbled. But she knew her sister was right. Even their mother had left an hour ago for a mandatory church meeting.

"Hold up! Let me take a picture so I can send the dress to her." Sage reached down for her new cell phone, aimed it in front of her, and snapped off enough pictures to satisfy her mother.

"Okay, Gigi, get on over here so I can see you in that gown."

"Okay, just as long as we hurry this along because a sistah is hungry!" Stomach growling, Sage rose from the chair and sauntered up the stairs onto the platform in a pair of rhinestone pumps.

Hands planted on narrow hips, Sedona cast an appraising look before saying, "Oh damn. Gigi, you look so good."

"I do, don't I?" Sage replied with a saucy grin. She spun around, taking in the long, off the shoulder, crepe, and satin Vera Wang gown at all angles. "But did you have to pick orange?"

Sedona pursed her painted lips. "It's not orange. It's persimmon."

"Looks like orange to me." She struck a pose with her hands at her waist, and her leg slipped out from between the high split in the floor-length dress. "But I still look good."

"I know, right. Wait until Cser sees you coming down the aisle in this."

Sage waved a hand and issued a dramatic sigh. "Sure, not that it's going to make a difference," she said grudgingly. "Besides, he might not be back from Afghanistan in time."

"Never say never," Sedona said, turning left and right in the mirror.

Sage drew another sigh as she stared at Sedona's reflection in the mirror. "How'd you do it all those years? You know…, watch Webb leave to go out at sea for months at a time?"

She gave a thoughtful expression. "It wasn't easy. I missed my fiancé like crazy, but a military wife has to learn to be strong. You gotta be for your man's sake."

"You've *always* been strong."

Easing back, Sedona turned to her. "No, I haven't. I was scared. But I loved that man with all of my heart, and while he was away, I made sure there was no doubt in his mind I was at home holding it down and waiting for him to return."

Her words caused Sage to frown. If only she could get Cser to buy into the idea.

"Ladies, have you decided yet?"

They both turned toward the perky sales assistant. Sedona was the first to speak.

"Yes, *this* is the dress."

The short, stout woman clapped her hands together. "Excellent, it looks beautiful on you!"

Sage beamed. "I agree. My sister is going to make a beautiful bride."

An hour later, they were seated at an Italian restaurant in downtown Richmond eating lasagna.

"When are you heading back to Hampton?" Sage asked as she speared a tomato.

"Not until after New Year's Eve. I figured I'd spend time picking out china with Mom," Sedona added with a dramatic eye roll.

"Sounds fun," she replied sarcastically and took a bite.

Her sister pointed her fork at her. "You know I'm waiting to hear about Remy finding out about you two."

Sage's eyebrows lifted a fraction. "What's there to tell? He showed up when I was running around in one of Cser's t-shirts."

Sedona laughed, the sultry sound floating across the restaurant. Reaching for her wine, she sipped while Sage gave her the Reader's Digest version. "Good for you! I'm just glad you finally got you some."

Sage couldn't believe she was blushing. "Me too." She caught big sister studying her.

"How do you feel?" Sedona probed.

A sad smile touched her lips. "I feel like I've never felt before. Now that we've made love, I love that man more than I've ever loved him."

"Have you told him?"

Eyes narrowing, she replied, "Hell no. You know I can't put

myself out there like that."

There was a pregnant pause before Sedona asked, "Has he told you how he feels?"

Slumping back on the chair, Sage said, "Other than telling Remy he cares about me, that's about it."

Sedona shrugged. "Hey, that's a start."

"Not really." She wanted more. Groaning inward, Sage stabbed a noodle with her fork. She wanted a lot more from him. "He's leaving the day after Christmas." She felt the tears threatening her eyes.

Leaning over the table, Sedona replied, "You need to tell him. Do you know how many things I wished I'd had a chance to tell Webb before he died??" She shook her head. "You can't let Cser leave without telling him how you really feel."

Sage chewed and nodded her head. Sedona was right. She had to tell him. That way, she would at least know where she stood before he left. Six more months of not knowing would drive her insane.

"You're right, but I don't know if it will make a difference. He is adamant about staying away from commitments because of how unpredictable and dangerous his job is."

"I can understand why he feels that way. Getting over Webb was hard," Sedona revealed between sips from her glass.

"How were you able to finally get over him?"

She pushed out her lower lip. "I don't think you ever get over it. I loved Webb with my every breath and didn't think I could ever love anyone as much as I had loved him. I learned that if I loved once, I could love again but only if I opened my heart and allowed someone else a chance." She gave a sad smirk and brought a forkful of pasta to her mouth. "But then I met Keith and discovered I love him so much more."

Sage sucked her teeth loudly. "Damn, if I can just get a

piece of that from Cser, I'd be happy."

"It's there for the taking." Sedona winked. "You just have to find a way to convince him you're worth the risk."

Cser pulled into the parking lot and was pleased to see piles of snow had been pushed to the rear of the building, clearing enough spaces for the regular patrons to park their vehicles without fear of slipping on the ice and snow. Based on the number of cars in the lot, customers seemed anxious to get out from being cooped up in the house.

Cser parked his truck beside a red Honda Accord and climbed out. The second the cold air hit him, he lifted the collar of his leather jacket and headed into the establishment. The bell overhead rang as he went inside.

His eyes scanned the inside. The dim place was decorated with a string of blinking Christmas lights. And knowing Mack, the owner, the place would probably look that way until Easter.

Washington was playing the Eagles on every television mounted overhead. Customers were sitting on stools along a long wooden bar, cheering their team while others were ranting, eating hot wings, or sipping from frosty glasses.

There were bar height tables throughout the restaurant, and after another quick sweep of the establishment, Cser spotted a tall man with long, shoulder-length hair seated in the far corner. He had expected all five Beaumont brothers but was pleased to see only one at the table.

Squaring his shoulders, Cser maneuvered his way through the crowd of customers and headed his way.

"That was pass interference!" Remy shouted to the screen.

"Tight game?" he asked and pulled out the chair across from him.

"Yep, the refs are on one tonight." Remy brought the glass bottle to his lips and took a sip. "The last two plays have been straight bullshit."

Cser noticed Remy had yet to look his way. He decided to play along and focus on the game. A waitress came by, ordered another round, and then reached for the bowl of peanuts on the table. It wasn't until half-time that Remy finally looked at him and said, "What did you want to talk about?"

Another round of beers arrived. Cser took a sip, stalling, letting Remy know he was controlling the conversation, not him. "I want to talk about the other day."

Remy shrugged nonchalantly. "What's there to say? You're screwing my sister."

Possessiveness surged through him. "That was not the way I wanted you to find out. But I'm not going to apologize for being with Sage."

He noticed the way Remy's fingers tightened around the glass.

"And that's supposed to make it right?"

Cser drew a deep breath that burned at his lungs. "I don't know if anything will ever make it right again, but I wanted to go on the record by letting you know I care about your sister and would never do anything to hurt her. You should know that."

Remy turned his head to stare up at the game. "I don't know anything anymore."

Cser took another swallow of his beer.

"So, what now?" Remy prompted with a hard dead stare.

"I leave to go back the day after Christmas."

They held eyes for a moment.

"So, what was Gigi to you, just a fucking way to pass the time?"

His tone was low. "You know she isn't that."

"Then, if that's the case, why are you treating her like all the others?" Remy inquired.

"I don't want her waiting on me," Cser admitted, heaving a sigh of regret.

A savage curse escaped Remy's lips. "I always knew you could be a selfish prick, but I never realized just how much. You come, and you take." Their eyes locked. "Trust me; I *know* what you took. Now you want her to forget about you while you trot back off to the desert. Do you see what position you've put me in?" he added in a deadly voice.

When he put it that way, it did make him feel like a selfish prick.

"From what I'm hearing, Gigi cares about you. She's had a crush on you for God knows how long. And when you finally decide to give her the time of day, you wanna treat her like the last trick."

"I've never treated her with anything but respect!" Cser barked in protest.

"Really? So, you think it's okay as long as it's done with *respect*?" Remy emphasized with his fingers making quotation marks in the air, "And why shouldn't I put my fist in your mouth?" Remy looked at him, eyes smoldering with lethal fury.

"Try it. The last time I let you get one in, but the next time I'm not going to be so nice." His muscles were ridged, primed for a fight. "You're making a scene. So, either we're gonna work this out, or I'm out this bitch."

"What's there to work out?" Remy paused to take a thirsty swig from the bottle. "I'm not hearing none of that bullshit you're saying about leaving my sister hanging while you go off to play soldier. I know you ain't that heartless."

"I've been alone my entire life. It's been better for me that way. Nobody gets hurt."

Remy's mouth twisted cynically. "And how's that worked

out for you so far?"

He was trying to keep it real, and Remy was a smart-ass.

"My sister expects more. Hell, even I expected more out of you." The disappointment was etched on his face.

Cser shook his head. "You don't understand."

"Then bruh, help me out."

"I can't have her worrying about me, wondering if I'll come back alive or in one piece. I see too many soldiers returning home, broken or even in coffins. I can't do that to her. I can't have her worrying about me."

"That's her decision. You can't tell people how to feel. Hell, you think I don't worry about your dumb ass every time you ship out!"

"Why I gotta be dumb?"

"Cause the shit you're saying don't make no sense. Every time I hear on the news about another fallen soldier, you don't think I'm holding my breath until the name of that man has been revealed. Like it or not, some people do care about you. My family, and *especially* Sage. I just don't know how I didn't see it before.

"You can't keep running and thinking you're all alone in the world because you're not," he added with quiet conviction. "And I'm not gonna allow you to hurt my sister by popping in now and then, getting her all excited."

Remy's eyes shifted toward the front of the bar. Cser turned and groaned with dread. Rance, Roman, and Rush were heading their way, along with Sedona's fiancé Keith.

Fuck!

He sipped his beer. When they reached the table, and each gave him a head nod, which he returned, he felt a little hopeful. Good thing they were in a public place.

"What we miss?" Rance asked as he struggled out of his coat.

"The Redskins are getting their asses kicked. But Cser's getting ready to tell us about his intentions with Sage."

All eyes were on him.

Cser's eyes shifted from one to the other. "What is this, intimidation?"

"Call it what you want, but we want to know what the hell's going on?" The NBA player straddled the seat beside him.

He answered Rance without hesitation, "If I had my way, I'd spend the rest of my life with her."

"So, what's the problem?" Roman probed.

Rush signaled for another pitcher of beer, but all eyes were still on him.

He sighed heavily. "My life doesn't belong to me. I'm property of the United States government."

Roman chuckled. "Dude, do you know how ridiculous you sound?"

"Exactly," Rance chimed in.

Keith shook his head in agreement. "Nothing makes those deployments easier than knowing you have someone back at home waiting on you."

Remy pointed. "Remember, Keith did over twenty years in the navy."

The retiree nodded in agreement. "And I spent more time on the sea than anything else. Do you know how many nights I wished I had someone back at home? My shipmates, all they talked about was getting back to their wives and girlfriends. Trust me. Sage will be your motivation. Every letter and phone call will give you a newfound determination to take fewer risks, be safe, and get your ass back in one piece."

"Oh damn! Y'all giving my boy a motivational speech." Remy cringed.

Rance slid his chair closer. "Yo, Remy is the worst person for you to take advice from on or off the radio. You need to talk to a man with years of experience. I'm here to tell you; the right woman can turn your world upside down."

"Hell yeah! Ain't nothing like the love of a woman," Keith chimed in.

Remy fumed. "I'll stick with just the lovemaking."

Roman laughed. "I'll second that."

"I'm with you two," Rush added with a dramatic shudder. "The last thing I'm looking for is a commitment."

Rance shook his head. "That's because you're married to your work."

"And you see where that got him," Rance muttered. The others laughed. Cser's brow rose, and Remy took a moment to explain.

"Gigi's dealerships are the top performers of the year."

Cser grinned. "Good for her."

Rush pulled his gaze away from the television where the Eagles were seconds away from scoring another touchdown. "Yeah, I had to accept defeat. But I have to admit she's a beast."

Cser wondered why she hadn't told him and remembered why. He felt a second of emptiness followed by panic. Would he lose her before he returned from Afghanistan? He didn't want to love anyone—but he did.

He had been content with his life the way things were with casual sex and conversation. His focus had been his military duty, and he'd understood that he was not ready for forever at this time in his life. He dated many women, but none lasted more than a few days, which worked out perfectly—until now.

He had fallen in love with Sage.

Realization hit Cser square in the chest. It had been inevitable because there was something about her that stirred him deep inside as if waking him up from a long nap—*no more walking dead among the living.* And now, there was no turning back. It was time to quit fighting and accept the truth. He loved

Sage and didn't want to lose her. If he came home to find her with another man, he would lose his damn mind. He had to tell her because he wasn't willing to take that risk.

She's mine. Sage belongs to me.

He knew his life would never be the same without her because they were meant to be together. Cser dragged a hand down his face. Searching his brain, he recounted something Laverne had once said to him.

Don't give up on someone you can't go one day without thinking about.

That was Sage. Tomorrow wasn't promised, but he had to live each day as if it was his last. He paused, startled by another realization. His life as a loner was over. How in the world could he have been so stupid? His future had been right in front of him.

"Sage and I will talk before I leave. I'm going to make things right," he promised.

Remy's brow rose. "You better."

CHAPTER 10

" Merry Christmas, everyone!"

Sage waved farewell to her employees as they began to file out of the building. She'd closed the dealership at noon and had lunch catered that included smoked turkey and all the trimmings. Afterward had been a gift exchange before the day was officially over. She, too, would be leaving shortly. As soon as she straightened her desk, she'd head back to her condo for a miserable evening alone. Tomorrow the family was dining at her parent's house.

"Have a great holiday, Clara," Sage called as she spotted her coming down the stairs bundled in her coat and hat.

"Merry Christmas to you, too!" Her eyes were sparkling. She was headed to pick up the presents she had hidden at her mother's for her six-year-old daughter to put under the tree in the wee hours of the night. As Sage climbed the stairs to her office, she thought about how amazing Christmas had been growing up with six siblings and mountains of presents under the tree. It was like having their own toy store.

While she walked along the thick Berber carpet, her thoughts shifted to Cser.

She hadn't heard from him since he'd dropped her off at her condo that morning. That evening, she'd glanced out the window, spotting the F-150 in the driveway, but hadn't bothered to call to thank him. Hopefully, she will get a chance to see him at the Christmas party tomorrow. Tears pricked her eyes that she pushed away. She'd cried enough already over that man. How could she have been so stupid to have fallen in love with him? But Sedona had been right. They needed to talk. If there was no hope for them, then she needed closure.

Sage heard a rap at her door and glanced up. As soon as she spotted the man standing there, a smile escaped her lips.

"Dad, come on in!" she said, excited to see him. Swiveling on her leather chair, Sage hurried over to his big embrace. One look at the man's dark complexion and sable eyes, and you knew he was a Beaumont.

"What are you doing here?"

Standing at six-eight, Richard Beaumont towered over Sage as he stared down at her adoringly. "I thought I'd come and see my daughter."

"No, you came to check on your investment."

"Yes. That, too." Chuckling, he nodded his salt and pepper head. "Please sit."

Smiling, she stared in admiration at her father as he lowered onto one of the leather chairs across from her desk.

Her father had begun his first Toyota dealership long before she was born, and then the company grew to become one of the most prominent auto sales groups on the East Coast. Her father knew early on expansion was one way of staying ahead of the competition. After Toyota, he became Ford, Lincoln, BMW, Mercedes, Nissan, and Volkswagen with nearly two dozen Beaumont dealerships.

Sage walked back around and flopped onto her executive chair. "If I had known you were coming, I would have invited you to our luncheon this afternoon."

"Your mother had me out at the country club for their holiday party," he said and scowled. She had to resist laughter. Her father hated social functions and preferred the simple, quiet life. Nevertheless, he adored his wife of forty-five years and would do anything to keep her happy.

"I spoke to Bianca this morning. She and Sheyna have started working on the family reunion again."

She noticed the way her father's eyes darkened as he said stubbornly, "I'm not going."

As she watched him, Sage shook her head.

There had been an ongoing feud with his brother Roger Beaumont for two decades that none of them understood. She and her cousin Bianca and her brother Jace's wife Sheyna had been trying to get the two together for the last four years with absolutely no success. Was she ever going to be able to get to the source of the problem?

Uncle Roger was the genius behind the Beaumont Hotels, one of the most prestigious hotels in the country, with locations dotting the map from coast to coast, offering every amenity imaginable. She adored her cousins Bianca, Jabarie, Jaden, and Jace and wished they had a chance to see each other more often. Unlike them, Richard never allowed his children to grow up feeling privileged. Everything they had, they'd worked for. It wasn't until her twenty-first birthday that her father revealed a trust-fund left to her by their millionaire grandfather. She'd never have to work another day in her life if she'd wanted, but nothing gave her more pleasure than being around cars.

"There's a reason for my visit." Sage heard her father say, and his expression became so serious, he had her sitting upright on the seat.

"What's wrong?" She was suddenly afraid it might have something to do with his health.

He drew back on the seat, sticking out his long legs in front of him. "When I first started this business, I was certain all of my children would follow in my footsteps. I started this legacy for all of you, but you and Rush were the only two who seemed interested. I figured you'd get a degree in business and help me run that side of the house while he ran and oversaw the day-to-day operation of the dealerships. But then you surprised me by showing an interest in all the insides and outs, especially mechanical engineering."

She propped her elbows on top of her desk and steepled her fingers. "Hey, that's what I like to do."

"Yes, and your mother saw it, too, and made me promise to never leave the business to you."

"What, but Dad, I—"

"Let me finish." He held up a hand, stopping her, and then there was a knock at her open door. Sage looked up to see Rush's towering presence.

With uneasiness, she looked from him to her father. "What's going on here?"

Grinning, her brother entered with long strides. "Is that any way to greet your favorite brother?"

"I see you got jokes." She tilted the chair back slightly and folded her arms across her breasts. "Don't you have work to do?" she asked suspiciously.

"Like you, I've closed my dealerships for the holiday weekend."

"Come on over, son, and have a seat." Her father signaled with a sweep of his hand and pointed to the chair beside his.

"Dad, what's going on?" Sage asked, dumbfounded.

He waited until Rush was seated before saying, "I asked Rush to come because I wanted to say this in front of both of you."

She glared across the desk at the sinister smirk on her brother's lips.

Her father's dark eyes softened as they shifted from one to the other. "I have been giving this a lot of thought, and I finally decided who I want to hand the business over to, but I need you both to understand my decision." He swung on the seat so he could see both of them as he spoke. "Rush, you've proven yourself as a businessman and a leader. And you, princess, I've seen more of me in you than any of my other children." She gasped and couldn't believe what he was saying.

Even Rush was nodding in agreement. "Yeah, I have to admit, Gigi is a chip off the old block."

With a nod, her father said, "Princess, I have decided to let you manage my two other dealerships."

"What? Toyota *and* Honda?"

Rush nodded and stretched out his long legs. "That's what's up, Gigi. I know you can handle it."

Sage pushed out a long-ragged breath. She was so moved she didn't know what to say. Had her father really decided to let her run two more dealerships? She scrubbed a trembling hand down her face. "I can't believe it."

"Well, believe it, young lady. You have truly proven yourself."

"Thank you, Dad!" Sage clapped her hands as she'd done when she was a child.

"As for the Beaumont Automotive Group ... I'd like the both of you to run it together."

"What?" Sage felt the pulsing excitement heating her blood as her frantic gaze shifted to her brother. "And you're okay with this Rush?" she inquired, finding that hard to believe.

He gave her his signature crooked smile. "In the last year, I've figured out I can't run this business without you. Instead of competing, I would like us to start working as a team."

She nodded mutely. "I'd like that, too."

"Well, then it sounds like it's settled!" Her father slapped his palms together and looked quite pleased.

Rush smiled and nodded this head. "Merry Christmas, Gigi."

"Merry Christmas, Rush," she replied, still reeling with shock.

While leaning over the desk, her father's expression became serious. "Just promise your mother you won't allow the dealership to stop you from finding a man and settling down."

Rush erupted with laughter. "Dad, I don't think we have to worry about that. The way Remy was going off, I think this little woman here has already found a man she's interested in." Her brother gave her a knowing look, but she could see the sparkle in his eyes. "Good thing it's someone I like."

"Is there something I need to know about?" Her father asked, brow raised.

Sage quickly shook her head. "Dad, no, but as soon as it is, you'll be the first person I call."

His smile returned. "Sounds like a plan, young lady. In the meantime, how about the three of us going somewhere and celebrating?"

"You're on," Sage replied with tears of joy.

CHAPTER 11

By Christmas afternoon, Sage still hadn't heard from Cser, and she was afraid he might try to leave without saying goodbye.

Who could blame him after the way you went off on him!

As soon as her time with family was over, she planned to appear at his doorstep. Already, she was praying for another snowstorm.

They were all gathered in the family room of her parent's sprawling house: with twelve-foot ceilings, colorful handwoven rugs across the dark wood flooring, and tapestries covering the sofas and chairs inside the massive room. After dinner, they had all gathered for a gift exchange. As always, Sage received several fabulous gifts from her family, but nothing came close to what she wanted most.

When she spotted the designer purse Sage had purchased for her during a weekend shopping spree in Virginia Beach, Dominique exclaimed, "Thank you so much!"

"You're so welcome."

Her brother Reese and the curvy beauty had arrived last night. With a smile, Sage's eyes traveled down to Dominique's tiny baby bump. The couple was having their first child in June. While Sage sat on the sofa drinking homemade eggnog, she chatted with Dominique about her upcoming visit to Hawaii during Easter.

"When you fall in love with Waikiki, don't be trying to move in."

She gave Reese, who'd just walked up interrupting their conversation, the stank-eye.

"You know you miss me, so I don't know why you're playing."

She adored her big brother with his handsome toasted, almond-colored face and chiseled jawline with the neatly trimmed goatee.

His dark gaze softened. "Congratulations. Dad just gave me the news."

"Thank you." She blushed while her brother recounted his conversation about her partnership to Dominique, who hugged her with excitement.

"You are a true boss!" she screamed.

Sage was laughing when her mother sauntered over and took a seat on the sofa beside her.

"Mom, aren't you proud of Gigi?"

Sage turned and met her mother's lovely, amber-colored eyes and waited for her response.

Bettye Beaumont placed a comforting hand on her daughter's knees. "Yes, actually, I am very proud of her."

"You are?" she asked around the constriction in her throat.

She nodded. "You are a strong black woman. Maybe a little *too* independent, but a woman any mother would be proud to call her own."

Her eyes welled with tears.

"I know I have been hard on you, but that's because I was raised a woman did two things—cater to her husband and raise his children. But you've always been rebellious with a mind of your own," she added with a wag of her head.

Reese chuckled. "So true."

"Shut up. Who asked you?" Sage playfully stuck out her tongue.

Dominique giggled.

"Anyway, Gigi, I just wanted to let you know I'm so happy about your father's decision."

"Thank you, Mom." Sage leaned over and kissed her smooth cheek.

"But now that we've gotten your professional career together, how about we start working on finding you a husband?"

She had known it was just a matter of time before her mother started in on the husband's search again.

As she prepared to respond, the hairs at the back of her neck began to tingle. While she swung around, her heart somersaulted couldn't stop the rush of anticipation when she spotted Cser standing in the doorway talking to her father. He'd come! His serious expression made her pulse start to race.

"I heard you're headed back to the madness over in the Middle East."

Cser nodded at Richard Beaumont. "Yes, something like that, sir. My leave ends tomorrow."

The older man brought a hand to his shoulder. "You be safe."

"Thank you, sir."

"Well, come on in." He motioned with a sweep of his hand. "The gang's all here."

Cser stepped inside and looked around. He knew it had been a bold move showing up here. He and Remy had squashed their little beef, but it would be a while—if ever—before the two of them got things back on track. His involvement with Sage had been a risk he'd been willing to take, and he had no regrets. Not anymore. What had happened between him, and Sage had been inevitable. He'd spent too many years trying to pretend that something didn't exist when it was crystal clear it wasn't going away.

The last two days he'd spent trying to come up with the best way to tell her how he felt, and nothing came remotely close to honestly telling her how he felt. Expressing his emotions was something he had never been good at. So, he'd decided just to show up and take his chances by simply putting his feelings out in the open.

"Sir, may I have a word with Sage in private?"

Her father's eyes studied him, and after a moment, a slight grin turned the corner of his mouth. "So, *you're* the one."

No explanation was needed. "Yes, I'm the one," he replied with a nod. "At least I hope so."

The statement caused Richard Beaumont to chuckle as he gave him a hearty thump across the back. "Sure, son. Take all the time you need." He pointed, and Cser followed the direction of his finger across the room. As soon as he saw Sage sitting on the sofa beside her mother, he forgot to breathe. She was beautiful. The beautiful woman wore black leather pants and a matching jacket. On her feet were sexy red stilettoes.

Lawd, have mercy.

His eyes never left hers as he shrugged out of his jacket and hung it in the closet. He then wasted no time stepping into the room. The music was playing, and everyone was laughing and having a good time. But the moment Sage looked up and saw him coming, it was as if the room had grown silent. The closer he got, the stronger his heart raced. He felt more alive than he had in the last few days.

"Merry Christmas, Bae."

Slowly, Sage rose to stand in front of him. Before she could open her mouth to respond, Cser drew her into his arms, smothering her with a long sensual kiss. Sage resisted for only a moment before melting against him, reaching on tiptoe and leaning into him. After a long breathless moment, he drew back, leaving Sage panting heavily.

Looking down at a pair of curious eyes, he said softly, "Mrs. Beaumont, may I have a word with your daughter alone?"

The ageless beauty's eyes were dancing with delight. "Yes, absolutely."

Sage brought a defiant hand to her waist. "What makes you think I want to talk to you?"

"Then don't talk, just listen." Taking her hand, Cser led her out of the room, away from the spectators, and down the expansive foyer toward a sitting room at the rear of a massive eat-in kitchen. He'd been at the house enough times he knew the layout. Family and friends were everywhere, and Cser was sure Remy had called out to him, and yet he didn't stop until they had stepped into the room. As soon as she shut the door and turned around, Cser scooped Sage into his arms again, sliding his lips across her cheek and down to nuzzle her neck.

"Didn't you say you wanted to talk?"

It was her turn to pull back—putting some distance between them—and it was a good thing. It gave him a chance to get his head on right.

"Have a seat."

He led her to a navy-blue sofa, and Sage settled down on the cushions. Cser remained standing. Gazing down at her caused his loins to stir. The jacket was cut low and showed off the swell of breasts that he itched to hold in his palms. Her hair was wrapped in a scarf. There was no make-up on her face, and yet she was gorgeous like no other. At that moment, he wanted her in his arms, holding her, kissing—

"You said you wanted to talk," she repeated, abruptly putting an end to his sexual thoughts.

"Oh yeah, right," Cser mumbled and began pacing the

length of the floor. His stomach rolled with nerves.

In his mind, he'd rehearsed what he wanted to say to her. He wasn't sure how she would respond at this point and was even a little afraid she might throw his words back into his face, so he decided to get straight to the point.

"I love you."

"You what?" she whispered around the constriction in her throat.

Cser scrubbed a hand down his face and started toward her. "I love you, Sage. I can't say when it first happened, but I do." He laughed, realizing he was nervous as hell. "This is not at all how I planned this, the timing sucks, and you probably don't believe me. But I've wanted you in my life for a long time. I was just too afraid to allow myself to love, and with my job ..." He shook his head. "It just didn't seem right to lead you on."

"Keep going," she urged, crossing her arms and legs stubbornly.

His chest rapidly rose and fell as he stared at her. "This is all new for me. I am allowing someone in, letting you get close. But all I know for certain is that I love you, and I don't want to be without you in my life."

Sage bit her lip and choked at his confession. "I-I don't know what to say."

"Tell me you still love me."

"You don't stop loving someone that quick," Sage said softly.

He scowled. "Dammit, you're not gonna make this easy, are you."

Her eyes swelled as she shook her head.

"Then how about this?" Cser got down on one knee in front of her. "Sage Beaumont, I want you to share this adventure with me."

She just stared at him.

Gazing deep into his eyes, Cser said softly, "Will you take a chance on me?" Reaching inside his pocket, he pulled out a chain.

"What is that?" she whispered, as her dark eyebrows drew slightly together.

He gave a sheepish smirk. "A set of my dog tags. I would like you to wear them, like a promise ring."

"A promise ring?" The tears in her eyes began to slip down her cheeks, but she was laughing. "Does that mean we are officially dating?"

Cser smiled softly. "Yes, if you'll have me."

She brushed at the wetness on her face. "Are you sure this is what you want? Being with me means I will be worried about you every second you're gone and counting the days until you come back home to me. Can you handle that?"

Cupping her face, he kissed her mouth. Leaning back, he gazed intensely into her eyes. "After everything I've said, you might find this hard to believe, but yes, I can handle that. I was a fool for trying to deny my feelings for you. I would be an even bigger fool to not want a woman like you at home, waiting on my return."

"Yes, I will wait on you," she whispered, fighting back the tears.

He leaned down and gently kissed her lips, then carefully put the chain around her neck. Bringing Sage to her feet, he dragged her into his arms and held her closer.

"Look," she said and pointed.

Drawing back, Cser glanced up and smiled at the mistletoe hanging overhead.

"I don't need mistletoe or an excuse to kiss my girl," Cser whispered against her lips.

"I love you," Sage murmured.

"And I love you more."

They gazed at each other in quiet wonder for several moments. Cser's chest expanded with love and a dozen other unfamiliar emotions as he made their relationship official with a deep, searing kiss.

He hadn't left yet and already he couldn't wait to get back home.

ALL I WANT

~~The Beaumonts~~

Caramel Kisses Publishing

CHAPTER 1

"I can't believe Sage has finally snagged herself a man!" Sheyna Beaumont exclaimed as she ended the phone call.

"Sage?" her husband asked, curiously referring to his younger cousin. "Really? How'd she manage that?"

"That was Aunt Bettye on the phone. She's dating Remy's best friend."

"Let me get this straight..., Remy's *allowing* one of his friends to date his sister?" Jace said incredulously. "As overprotective as he is, that's hard to believe!"

"What's hard about it? C'mon. When have you known Sage to allow anyone to tell her what to do?" Sheyna pointed out with a laugh. That girl was as stubborn as it got.

Jace chuckled. "You're right about that."

"Aunt Bettye said Sage's been in love with him for a long time, and finally fate stepped in." Sheyna gave a dreamy smile. It was like out of a romance novel. The two had been stuck in a snowstorm together.

"Or maybe she put that brotha in a headlock," Jace joked.

"Stop it!" Sheyna scolded but found herself laughing. "Maybe it was just her time to fall in love."

"Maybe so." Jace tore his gaze away from the road long enough to give his wife an amusing look. "She's been in love a long time, huh? Come to think of it; Sage reminds me of you." Sheyna shifted on the upholstered leather seat and replied,

"What are you talking about?"

"You're both strong women, very independent, and you and I both know the only man you've ever wanted was me."

Injecting saccharine in her voice, she drawled, "How do you figure that?"

Her husband laughed. "The way you were sweating a brotha, everyone knew."

"*Everyone?* Are you serious?" she sputtered with laughter and playfully punched him in the arm. "I think it was the other way around."

"Mom, is that true?"

Swiveling around, Sheyna looked at her son, Jace Jr., sitting on the back seat, clearly entertained by Jace's fabrications. He was ten and the spitting image of his father with smooth dark skin and thickly lashed sable-brown colored eyes.

She chuckled dryly. "JJ don't believe anything your daddy says. He was in love from the second he first saw me."

"Really, Dad?" he asked. Dimples framed his happy smile.

Jace pulled up to a stoplight before he turned, and his eyes roamed across Sheyna's face. While she waited for him to share his humorous version, their eyes locked, and the very air she breathed seemed snatched from her lungs.

"Your mom's right. The second I laid my eyes on all that smooth melted chocolate, I knew I had to have her in my life," he stated, then grinned in a smoldering way that shook her to the core.

"Yuck!" JJ drew back on the seat as if they were both contagious.

Jace laughed, a deep, pleasant rumble. Reaching over, he placed his hand over hers, his thumb slowly stroking the delicate flesh at Sheyna's wrist.

She smiled as they shared heated looks in the shadowy

interior of his Jaguar. Jace Julius Beaumont was nothing short of handsome. He had a broad nose, an attractive cleft in his nutty brown chin, and gorgeous full lips surrounded by a neatly barbered goatee. Could she possibly have loved that man any more than she already did? They had been married twelve years, and every anniversary, she thanked God for bringing him into her life.

"Mom, can I stay over to Uncle Dee's tomorrow? He says he has a surprise for me!" JJ asked eagerly.

They had spent Christmas at her father's house in the country. Her brothers, Scott and Darnell, had joined them along with their families, bearing gifts. *He's so spoiled.* For years, JJ had been the only grandchild, but to her joy, that had finally changed. Darnell now had two of his own, and Scott and Zanaa were due to have their first baby in the spring.

Sheyna nodded and smiled over her shoulder. "Sure, you can go. I'll call and talk to your aunt Liberty in the morning."

"Yes!" he cried, voice bubbling with excitement. "They're taking Chance and me to the movies."

Not only were the kids out of school for winter break, but Darnell had also taken time off from his law practice to spend the holiday season with his family. It was hard to believe that not only was the former playboy married, but he had a wife and two children—a six-year-old son, Chance, and one-year-old Nona.

"Was Sage the only reason why Aunt Bettye called?" Jace asked, breaking into her thoughts. "How's everyone doing?"

Just as they were pulling away from her father's house, Aunt Bettye called with season's greetings. As always, they'd spent time catching up before the timeless beauty got to the reason for her call. "Everyone is doing great. She asked if we're planning to attend Jabarie's New Year's Eve party."

His brow cocked with curiosity. "Why? Is she coming?"

Nodding, Sheyna replied, "Yes, she said Remy and Sage are planning to drive up, and they're going to try and get your uncle Richard to come."

"Yeah, right. I'll believe that when I see it!" Jace sputtered with disbelief.

Sheyna shrugged. "Maybe he's finally ready to talk to your father." When Jace released a rude snort, she sighed dramatically and replied, "I know...I know. You're probably right. I've been trying to plan a reunion for forever that still hasn't happened, but maybe he's caught up in the spirit of the holiday and had a change of heart."

There was an ongoing feud between the Beaumont brothers—her father-in-law Roger and his younger brother Richard—that had been going on for over two decades that no one understood. Sheyna and Jace's sister Bianca had been trying to get the two together for the last four years with absolutely no success until she'd finally given up. Sheyna scowled inwardly. Were they ever going to get to the source of the problem? Even Aunt Bettye had no idea what the feud was about.

Sheyna shook her head with confusion because she could never imagine her father and Uncle Jimmy not speaking. Those two spent every possible Sunday they could either fishing or watching sports while Roger and Richard Beaumont wouldn't be caught dead in the same room.

Roger was the genius behind the Beaumont Hotels, one of the most prestigious hotel chains in the country, with locations dotting the map from coast to coast, offering every amenity imaginable. His children Bianca, Jabarie, Jaden, and Jace, had lived a privileged life. Richard, who owned car dealerships up and down the east coast, never allowed his seven children to grow up feeling privileged. Everything they had, they'd worked for, although, on their twenty-first birthdays, they were each given access to a trust fund left by their millionaire grandfather. Nevertheless, even then, they continued to live a modest lifestyle. She loved all of them because regardless of how they were raised, none of the children ever allowed money to define them.

"Well, let's just hope for the best," Sheyna added and let their fingers twine sensually. Jace nodded, but she could he wasn't going to get his hopes up. In all honesty, neither was she.

Sheyna gazed out the window as they pulled into a residential area. The snow was coming down heavily, blanketing the manicured lawns. The light was twinkling in windows. The sight always caused a feeling of holiday cheer to fill her belly. Winter was indeed her favorite time of the year.

Jace pulled onto the private wooded road. As they traveled around the windy path, a grand farmhouse with a circular driveway came into view, and Sheyna's heart warmed with pride. The large white house had been an engagement present from Jace, and they'd been adding wings to it ever since. Tiny white lights circled the posts and nearby trees, casting a glow over everything.

Jace reached up and pressed the remote, and up ahead, one of the garage doors raised. As they drew closer, a smile tipped Sheyna's lips at the Christmas tree twinkling in the front window of their home. Jace had positioned it just right so that it was on full display from the road. Her eyes scanned the electric candles in the center of each front window of their forty-two hundred square foot home. White holiday lights adorned the manicured shrubs and the railing of the wraparound porch. A massive holly wreath she'd found during a shopping spree in Philadelphia was hanging on a red front door.

Jace pulled into the five-car garage and killed the engine.

JJ dashed out of the car and into the house with a bag of presents. Smiling, Sheyna shook her head. She knew Jace was heading to the entertainment room, where he mounted a seventy-five-inch television on the wall. Scott, a video game designer, had given his nephew one of the newest releases before it hit the shelves New Year's Day, and JJ was anxious to play it on a big screen.

Jace climbed out and came around to open the door for her. Taking Sheyna's gloved hand, he helped her to her feet. Standing at six feet in heels, Sheyna still tilted her head and found his dark, sable gaze already fixed on her face. Eyes locked, crackling with awareness, heat ignited and spread to every part of her body.

"Precious, go on inside and get comfortable," he growled, and his words sounded almost like an order. "I'm going to grab the bags out the trunk and toss salt on the driveway."

"You won't get any argument out of me." A smile tugged at the corners of her lips. Jace slanted his head and seized her mouth possessively. Sheyna arched into him, and he deepened the kiss, devouring her mouth until she was breathless and aroused. Soon they were both breathing heavily. Sheyna swayed on her feet and was gratefully for the hand at her waist that kept her steady.

That man still can bring me to my knees.

She felt the deep timbre of his voice vibrating through her body when he drew back and groaned, "Dammit, go inside." There was raw hunger in Jace's gaze as he stared back at her. She had seen it all evening, but it had since magnified.

With a nod, she reached for her purse then went inside, where it was blissfully warm and cozy. Stopping in the mudroom, she hung the winter-white wool coat on the hook then tugged off her leather gloves. Taking a seat, she removed the high-heel boots from her tiny feet. As she wiggled her toes,

Sheyna sighed with relief. *The price for looking cute meant sacrificing comfort.* A pair of blue memory foam slippers were on the lower shelf waiting for her. She slipped her feet inside then padded across the Moroccan wooden floors through an enormous modern kitchen. The six-bedroom home had an open floor plan with large living areas, several screened porches with decks, providing great breezes from the lake in the summer. Sheyna stepped out into the foyer. Exposed beams accented the living and dining areas while drawing attention to the dramatic crystal chandelier. As she climbed the custom-crafted mahogany spiral staircase, Sheyna breathed the intensely fragranced tree appreciatively. Staring down at the twinkling lights, she grinned. The holidays always had a way of making her feel better.

As a family, they had gone out to the nursery and had found the perfect tree to bring home. The balsam fir stood twelve-foot tall and carefully decorated with glass ornaments that once belonged to her mother. Christmas had also been her favorite time of the year.

Sheyna still had fond memories of the holidays with her family laughing and her brothers arguing. Holiday music was constantly playing in the background, and the scent of fresh-baked sugar cookies filled the air. Their Christmases had always been perfect because her mother made sure that their holiday was special no matter what was going on.

As she climbed the stairs, Sheyna pressed her lips together. She was determined to form a similar tradition in her own home no matter what was happening, good or bad.

She moved up to the third level, where a spacious master suite took over the entire floor. There was also an office and a private sitting room. The blinds were open, and immediately her eyes were drawn to the French doors that lead out onto a private deck, which offered direct views of the lake. Those views were one of the reasons why she had fallen in love with the place. Sheraton Beach, a beachfront town with a population of fewer than eight thousand residents, was the only home she'd ever known and loved.

Sheyna tugged at the skinny designer jeans, peeling them down her legs. She reached for the hem of her sweater and dragged it over her head, then disappeared to shower and get comfortable before Jace made it upstairs.

A few moments later, she emerged from the ensuite, freshly showered, and slipped into a sheer gown that was flattering to her long legs. After a long day of holiday festivities, she could finally try to relax.

Sheyna twisted her shoulder-length hair in a loose knot at the top of her head. As she secured it with a hair clip, she stared at her reflection in the mirror. A sweep of mascara had lengthened her lashes, emphasizing her amber eyes. Despite the dark circles and the red bruising above her left cheekbone, she gave a faint smile. It was the holiday season, and no matter what, she wasn't going to allow what had happened to her to ruin her holiday spirit.

Plush oatmeal-colored carpeting silenced her steps as she made her way toward the window. Usually, staring out into the water made everything in her life better. However, instead of watching the soft, white snow blanketing the frozen lake, thoughts of the evening she was attacked clouded her mind.

Jace had left the office early that evening to take JJ to hockey practice, and she'd decided to work late. She knew better than walking out after dark alone, and yet she was parked so close to the building she didn't think it would have mattered. However, just as she was about to climb into her Volvo, someone had called her name. The moment she glanced over her shoulder, everything had gone black. It had been three weeks, and yet her heart clutched painfully at the memory of waking up in the emergency room with Jace standing over her. In all the years she had known him, she had never seen him so afraid.

According to him, someone had jacked her purse. She didn't care about the money—credit cards she'd canceled. Other than being attacked, the worst part was having to stand for hours at the DMV.

Jace had been livid. Unfortunately, the security cameras surrounding the Beaumont Corporation hadn't picked up a thing. She could still hear Jace's voice. He had been outraged, and the entire corporation knew it. For days he refused to leave her side. He was loving, attentive, and after two weeks of hiding at home, Sheyna thought she would lose her mind. Now she needed to be back at work.

"Hello."

His deep masculine voice pulled her away from her thoughts and caused her to swing around. Sheyna looked at Jace standing a few feet away. His face and nose were both red from cold.

"It's freezing out there," he said, shrugging out of his coat and draping it across a navy-blue settee. Just the sight of the sweater hugging his broad chest and defined biceps made her libido want to do a happy dance.

He turned, met her eyes, and frowned. "Why do you have that troubled look on your face?"

"No reason." She hated worrying him.

"Don't lie to me, precious." Jace looked grim and fierce as he crossed the length of the room. Her stomach fluttered as he drew closer. "Talk to me." Standing beside her, Jace stared into her eyes as his fingers grazed her dark mahogany cheek.

"I was just thinking."

His gaze burned hers. "You're thinking about that night." She dropped her eyes. It wasn't a question because her husband knew her all too well. He grabbed her waist with both hands and eased her closer.

Sheyna nodded and felt the pain in her stomach twist. Her gaze shifted to his, and she drew in a shaky breath. "I wish I knew who it was." All she could remember was that nauseating smell.

Jace lifted Sheyna into his arms and carried her over to the bed. Taking a seat, he lowered her onto his lap, where he cradled her close to his chest. "Don't worry about that. No one will ever hurt you again." There was an air of power radiating in both the timbre of his voice and in his eyes.

Sheyna drew a soft, shallow breath. "Why are you so good to me?" Her voice broke on the words.

"I love you, and I'm supposed to protect what's mine." Jace held up his hand and pointed at the platinum band on his finger. "This here makes you my responsibility. I swear to you I'm going to find the person who did that to you," he said, pointing at the bruise on her face. "You can count on that." His lips were soft, questing on hers. He tasted, exploring the contours of her mouth. When he reared back, Jace brought his hand up to cup her face, thumb brushing over her bottom lip, and she shivered.

"I keep thinking it's just a game someone was playing," she said while watching him from the veil of her lashes.

"Well, they're playing with the wrong man's wife."

As Jace stared, possession raged in his gaze, and her heart skipped a beat. She loved when he talked that way.

"Maybe you should stay home until after the first of the year."

Quickly, she shook her head. "No, not at all. I told you. We've got too much going on this week."

He drew a breath. "I'm not going to argue with you, but I *am* going to heighten security in the building."

Lovingly, she reached up and stroked his wickedly handsome face. "No need. I'll be at work." She smiled, bringing his heated gaze to her parted lips.

"It's not up for discussion," Jace warned.

"You worry too much," she murmured.

"Damn right, I'm worried." He scowled and blew out a breath. His warm lips were close as he moved even closer and kissed her. He tasted as he had just snatched a peppermint candy cane from the tree. As he eased back slightly, Jace whispered, "I'm going to jump in the shower. Don't fall asleep." He gave a playful wink then kissed her once more. Slipping his hands beneath her, he lifted Sheyna from his lap and lowered her gently onto the bed beside him.

Once he disappeared into the ensuite, Sheyna released a slow breath, then climbed underneath the covers and clicked on the television, pushing her worries aside. She was going back to work. Teleworking had gotten old. Besides, she wasn't about to let somebody scare her. She had done nothing. *Or at least I don't think so.* For weeks, she'd searched her memory catalog, trying to remember if she had pissed anyone off if human resources had fired in the last few months. One employee was caught stealing hotel robes that her son had been selling on eBay. She was fired, given a month's pay, and sent on her way. *Maybe her son's responsible,* Sheyna wondered and then became so consumed that she missed the beginning of the television show. *Not tonight,* she told herself. She couldn't think about that; otherwise, she'd find herself spending another week at home. Nope. She was going in to work on Tuesday. It was the holiday season, and the Beaumont Corporation would be quiet. Only essential personnel or the ones who wanted to save their leave would be in the building. Nope, she was going to ease herself back into the office so that after the New Year, she would be in full swing.

Shivering, Sheyna rose to place a log in the fireplace. By the time she heard the running water stop, a fire had crackled, and embers glowed beneath a row of silver garland that strung the length of a wooden mantel. She was back under the covers, laughing at an episode of *Black-ish* when her husband stepped into the bedroom wrapped in a thick, thirsty bath towel.

Have mercy!

Her heart skittered in double time. Water was dripping from his short-cropped hair, down onto a strong, dark shoulder, then trickled slowly across the peak of his nipple, causing her throat to dry. Her tongue slipped out of her mouth as she watched the droplets travel further down across the taut line of every hard muscle and then disappear inside the waist of the towel.

"What are you watching?" Jace's expressive eyebrows lifted a fraction.

She gave him the truth. "You." Her response caused him to smile as well.

"Is that so?" His voice was deep and intimate.

Jace yanked the covers away, then reached for Sheyna's ankles and dragged her down toward the edge of the bed. Looking up, she met his eyes. She watched his searching hers then drift over her face. Leaning forward, Jace pressed his mouth to hers. She drew in a shallow breath and parted her lips. The kiss was hungry and demanding. She met his strokes with her own selfish need. All too soon, Jace eased back and kneeled onto the plush carpeted floor in front of her.

Moans began to spill from between her lips as Jace rubbed her feet, then her toes. He drew them into his mouth, gently sucking, making her squirm, and she began to whimper. "Oh, that feels wonderful," she whispered. He always knew how to make her forget about her worries.

His tongue slid across her calf, then her knee, and upward along her inner thighs in a slow torturous speed that made her cry out in desire. Jace's lips grazed her curls, and she shuddered hard before he moved up to her stomach. She was pulsing, aching to feel his tongue buried between her throbbing folds, but instead, he nipped and kissed at her belly button. Sheyna reached out, resting her palms onto his shoulders, spreading her fingers against the warm flesh. Jace continued caressing and nibbling, his tongue heating its path as he traced, outlined, and possessed. She was on fire. The feel of his warm breath sent her quivering and yearning for much more.

Jace slipped a nipple into his mouth. His tongue lavished first one and then the other with a slowness that stretched her nerves taut. Her hands cupping his shoulders tightened and eased, then squeezed again. As he moved toward her neck and shoulders, his goatee slid across her sensitive skin, and she whimpered, "Jace," softly under her breath.

Dipping his head, Sheyna released another slow moan of pleasure as he slipped a nipple between his lips again. Desire raged through her body. He applied just enough pressure to drive her crazy, yet his lips and tongue were gentle and arousing. With him sucking, nibbling, and then his teeth lightly grazing the hardened peak, Sheyna jerked, lifting her back off the bed and leaning further into his mouth.

He shifted to the other, and she whimpered and moaned, practically begging him to take her.

"Now, Jace!" she cried.

"Shhh, be patient, love," he told Sheyna as she continued to squirm beside him. When he finally eased back, she whimpered in protest and opened her eyes to find her husband staring down at her.

Jace's lips curled into a saucy grin as he slid the straps of the nightie over her shoulders, causing her to shudder.

"Relax, we got all night," he told her.

When she responded with a disgruntled frown, he added, "I want to make you feel good."

"I *do* feel good."

"You know what I mean."

Sheyna smirked. "No, I don't know. So why don't you show me?" she added with a smirk, then leaned back, resting her elbows on the bed and parted her thighs. The nightie slipped lower, revealing her large breasts.

With eyes locked, Jace slid his palm along her nipples then down her body until his fingers lightly combed the hair at her apex. Sheyna sucked in a long breath. The corner of his mouth tilted upward when his fingers traveled along her moist slit. On contact, Sheyna jerked and shuddered. He had barely touched her, but it had been just enough to make her body come to life. Jace's fingers slid across again, first up and then down, teasing her pulsating clit. The impact, she felt right smack at her core.

"Yes," she whispered, rocking her hips. "Yes, please."

Jace leaned forward, parting her thighs further apart, and then settled his wicked tongue to her softness. At the feel of his hot mouth at her pussy, Sheyna's lungs seized, and her wits scattered. He licked, probed, and she was lost. Her body and her senses all belonged to him. Sheyna brought her hands up to cup his head. Her fingers were there to aid him, but her husband required no assistance. He caught one of her knees and draped her leg over his shoulder. His large hands cupped her butt, spreading her wider, allowing him deeper penetration. Her head tipped back, and her eyes were closed as his tongue stroked her most maddeningly. Jace knew what she liked. He knew what it took, and he held nothing back. Her body felt heated by flames licking over her vagina. The pleasure was building at a rapid speed, and she struggled even to gasp. She was drowning as he refused to ease up no matter how much she whimpered and withered beneath his lips.

It was the faintest sound, but she heard him suck in a breath and groan as he slipped his fingers between her lips and eased inside her.

Her body shook, and her lungs exhaled. His tongue found her clit and sucked hard, and at the exact moment, he pushed deeper inside, sending blood raging through her veins. And when he turned his fingers in a corkscrew motion and found her spot, spine arching, she ignited and screamed with release. "Yes...Yesss!" However, Jace refused to let up, not until the last wave had passed and her hips had lowered back onto the bed. Sheyna was panting, and her body was still hot and wanting more.

"I need you inside of me," she told him as she tried to lift him on the bed, but his hold was unbreakable and strong. "Please, baby. Fuck me, Jace!" she pleaded and arched into his hand.

Finally ready to give her what she desperately needed, Jace moved on top of her, his muscular thighs pushing her legs wide part. She clutched his arms and looked up to search his face. He was looking down at her as he drew her hips to his. In that instant, she felt the head of his erection parting her slick folds. Tilting her hips closer, she lost her breath as he thrust into her core. He was hard, hot, and large, filling her. Her need for him became savaged. She locked her hands at his shoulders, rocked with him, meeting his downward thrusts as he served her. With relentless intent, he drew her hips to him, held her there, and pushed even further. And she was lost by the intensity and the power of his strokes. Wrapping her legs around him, she forced him deeper.

Shifting, Jace began a series of what she considered her

favorite position. His weight rested on his forearms while he moved between her thighs in a push-up motion. He lifted, drawing his cock from her, only to slide home again. He was driving so deep, Sheyna cried, "Jace!" She began pleading with need, desperate for release. It was intense. It was greedy and quick. But sometimes, that was all she needed. Tonight nothing drawn out was required. She just wanted to feel and take her mind off her worries.

Holding her hips immobile, Jace set up a driving rhythm that sent her sobbing and thrashing her head from side to side.

When another intense wave hit her, she sucked in a gasp and clamped hard, closing around his penis so snuggly. Her breath came out in panting gasps as the tempo increased and Jace pounded into hers. Sheyna's spine arched, and her body seized. She could feel his erection swelling, and then she came apart. Ripples cascaded, rocked her, and then shattered. But Jace wasn't finished. He released her hips and gripped her ass, holding her steady as he increased his pace. He continued to move inside her while her body sizzled.

"Yesss.... yesss!" Sheyna whimpered.

Harder. Faster, more profound, and steady. Jace pumped repetitively, penetrating her further. His breath came out shaky, and he shuddered. She felt the tension winding tight then she heard him drag in a huge breath.

Their lovemaking had always been glorious and perfect. The love they had for each other made her heart ache.

She loved the life they had together.

She loved Jace.

And there was no inkling of doubt that her husband loved her.

Breathing heavily, Jace collapsed on the bed beside her and then pulled her into the warmth of his embrace. She needed this. His warmth. His comfort. He tugged the blankets over them, and she snuggled closer with her nose and cheek against his chest. His arm rested protectively just below her breasts. Inhaling, she took a deep breath, filled her lungs with the scent of him, and sighed before falling into a peaceful sleep.

CHAPTER 2

"I want to be on Uncle Jaden's team!" JJ bellowed. "Traitor!" Jace cried.

Jaden rumbled with laughter. "My nephew knows a winner when he sees one."

Sheyna stood to the side of a cluster of snow-laden evergreens along with Brenna and Danica. Together, the Beaumont wives watched as their husbands behaved like teenagers.

After an insatiable night of lovemaking, Sheyna had awakened and prepared breakfast before the family met over at Bianca and London's house for the Beaumont Winter Olympics. Snowman building. Snow angels. A shoveling contest and now a toboggan race. A few years ago, Jaden had propositioned his brothers and had been the champion ever since. The three never backed away from a challenge, especially Jace. And this year, he was determined to win.

"I'm ready," Jabarie announced as he moved to the top of the hill with his sled.

"Hold your horses." Jaden lowered onto the toboggan behind his five-year-old daughter Kimora.

"Y'all are way too slow," London replied and laughed.

Julian and Justice, Jabarie's seven-year-old twin boys, who had been dubbed double-trouble, were on a toboggan beside him, holding the reins.

JJ had one of his own and moved into position. Smiling,

Sheyna shook her head. That competitive urge had rubbed off onto their only child.

"Okay, family. Are we ready to begin?" Danica said with amusement. The former runway model was six feet barefoot, with long reddish-brown hair, hanging low on her shoulders beneath the faux fur hat. She held up a horn in her hand, ready to start the race.

"Wait, just a moment." Jabarie zipped his coat just below his neck and then tossed the hood over his ears. "Okay, now I'm ready."

They looked so boyish, Sheyna couldn't help laughing again. The Beaumont brothers were kids at heart.

Danica raised her arms. "On your marks, get set..."

The second she blew the horn, they each took off, sliding fast down the hill. London fell off the back of the toboggan and skid onto his butt on the snow. Kimora continued without him. The twins lost control and ended up in a bush, and everyone else went down like out-of-control bobsleds. Sheyna watched as JJ swerved in front and beat his father across the red cones by mere seconds.

"I won!" he cried.

"No way! You cheated!" Jaden said.

"No, I didn't, Uncle Jaden. You're just slow!" JJ's response caused everyone to laugh.

"We have been at this for the last two hours," Brenna said, teeth chattering as she tried to hug herself.

"You know how they are when they get together. A bunch of big babies," Danica added. She was married to Jaden.

Sheyna shivered. "I think they will stay out here until their limbs fall off."

"Then they are going to freeze to death by themselves," Brenna retorted. "I should have stayed in the house with Bianca."

"Me too!" It was a cold Delaware afternoon, and Sheyna found she couldn't keep a positive attitude with frozen toes.

When the racers made it back to the top, breathing heavily against the cold wind, Brenna said, "Don't you think you guys have had enough?"

"Yes, we do," Jabarie replied and couldn't stop smiling at his gorgeous wife.

Jaden nodded in agreement. "We decided it's now our wives turn."

Sheyna glanced up in surprise. "Huh?" They've never participated.

Jaden's long dark lashes held a few snowflakes as he said, "Yes, I want to see if my wife can represent the family."

Danica gave a rude snort. "That isn't an issue."

Brenna laughed. "We'll see about that."

"I hate to embarrass you two," Sheyna replied as she took the red toboggan from Jace.

"Embarrass?" Danica's brow arched.

Brenna rubbed the round baby bump hidden beneath the coat. "If I weren't pregnant, I'd give you both a run for your money."

"Yeah...yeah. I think you've been using your pregnancies as excuses for the last fourteen years." Laughing, Sheyna thumped along in oversized boots to stand at the top of the hill.

"Mommy, I'll go for you!" Arianna said and moved beside her aunt. Sheyna saw the eager face of Jabarie and Brenna's thirteen-year-old daughter.

"Good for you, Arie. Make me proud," her mother said with warmth.

"I'm going to do more than make you proud. I'm here to win!" she challenged.

Brenna exchanged an amused glance with her husband, sending the group into a fit of laughter.

"Me too." Briana, their twelve-year-old daughter, took the toboggan from the twins and moved into position beside her older sister. The two beautiful girls often made Sheyna yearn for a daughter of her own before she remembered how difficult she had made life for her father growing up. Years ago, she and Jace had decided they were happy with their family the way it was.

The men made wagers, and then JJ had the horn in his hand.

"Mom, please don't embarrass us," he whispered, then shook his head the way his father does.

The horn sounded, and the racers went sailing down the hill. Sheyna held on, laughing, and the cold air beat across her face. From behind, she could hear the men shouting and urging them on. Briana was in the first place, and Arianna was behind her. Sheyna was moving to third place when she felt a bump from behind and went sailing, landing on top of a mound of snow. Hearing laughter nearby, she looked up to see Danica lying on the ground beside her. "Oh no! Are you okay?"

"I guess we aren't meant to represent the family," she teased.

"I agree. This is one time I don't mind the brothers saying a woman's place is in the kitchen. I should have stayed inside and helped with lunch."

Laughing, Danica nodded as she brushed snow from her hair. "I agree."

Sheyna was moving into a sitting position when she spotted Jace and Jaden racing down the hill.

"Sheyna, you, okay?" her husband asked. There was no mistaking the humor in his tone.

"You think you're funny." She picked up a clod of snow and tossed it at him. It missed him by a mile, but that didn't stop him from scooping some in his hand and packing it firmly with his gloves.

"You wouldn't?"

She was mildly alarmed when he threw it hard at her shoulder.

"Ow!"

"How dare you hit my sister," Danica said and tossed snow, hitting him smack in the back of his head. Jace retaliated.

"Yo, bro! Don't hit the mother of my children!" Jaden sputtered with laughter, tossing a snowball at him.

"Then tell her this here is between my wife and me." Jace ducked and sent one flying that caught Danica in the side.

"Don't hit my mommy!" Kimora chimed in as she and her nine-year-old brother Joshua raced over, tossing snowballs.

JJ sent one hurling through the sky, hitting Arianna in the back. Following that, laughter rang through the air, and it was a full-fledged snowball fight.

When Jace wasn't looking, Sheyna launched herself at him, and they both fell back onto a bed of snow. She landed on top, covering his cold face with warm kisses.

He gazed up at her, eyes sparkling with mischief. "Did you ever think you'd be married to such a crazy family?"

She smiled lovingly down at her husband and whispered, "I wouldn't have it any other way." Tipping her head, she lowered her mouth over his.

While the Beaumont Winter Olympics continued, the women went inside to assist Bianca with lunch. Sheyna stepped out of the mudroom wearing fluffy socks and leggings and an oversized cable knit sweater that she had borrowed from Bianca. Her wet ponytail dampened her neck. Lifting it away from her skin, she twirled it around in a bun and used a hair-tie to keep it firmly twisted in place.

Inside, Bianca's home was charming. It was two-story with glass walls and located on the ocean with breathtaking views. Multicolored lights decorated a fourteen-foot tree in the corner of the massive foyer. Holiday decorations filled every room. She stepped into the enormous kitchen with a generous eating area, stainless steel appliances, and a large island with six barstools.

Bianca was married to London Brown, the owner of Clarence's Chicken & Fish House, with locations around Delaware and Philadelphia. They were also the proud parents of seven-year-old Sierra.

London had homemade tomato soup and pre-buttered grilled cheese sandwiches delivered from the restaurant. Bianca was standing in front of the island, lining the sandwiches on a foil-covered cookie sheet.

"What can I do to help?" Sheyna asked as her eyes traveled around the beautifully decorated white and gray kitchen. Brenna was pouring potato chips into two large bowls. Danica was already filling Styrofoam mugs with warm apple cider.

"Nothing for now. Just take a seat. It will probably be another hour before they finally decide to come in the house." Bianca laughed.

"You are so right," Brenna chimed in. "They're not going to stop until the competition is officially over."

Bianca's walnut-colored eyes beamed with delight. "Or someone's toes fall off."

"So true," Danica cosigned with a playful eye roll.

"How are you doing?" Bianca asked, studying Sheyna with a squinty-eyed look.

Sheyna took a seat before answering truthfully. "Ask me after my first day back in the office." At the sympathetic looks, she added, "I wish they would find who'd attacked me so I can move on."

Brenna angled her head to the side. Her long honey-brown hair bounced with the gesture. "Jabarie said they didn't have any leads yet."

Shaking her head, Sheyna replied, "No, they don't, so every time I step out the house, I feel myself tensing up like I'm expecting to be ambushed again."

Bianca gave her a sympathetic smile. "It's only natural to be still nervous. I mean, it just happened."

Danica had bundled her damp hair into a loose braid that she flipped over her shoulder as she chimed in. "She's right. You have every right to feel still uneasy."

Opening the door to the stove, Bianca slid the cookie sheet inside then turned around. Resting her hip against the countertop, she tossed her a look. "Whatever you do, just promise me you'll watch your back."

Sheyna waved off her worry with a manicured hand. "I refuse to live my life in fear."

Her expression softened. "Good for you. You shouldn't, but at the same time, we have to be careful out here."

Brenna touched her comfortingly. "You're going to get through it."

Sheyna leaned forward, resting her elbows on the island. "Sheraton Beach isn't as safe as it used to be."

"That's not true!" Danica insisted.

"Why would you say that?" Bianca asked.

Brenna slowly shook her head, hazel eyes narrowed. "I understand what Sheyna means, and that's because folks from Philadelphia are trying to migrate to this area, but the mayor is not having it. He's got the police department patrolling the streets at night and keeping a tight watch on our small town."

Crossing her arms under her breasts, Danica breathed,

"Thank goodness! I love this town. It's the safest place to live in the state. I hate to see that change."

"Sheyna, I'm sure whoever stole your purse is probably long gone by now," Bianca said with confidence.

"I sure hope so because I'm returning to work." She wanted things back to the way they used to be. Ever since the attack, she refused to drive the Volvo. The car had been a birthday present from Jace, but she feared her assailant would recognize the vehicle and her.

"Speaking of the police..." Danica glanced over her shoulder, checking to see if anyone was listening before saying, "Have you seen the new chief?"

Bianca nodded and smiled. "Yes, I have. He already has the single women in this town going crazy."

Sheyna grinned knowingly. "Jace and I ran into him at the grocery store last week. He's eye candy." He was tall and wickedly gorgeous. Danica gave a description filled with adjectives, and the women laughed. Sheyna was glad her in-laws were around, taking her mind off her troubles.

"Well, since you're going to be back at work on Tuesday, we have to go to that new restaurant, Camellia. She has this seafood pasta. OMG! It's to die for."

Sheyna nodded. "I'm game. I have a conference call, but we can go early."

The others agreed.

By the time the men and children trooped inside, stomping the snow from their boots, lunch was ready. The entire family gathered around the room. So far, the teams were tied, but both Jace and Jaden had already declared victory. They debated and went back in forth until the conversation shifted to them all being competitive teenagers. The children loved hearing stories about their parents growing up in Sheraton Beach.

After everyone had finished eating, the children rushed to grab their coats, and the Olympics resumed. Determined not to go back out in the cold, Sheyna and Brenna offered to help with the dishes. One washed and the other dried. Danica focused on the floor. When everything was spotless, the ladies moved to the sunroom at the rear of the house lit up by the bright winter sunlight pouring through the floor-to-ceiling windows. A warm fire crackled invitingly in the hearth. Sheyna curled up onto one of the couches. Brenna lowered on the cushion beside her.

"I'm taking Arie bra shopping this weekend."

Danica registered surprise for a split second before she gave Brenna a knowing look. "I told you it was time for a bra."

Brenna lovingly stroked her pregnant stomach as she shook her head the way a parent does when they realize their child's growing up, whether they're ready or not. "I agree," she admitted with a sheepish grin. "She came down to breakfast wearing a t-shirt that was showing way too much. You should have seen my husband's face." She giggled because Jabarie didn't want to believe Arianna was now a teenager.

"I bet that changed my brother's tune real quick." Bianca chuckled heartedly.

The petite beauty laughed. "Quick, fast, and in a hurry."

Smiling, Sheyna thought about her beautiful niece, her lengthy hair still in pigtails. With her mother's caramel complexion and hazel eyes, Arianna already had the little boys sniffing around her.

As she focused out the window, she saw the children having another snowball fight. *So much for the Beaumont Winter Olympics.* From a distance, she could hear the roar of a motor quickly approaching. "What's that?"

"Probably the last event of the afternoon." Bianca met her gaze. "That's London. He's on his snowmobile."

They moved over to the window where icicles were hanging outside the frosted glass to see him jetting across the blanket of white snow on a red bike on skis. The children shrieked with excitement and ran over to see Uncle London.

"He just started something," Sheyna murmured and shook her head. Everyone wanted a turn on the snowmobile. The other men joined them, and then within seconds, they went dashing toward the rear of the yard. "Where are they going?"

Bianca groaned. "The garage. London has two more snowmobiles inside."

Moments later, Jace and Jaden were jetting across the snow. Danica shook her head. "Men and their toys."

The women erupted with laughter.

CHAPTER 3

Jace moved down the carpeted corridors of the Beaumont Corporation with wide strides and a grim expression on his face. Even though it was the holiday season, a few of the secretaries were on duty and seated at their workstations. As soon as the women spotted him heading their way, they dropped their headsets from their ears and rose, greeting him with a chorus of good mornings.

Despite how he was feeling, Jace flashed a sincere smile and a "Season's Greeting." However, he didn't stop. He kept moving until he was in the conference room. Jabarie was seated at the head of the table. As soon as he spotted his older brother stepping inside the room, he looked up from the stack of papers in front of him and grinned; identical sable-colored eyes were gleaming with pleasure.

"I just finished a conference call with Pierre." He was the general manager of the Beaumont Hotel in Biloxi, Mississippi. "I think we finally have their labor costs under control for next quarter."

"Sheyna's still having the nightmares," Jace blurted as if he hadn't heard him.

Jabarie quirked an eyebrow. There was no need to explain.

Jace dropped onto the seat across from him. Something on his face must have gotten Jabarie's attention because his shoulders tensed, and he lowered his pen.

"I was hoping they would have stopped by now."

"So did I." Jace shook his head. "She rode into work with me this morning, and so far, she seems to be doing fine. I keep telling her it was an isolated incident and that I am confident it won't happen again, but how can I be sure?"

Sighing deeply, Jabarie pushed back from his desk and rose from the executive chair as if he'd been seated far too long. "You want some coffee?" he offered as he moved from behind the large mahogany table.

"Sure. I'll take it black." Jace leaned back in the chair. His eyes followed his brother as he moved to a coffee bar to the far corner of the room. Who needed Starbucks when they had everything, including a cappuccino machine.

Like him, his brother was dressed in crisp white shirt and black slacks. Since it was the holiday season, he hadn't bothered with the tie, but Jabarie was wearing a black one, festively decorated with silver Christmas bells, a present from his daughter Briana.

"I believe the fear will go away. It's going to take time. But if being back at work doesn't help, maybe you should take her to a therapist," he suggested. "It might help."

Jace flinched and blew out a breath. "I tried to convince her, right after the nightmares began, but you know how stubborn my wife is."

"Yes, I know. About as stubborn as mine." Chuckling, Jabarie put a mug under the spout and hit the button.

"Dammit! I feel so helpless."

Jabarie's eyes met his from across the room. "I know how you feel. Remember when Arianna went missing and I couldn't find her? Well, that was probably the scariest moment in my life because there was absolutely nothing I could do to get that look of panic off Brenna's face. So, I understand."

He would never forget that Jabarie had been just as afraid as Brenna when their oldest child had gone missing. The entire family had jumped into action, searching the town, including the surrounding woods, for her. Luckily, they had been able to bring her home without incident.

Within moments, Jabarie carried two mugs over to the table and handed one to Jace. He instantly brought the coffee to his lips as he stared at his brother over the rim.

Jabarie still wore his thick curly hair low on top and faded on the sides. The only difference was the generous strands of gray. He often wondered if his turning gray prematurely resulted from the stress of being the CEO of the Beaumont Corporation.

After their father had stepped down, he had appointed Jabarie, not his firstborn son, to take over. Jace had known even back then Jabarie had what it took to run the corporation.

"What's security saying?" Jabarie asked as he lowered back onto his chair.

"The same as before...there's nothing wrong with the system. But if that was the case, where's the footage?"

Jabarie took a sip then frowned. "I still don't understand that. Do you recall any glitches in the system before?"

Jace shook his head. "Nope. It's as if the camera was turned off right before it happened and turned on again right after Sheyna's incident."

He gave his brother a look. Jabarie nodded and replied, "I agree. Something about that doesn't quite sound right to me. I think someone turned off that camera."

After the incident had happened, Jace was sure one of the staff was responsible. He'd been ready to fire every security officer on duty that evening until Jabarie had been his voice of reason, which was a prime example as to why he was the CEO, and he wasn't.

Jabarie was just that good at what he did. A few years ago, after the corporation had suffered a significant financial hit that threatened the jobs of hundreds of their local employees, Jabarie had come up with a way to save every single job. Because of that, their employees were loyal. At least Jace had thought so before his wife's attack.

Jabarie's sable-colored eyes burned over at him as he said, "What's Troy have to say?" He was their head of security.

"The same as before, he interviewed everyone on that shift, including anyone who called in sick, and no one remembers anything out of the ordinary or remembers a camera not working."

"Interesting." By the tone of Jabarie's voice, he wasn't buying it either.

As he sipped his coffee, Jace drummed his fingers against the table with increasing agitation. Someone knew something that he was sure of. "I think someone wasn't manning the station, and while they weren't looking, someone slipped into the security office and turned that camera off."

A muscle ticked at Jabarie's jaw. "But why? Who would want to hurt Sheyna?"

That's what he wanted to know and was determined to find out.

"In the meantime, engineering added new cameras, and we assigned security to escort employees to their cars after dark. Another was detailed to patrol around both the employee and guest parking lots," Jabarie offered between sips as if it were any consolation.

Jace brought the mug to his lips again as he stared over at his brother. Even though there had been no recent attacks, it still wasn't enough as far as he was concerned. He wanted the person responsible found and hung by his necktie.

"Relax. If they are still around, we're going to catch them," Jabarie reassured him.

"We better because I'm not going to rest until we do."

"He is just too freaking gorgeous."

Sheyna looked up from her desk and followed the direction of Bianca's eyes out into the reception area, and grinned. Even before she'd spotted him, she knew who Bianca was referencing.

Chavez Berry.

He was coming across the floor with enough swag he had all the ladies in the secretarial pool salivating. He was tall, six-four maybe, muscled and raw with olive-toned skin with dimples at each cheek. There was a diamond in each earlobe. And his hair cut close to his scalp. Today he was wearing a designer gray suit with a crisp white shirt underneath. The outfit looked tailor-made.

"Yes, all the single women in this building think that man is gorgeous."

"*Single*? I'm married, and I even think he's yummy." Bianca was fanning herself. "If I was single—"

"If you were single, you'd still be in love with the same man." She grinned. Bianca had eyes for one man. That was London Brown.

"They didn't make them like that back when I was single," she replied. Her glossy dark hair was swept over one shoulder. Bianca crossed long legs as she leaned back on the chair and glanced again out onto the floor.

"Ain't that the truth," Sheyna agreed. Although, she had eyes for no one but Jace. It had always been that way. When she was single, he'd been all she wanted, even when she refused to admit it to herself.

"Is he dating?" Bianca asked, arching a perfectly sculpted eyebrow.

Sheyna frowned at her. "Why, you want to date him?"

"No, but I might know someone who would." Sheyna could see the wheels turning.

"You are bad."

Bianca giggled like a schoolgirl. "Hey, I might as well help her out."

"Who is it?"

"She works at Sierra's after-school program. Smart, beautiful, educated, and single. What man doesn't want that combination?"

Following a long, thoughtful look, Sheyna replied, "You never know." His personal life was still a mystery.

On cue, Chavez walked up to her open door and rapped his knuckles. "May I come in?"

With a smile and a wave of her hand, she signaled for him to enter. "Sure. Bianca and I were just talking about you."

Bianca gave her a side-eye glare that Sheyna ignored.

"What about?" he asked, and she smiled at his lazy, sensual appeal.

"I was feeling guilty for not reaching out and inviting you to join our family for a holiday, being that you're new to the area. I hope you were able to have Christmas dinner with someone special," she added with a sly smirk.

"I did." His grin was easy. "I served dinner at the local homeless shelter."

"Oh, my goodness! I'm in love with him," Bianca mumbled under her breath. "I'll see you at lunch." She rose, gave him a slow, deliberate once-over, then strolled across the room in red bottom pumps. The moment he turned his back, Bianca gave an appreciative look before heading out the door.

It took everything Sheyna had not to laugh out loud as she swiveled her chair closer and rested elbows on the desk. "I'm glad you could come into the office. I hope I didn't ruin your holiday."

He smiled again. Chavez's face was a canvas of hard angles and sinful beauty from his long lashes feathering his dark eyes to his jaw, square and strong, shadowed with dark hair. "No, not at all. I wouldn't miss it. We've worked hard on this project."

"No, *you* worked hard. I was just along for the ride," she corrected.

The Coalition for America's Heroes was a comprehensive global network enhancing the quality of life, supporting well-being, and boasting soldiers' morale, families, civilian employees, and military retirees. It had been Chavez's idea to give back. It didn't take much convincing before Sheyna jumped on board, setting up a campaign for employees to contribute through payroll deductions. However, after months of watching his commitment to sponsoring military families, she decided to take it a step further and become a sponsor for the armed forces moral and welfare center. After weeks of meeting with the board together, they had come up with a way to show their patriotic support to servicemen and women.

With the help of Bianca and her team of marketing representatives, they built the Beaumont Military Vacation Club around the idea that heroes deserved the best. To honor members of the U.S. Armed Forces for their dedication and courage, the Beaumont Corporation would be offering two-night weekend hotel stays, including breakfast, for a flat rate of forty-nine dollars at any of the hundreds of resort locations. The CEO of Moral and Welfare Recreations was so eager to have the contract signed; she scheduled their meeting before the New Year's holiday to announce the merger at their next board meeting.

Chavez straddled the chair across from her. His long, lean face was serious. "So, what's the plan?"

"The plan is you'll lead. Bianca and I will be available to jump in if you need us, but I don't think you will." Sheyna smiled. She had lied and told Jace she needed to be here, but it had just been an excuse to come back to the office. Chavez was more than prepared to handle the final touches of the program. They were lucky to have him. The former military personnel officer had been with them for almost seven months and was a pleasure to work with.

"This meeting wasn't supposed to happen until after the first of the year, but you impressed them. The director was ready to head out of the country for a couple of weeks but decided she didn't want to waste time."

"I think she wants to lock this deal in before someone changes their mind," Chavez teased.

Sheyna laughed. "You might be right." The rate they were offering wasn't even available to their Platinum members. "Two o'clock this afternoon. She wants congrats signed before she leaves, and so do I."

"A woman who knows what she wants...I like that." Chavez gave her an irresistible grin.

"Well, let's just hope you can schmooze our servicemen and women, so they'll keep coming back."

Chavez winked. "You just leave that up to me."

CHAPTER 4

"Everything's all set," Danica announced with a smile. "My designs are already shipped, and I'm ready to leave." Her accentuated smoky gray eyes stared at Sheyna from across the restaurant.

"Have you told Jaden you're going to New York the day after New Year's?" Brenna asked as she chewed a roll.

Danica shook her head, her lashes sweeping shadows down across her freckled cheeks. "No, I was hoping you would do it for me."

"Are you crazy?" Sheyna barked. "Just tell your husband you're going to be the next Kimora Lee Simmons. He'll understand."

"No, he won't. He's just like Jabarie. Those brothers think a woman should be at home raising babies," Brenna stated with humor in her tone.

"Uh-uh, not Jace. He knows better than that." Sheyna pointed a French manicured nail at them. "See, the problem with the two of you is you've changed. For me, the same thing I was doing before I married Jace is the same thing I'm doing now." She shook her head, sending her curls bouncing. "Women try to change, and when you do, men expect you to keep being that person. I knew from day one I wasn't changing who I was for nobody," she emphasized with a finger snap.

Brenna replied with a snort. "Blah, blah. You're preaching to the choir. Been there and done that. Although, I have to admit that ever since I went back to running my bookstore, things have been different with Jabarie and me in a good way."

Sheyna looked over at her beautiful sister-in-law. Flawless caramel skin, hazel eyes, and honey brown hair. They had been best of friends since elementary school and fell in love and married brothers. She'd had one child; Brenna went on to have a handful of babies and became a stay-at-home mom. A few years ago, she decided she wanted to go back to work and run her bookstore. There was a little resistance at first, but eventually, Jabarie saw how important it was.

While listening to Brenna talk about a book signing, she had lined up for the Valentine's Day weekend, Sheyna's eyes lowered to her protruding stomach.

"I don't know how the two of you had time to make *that*."

Brenna lovingly rubbed her belly. "Easy, Jabarie and I both have private offices away from the prying eyes of our children."

Danica made an exaggerated show of rolling her eyes. "Uh-uh, you are so nasty."

Brenna laughed with pleasure. "Yes, we are," she agreed, and then they each exploded with laughter.

Six children...Sheyna and Jace could barely raise one, yet the couple seemed to have perfected childrearing.

Their server returned and lowered piping hot plates of seafood pasta in front of them.

"Mmmm, that looks good!" Danica said.

Brenna nodded in agreement. "Bianca said we would like this place."

A public relations fiasco at one of their California hotels required Bianca's immediate expertise, and she had been unable to join them for lunch.

Sheyna spun noodles around on her fork as she replied, "I think Jaden will be okay with your decision to go back to runway modeling, so tell him and quit sneaking around behind his back. *That's* what's going to cause the issues."

"She's right," Brenna chimed in. "You need to just talk to

him. And do it soon," she urged.

"I know," Danica said with a mouthful of pasta. "I'm just not ready for his reaction. I promised him I was done, but I have this overwhelming urge to get back out there one more time."

With the surge of plus-size clothing, Danica's Ujema Swimwear collection was getting ready to launch an entire line of swim gear just for the curvy woman. After giving birth to two beautiful babies, her curves were the perfect push for the line. Tyra Banks was quoted saying, "No one struts a runway like Danica Dansforth."

They engaged in a conversation about marriage, and the two women offered Danica insight into their demanding husbands and lessons learned over the years.

Brenna was patting her lips with a white linen napkin when she asked, "Sheyna, how are you feeling?"

"Oh my! How insensitive of me. How's your first day back in the office?" Danica asked as she sipped iced tea from her glass.

Sheyna noticed the concerned looks on their faces and shrugged. "It's not as scary as I thought it would be. When Jace first pulled up into the parking lot, I felt a moment of anxiety, but I was fine once we were inside the building."

"I'm surprised he let you drive to the restaurant by yourself," Brenna commented while nibbling on a roll.

"I was supposed to ride with Bianca, but when I found out she couldn't make it, Jace walked me out to his car. He parks close enough to the building that all I have to do is call security when I'm on my way, and someone will come out to valet the car."

Brenna smiled. "I'm just glad you felt brave enough to return to work. That's a big step for you."

She gave a shaky smile. "Yes, I'm fine. No, scratch that! It's the holiday season. I'm better than fine!"

"I guess so with that beautiful rock on your finger," Danica said, pointing down at Sheyna's hand.

Wiggling her fingers, she showed off the new bling. It had been her Christmas present. A five-carat princess diamond in a platinum setting. "I've put up with that man for more than twelve years. I earned this."

Danica exploded with laughter. "I know that's right!"

Brenna reached over and gave her a high-five.

By the time they were eating dessert, the conversation had shifted to their children.

"I'm going to try and make JJ's hockey game. Bree has ice skating lessons at five," Brenna explained between chews.

Sheyna bit into a slice of sweet potato pie and replied, "No worries. I'm sure all of his uncles will be there being loud and rowdy."

Danica laughed. "The way they behave, you would think *they* were on the hockey team," she complained, but there was no hiding the admiration shining in her eyes.

Their serving returned with the bill. Sheyna quickly snatched it off the table.

"What can I do to help with the party?" Danica asked as she tossed a sizable tip onto the table.

"Absolutely nothing. I hired a party planner," Brenna explained with a dismissive wave.

Sheyna scowled. "I don't blame you. After wasting the last four years trying to plan a family reunion, I'm worn out."

"It will happen. Like Sedona told us, just pick a date and get it scheduled and she and her brothers will try and get her father there." She was referring to Sedona Beaumont, Sage's sister. "Those two old men are so stubborn! All we have to do is not invite one, and the other is going to show up pissed because he wasn't invited."

Danica laughed. "Yes, that is probably a great idea."

Sheyna sighed. "I just don't have the energy to think about that right now. Besides, Aunt Bettye said she's going to try and bring Uncle Richard to your party."

Brenna's eyes sparkled. "You're kidding?"

"Nope. She told me herself. Jace said it isn't going to happen, but we'll see."

"We can only hope," Brenna replied and crossed her fingers.

By the time they'd left the restaurant, a frigid wind had kicked up. Sheyna tightened the belt around the narrow waist of a pink wool coat as the three women sauntered out of the restaurant. Flecks of white snow blew around them, promising several more inches. The parking lot had been cleared, but the snowplow would be back by morning. Sheyna slipped into Jace's Jaguar. She shut the door and put the key in the ignition. The moment the engine purred, and the air blew from the vents onto her face, and she went utterly still. Only the rise and fall of her breasts revealed she was breathing—that smell. A woodsy masculine scent she would never forget filled her nostril and caused her entire body to shake.

Oh no. It can't be!

Sheyna couldn't move. She couldn't reach for her phone. She was too afraid to turn around and see if she was in the car alone.

Tap, tap, tap!

She jerked, and her eyes snapped to look out the window where she saw Brenna standing beside the car. Frantically, she pressed the button and lowered the glass.

"Hey," Brenna began. "I almost forgot; I need... Are you okay?"

Sheyna was breathing heavily, trying to get her heart rate under control. She started to lie, but when she saw Brenna's eyes widen, she knew there was no point.

"He w-was here...inside my car."

Jace drove Jaden's Ashton Martin fast, whipping in and out of traffic, and was thankful to see so many green lights.

"Bro, slow down."

"I need to get to my wife!" he barked just before pressing down hard on the brakes in time to prevent hitting a white Sonata from the rear.

"You're not going to do either of you any good if you have an accident," Jaden told him as the tires slid in the slushy snow.

"He's right," Jabarie chimed from the rear. The three of them had been having lunch in the hotel's restaurant when he'd received the call.

"Would you both just shut the hell up!"

He accelerated again, hoping to make it through the streetlight before it turned red. However, the car in front of him slowed, and Jace slammed on the brakes. "Fuck!"

"Enough," Jaden said and opened the passenger door. "Get out, now!" He rose from the seat and walked around the front of the car. He stopped long enough to glare at Jace through the windshield and gestured with his thumb for his big brother to get out of the vehicle.

"I think you better listen," Jabarie warned him.

Jace muttered obscenities under his breath before he jerked the door open and stepped out. When Jaden came around with a smirk on his lips, he cut his eyes at him and barked, "Hurry up before the light turns green."

Jaden nodded and climbed behind the wheel. As soon as their seatbelts were fastened, he shifted the car into gear and took off like a rocket.

Somehow Jace managed a harsh laugh. "Why is it okay for him to speed?"

"Because speed is what I do for a living," Jaden told him with a cocky grin.

When he looked back, and Jabarie nodded, Jace knew there was no point in arguing.

His brother owned AutoBeau with locations across the country and used by professional NASCAR drivers. Not only could Jaden fix cars, but he built engines and had become sought after for his talents.

"Just get me to my wife," Jace muttered and rubbed his stubble-covered jaw.

Jaden nodded, then whipped around a car and took off like a torpedo down the road, missing every red light. He shook his head. "Bro, why the hell was he in your car?"

"I don't know." Jace tightened his fists until he felt his nails piercing the skin at the palm of his hand. "But trust me. I'm going to find out what the hell is going on." He sat taller on the seat when Jaden made a sharp right turn onto Main Street and rounded the restaurant into the parking lot. Up ahead, he saw Brenna's Mercedes parked beside his Jaguar. A police car was blocking it in with the red and blue emergency vehicle lights trolling.

The moment Jaden skidded to a halt, Jace jerked, opened the car door, and leaped out. He had to catch himself before he slipped on the snow in his leather shoes. However, that didn't stop him from getting to the woman he loved.

"Sheyna!" he shouted. Quickly, he walked around and peered inside the window of Brenna's car. Sheyna was in the front. Danica in the rear. The motor was running, and the windshield wipers were swinging back and forth, clearing the rapidly falling snow. As soon as Sheyna's saw him, she stopped mid-sentence. The wide eyes that stared up at him were wide and frantic with fear. "Open the door!" he shouted and rushed around to the passenger's side.

Quickly, she reached for the lock, and Jace pulled it open and crouched down on the ground beside her. "Sheyna, you okay?"

He recognized the stark fear in her expression, the trembling of her soft lips. Moisture filled her eyes, and at that moment, he was ready to murder someone. She visually swallowed hard, the delicate muscles at her neck working up and down.

"He was in your car. Jace, h-he was in your car."

Jace enfolded her in his embrace. The top of her head rested on his shoulder as he inhaled her fragrance. With long sweeps, he stroked her back gently, focusing on the fit and feel of her in his arms.

"It's not even the same car which means his target is...is me," she whispered.

He reared back and stared at her. Her bottom lip trembled, and terror blazed in her pupils. Reaching out, Jace brushed a strand of hair off her cheek. Her soft skin sent warmth spiraling through him. "We're going to find out who this is. I made you a promise."

Danica cleared her throat. "Jace is right, Sheyna. They're going to find him."

Jace shifted his gaze. "Thanks for sitting with her until I got here," he said. Brenna and Danica were both turned on their seats, watching him.

Danica shook her reddish-brown hair and said, "You don't have to thank us. There was no way we were leaving her alone."

"Exactly," Brenna chimed in.

He nodded appreciatively. His brothers had married amazing women. "Hang on, precious. Let me go and speak with the police." Jace brushed his lips against hers once more then walked around the car. Jabarie and Jace were already there, practically interrogating the male and female officers.

While two others came and investigated the crime scene, the first two police officers asked a series of questions then interviewed Sheyna again. Brenna and Danica were able to fill in what she was unable to say. The car was dusted for fingerprints and searched for any other evidence.

Jace moved back and forth from sitting in the Mercedes long enough to warm up and then was back standing out in the snow with his arms wrapped tightly around his wife, providing both body heat and comfort.

Jaden was fired up and determined to find out who was responsible. Jabarie focused on keeping everyone calm and in control.

They were in the parking lot of a new restaurant. Management was concerned and had come out to see what was going on. Police cars in the parking lot of a new establishment weren't good for business but were drawing the residents' attention driving by the restaurant. Jace groaned. In a town this small, the gossip was already spreading.

When Jaden spotted a yellow mustang driving slowly while someone on the passenger's side was taking pictures, he shook his head. "The rumor mill is going to have this story all over town before dinner."

"We're Beaumonts. Anything we do is news," Jabarie replied uncomfortably.

"One of the disadvantages of living in a small town," Jace added with a sigh. "I guess one of us better call Mother."

The Beaumont Corporation was the largest employer in Sheraton Beach and was responsible for the jobs of thousands of residents. As much as it made them feel uncomfortable, they were local celebrities. Beaumont Manor was on the highest elevation, with views of the entire town. Many joked that the Beaumonts were descendants of royalty. Anything they did, good or bad, was news. And Jessica Beaumont hated being the last to know.

While Jabarie called their mother, Jace moved to the car to check on his wife, who had climbed back in with Brenna. Sheyna was bravely holding it together. He slid onto the seat beside her long enough to stroke her back tenderly while he warmed up. "It shouldn't be much longer," he told her.

True to his words, a half-hour later, the police concluded, and the other two women said their goodbyes, promising to call Sheyna later.

"You good, Jace?" Jabarie asked after he checked on his wife. Jaden had done the same and was standing beside him.

Jace nodded. "Go ahead. I got this." He gave them each dap and watched them depart.

As soon as they were alone, Jace started up the engine. While waiting for the car to warm, his eyes moved back and forth across Sheyna's face. Over the years, he memorized every detail from the faint scar below her lower lip to the mole beneath her left ear. He could still see her causing havoc in their grammar school days. She'd had his attention then and held it ever since.

"You're shaking." He eased a forefinger beneath her chin. "I'm taking you home."

"No! I told you I have a teleconference this afternoon that I can't miss," she replied, even though she was struggling to regain control.

"Chavez can handle it." Hell, as the VP of Human Resources, Jace had hired him, so he knew Chavez was more than qualified to run things for a bit longer. "I'm sure you've trained him well."

She shook her head. "I don't want him to handle it alone.

This has been our project from the beginning."

"Precious, I'm not going to argue with you."

"Then don't. I'll be at work. You're right down the hall. I'll be fine," she countered. Intense heat flared her amber eyes.

He stared, studying her expression.

"I'm going to be okay." She straightened her shoulders and pouted the way she always did when she felt strongly about her decision. He'd wondered how long before the stubborn pride reappeared. "I feel safer at the corporation than I do anywhere else." There was no point in arguing with her. At least not yet. For now, he'd allow her to have her way.

Putting the car in gear, he headed back to the office and shifted the conversation to the good news he had received right before he had left. After months of negotiations, they finally signed Solange Knowles to perform twenty shows at their Beaumont Grand Chateau in Las Vegas.

"Yes, finally!" Sheyna was a huge fan, and as she expressed her excitement, Jace remembered the first time they had gone to Las Vegas together. It had been when he'd propositioned Sheyna to a no-strings-attached relationship, and she had agreed.

And look at us now.

Jace pulled onto the circle drive and asked the valet to park his car. Once they were in the building, he helped Sheyna out of her coat, and they stepped into the elevator. He removed his leather jacket and walked Sheyna to her office, holding her hand protectively. She wanted him to believe she had it under control, but he wasn't buying it. He knew her. Sometimes better than she knew herself.

Jace pushed opened the office door and waited until she was inside. Shutting the door with a click, he hung both coats on the hooks mounted on the rear side.

"You could have left it opened," she murmured.

"No, not until I know you're okay."

Sheyna gave a dismissive wave before walking around the desk and lowering onto her chair. Jace observed her.

"Look, I'm fine."

He came over, closing the distance between them, placing the palms of his hands on the arms of her chair as he leaned in so complete their foreheads were touching. "You're not fine. And if for any reason you decide you want to go home, you let me know."

Her gaze never lost eye contact. Sheyna swallowed, and then she did something that drove him insane.

She licked her lips, sending heat raging to his groin. Her mouth was generous and soft, and slightly parted, and did crazy things to his libido.

"What time is the teleconference?" He ached to hold that shapely body tightly against his frame.

Her palm swept the back of her neck wearily as she replied, "Two o'clock."

"Then I'll be back at three to take you home."

She slowly protested. "Jace—"

"No buts. The conference call, and that's it."

As she stared up at him, Jace continued to search her eyes. She had no idea how ready he was to scoop her into his arms, throw her over his shoulder and take her home. Once there, he planned to bury himself so deep, filling her, until fear would be the furthest thing from her mind.

She studied him and must have witnessed the desire burning in his gaze as she nodded. Her eyes spoke more than words as she said, "Okay."

"Good. Glad you see things my way," he mumbled and could see her begin to relax. Jace pressed his lips against her warm moist mouth, ensuring the kiss was both soothing and tender. A soft moan slipped from her throat that instantly made

Jace think of making slow, sweet love to his wife, waking up, and then joining their bodies again. His loins tightened painfully.

"I'll be back to check on you." Cradling her face between his hands, he brushed his lips over her forehead. He kissed her closed eyelids, nose, and cheeks before claiming her mouth.

"Okay," Sheyna barely managed when his lips left hers. "I'm too tired to fight you."

"Good, because I need you to save some of that energy for later," he added with a wink. She smiled at him, and his heart somersaulted.

Her office phone rang, and Jace took it as a sign it was time for him to leave. He turned and headed out, leaving the door slightly ajar. As he stepped away, he spotted Chavez coming toward Sheyna's office with long, vast strides.

"Let me talk to you," he said, signaling with his hand for him to walk around the corner so they could speak in private.

Chavez followed with his brow lifting with concern. "What's going on?"

Jace stared at him long and hard before saying, "Keep your eyes on my wife. If anything looks out of the ordinary, you are to notify me immediately."

"Absolutely. You have my word."

"Thanks." Jace nodded and walked away. He'd made it toward the bank of elevators at the end of the hall when he spotted Troy Burks, the head of security, getting off on the floor.

"Mr. Beaumont just told me someone followed your wife to lunch. Do you have any idea who it could be?" he asked, brow bunched with frustration.

Jace stopped walking and frowned. "If I did, do you think I would be standing here?"

"Yeah. Sorry, boss. You're right," he added apologetically. "I will keep patrolling the area. Everybody knows to report any suspicious activity to security immediately."

As Sheyna had mentioned, she was safer at the Beaumont Corporation than she was anywhere else. Security was something they took seriously even more now after the first incident in the parking lot.

"Where is she now? Do you think she's up to me questioning her?"

Jace shook his head. "Nah, she has a meeting, so she needs to prepare and clear her head. Don't worry. Chavez will keep his eye on her."

Troy shook his head, his receding hairline shining beneath the bright lights. "She doesn't deserve this. Your wife is one of the nicest women I've ever known."

"That she is." Jace dragged a hand across his head. "I'll bring her down later to speak with you, but it won't do any good. Whoever was in my car is gone."

"Maybe they were stupid and left fingerprints."

"Maybe." But Jace wasn't getting his hopes up.

"Let's hope the police find something. Since you have the keyless entry, someone must have figured out the code and got in."

He nodded. "Maybe so." With that, Jace promised to drop by the security office later and then headed down the hall.

His secretary called out to him, but he was oblivious to everything around him. Once he reached the executive office, he stepped in and slammed the door.

Sheyna heard a soft knock and looked up to see Chavez peeking his head inside.

"You, okay?" he asked.

She nodded and signaled for him to enter. Chavez stepped into the room, his presence overpowering the space, and strolled over slowly toward her desk.

"What happened?" He was watching her with a quiet, concerned expression.

She blew out a long breath of despair. "This time, he was inside Jace's car."

His brow rose with alarm. "How do you know?"

"I know the smell of that aftershave anywhere." It was a woodsy scent that made her feel nauseous. Even now, the stench was underneath her nose, seeping into her brain and in her thoughts.

"Shit! No wonder your husband was so pissed off."

His comment gave her reason to smirk. "Anything pisses my husband off."

"Especially when it involves you." He lowered onto the chair across from her desk, and she caught him staring. "You sure you're okay?"

"Yes, I'm fine. Really. What we need to be doing is preparing for our conference call."

Chavez leaned forward, and his gaze softened. "I'm more concerned about you."

Sheyna took a deep breath and released the thought that had been hovering in her mind for months, "Why are you single?" she asked and could tell by the way he blushed he was surprised by her question.

He chuckled soft and low. "Wow. You really wanna go there?"

Folding her arms, she leveled a look at him. "Yes, I do. I never see you with a woman. You never talk about one either, so yes, we have been working together long enough that I want to know more about you."

"Why?" he said and looked almost guarded.

Sheyna instantly held up her hands. "Don't take it the wrong way. I'm the Director of Benefits & Employee Relations for the Beaumont Corporation, so I make it my business to know our employees. If you haven't noticed, everyone around here is like family."

He met her eyes, and eventually, his gaze softened. "Yes, I have noticed."

"Good, because I want you to also feel like family around here. Now, quit stalling and tell me a little about yourself."

"There isn't much to tell," he guffawed and leaned back on the chair.

"I doubt that." Sheyna studied him with a slow smile.

"I joined the army while in college, did my twenty, and got out." Chavez shrugged. "I decided a long time ago, I wanted to find a small town near the water and found this place by accident."

"Sheraton Beach, huh?"

He looked amused. "It's a nice homey little town."

"Yeah, and everybody knows everybody's business." At her sheepish grin, he laughed and gave her a knowing look.

"Yes, which is why I am tight-lipped about my personal life."

Sobering after a moment, Sheyna drew a sigh. "Tell me at *least* one thing you. Pretty please."

He swallowed and finally answered, "I have a daughter."

"Really, where is she?" Sheyna saw the pain in his eyes.

"I don't know," he confessed huskily with emotion. And then, as if a light switch had been turned off, Chavez rose from the chair. "Come on. It's time for us to head to the conference room."

Sheyna reached for the file folder. As she followed him out of her office, she studied Chavez's rugged profile. Now, she wanted to know more about him than ever before.

CHAPTER 5

"Sorry, I'm late."

Sheyna looked up as Debra Beaumont plopped down on the bleacher beside her.

"No worries. They haven't started yet," she said warmly. She stared at the woman with the light butterscotch complexion and the greenest eyes she had ever seen on any black woman other than Vanessa L. Williams. Debra's round face was surrounded by a naturally curly brown afro that had been swept back with a jeweled headband, exposing the long column of her throat and the gold hoops dangling from her ears.

Debra was married to Jace's cousin Rance. The siblings were known as the Force MDs: Rush, Roman, Remy, Reese, Rance, Sedona, and Sage. Half African American and half Samoan, all educated and gorgeous doctors ... in their own unique ways. Rance was known as Dr. Dribble. The NBA player was a center for the Philadelphia Sixers.

"I was late closing the store tonight. Everyone wants cupcakes for the holidays." There was pride in her eyes. She was the owner of *DebbieCakes*, a popular bakery on Main Street with pastries to die for.

"I hope you're making some for the New Year's Eve party."

Nodding, Debra stretched her jean-clad legs as she said, "Of course I am."

"Where's Tyrese?"

As soon as she mentioned her son, Debra's expression

sparkled. "He's with Bianca and London." The two of them were best friends. It had been Bianca's idea to set Debra up with her cousin. Unknowing to either, they had been booked on a cruise and hadn't realized they were sharing the same cabin until it was too late. By the time the cruise was over, the two were in love, and Tyrese conceived. Before he was born, Debra and Rance had gotten married in a private ceremony away from the media frenzy.

Debra's gaze riveted over the rink. "Have you seen my husband?"

Sheyna folded her arms beneath her breasts and snorted. "Yep, along with mine and all the others." She pointed. "They're over there telling the referee how to do his job."

They shared a laugh.

When JJ had announced he wanted to play hockey, she had known practically nothing about the sport. Neither had Jace. Since then, they'd attended a few professional NHL games and had even watched the Philadelphia Flyers on television. After that, Jace became obsessed with learning everything there was to know and never missed a practice.

Sheyna propped her feet on the empty bleacher in front of her. She was wearing thigh-high gray boots that were too cute to leave in the store but were not designed for warmth. She suddenly wished she had worn the UGG boots instead.

Her eyes shifted to the bottom of the bleachers, where she spotted Jace's eyes blazing up at her. She drew in a breath. His gaze was dark and focused. A shiver of arousal rippled through her. He was wearing a navy-blue hooded sweatshirt and blue jeans that hung low and relaxed on his hips. Jace worked out five days a week, so his shoulders were broad, his stomach and waist trim, and his legs were large and toned. He'd started growing a goatee a few years ago, and it was beginning to turn salt and pepper. The look was so incredibly sexy; she felt herself swallowing hard.

Sheyna blew him a kiss which softened the hard edges of his expression. He smirked, causing her nipples to tighten. Their gazes stayed locked for several charged seconds. Rowdy, loud laughter from the group, eventually drew his attention away.

"I heard what happened to you," Debra said, breaking into her thoughts.

Self-consciously, Sheyna reached up and fingered her hair. It had been two days, and the fear had begun to subside. It wasn't easy. That man had been in the now parked in their garage at home. She'd felt so violated it might be a long time before she felt comfortable driving Jace's car again.

She tore her eyes from her husband's profile and turned to Debra. "I'm fine. Really."

"How can you be fine when someone is stalking you?" she asked her.

"I'm not going to live my life in fear, so whoever needs to reveal himself because I refuse to hide."

"Yes, but you have to be careful. I had a stalker once."

Sheyna raised a brow. "Really? And how did you handle it?"

"The police couldn't help me, so I set up my own sting. I announced on social media I was going to the library to study, then hid in the bushes and waited."

"Did you find out who it was?"

"Yes, girl. It was the pizza delivery guy. He had a huge crush on me," Debra replied, leaning back on the seat with a far-off look.

Sheyna chuckled. "Oh, my goodness! What did you do?"

Debra patted her friend's hand. "I kicked his ass and started ordering pizzas somewhere else."

Sheyna tossed her head back in hearty laughter, and Debra joined.

Looking down at the ice, she caught Jace watching her, his eyes momentarily holding her captive again. She shook her head to scatter her thoughts and gave him a dismissive wave. "Jace is driving me crazy! Watching my every move and won't let me out of his sight. I'm surprised he's not up here on the bench beside me."

Debra frowned. "You're lucky to have a man who cares that much about you."

Smiling softly, Sheyna replied, "Debbie, don't act like Rance wouldn't do the same for you."

"Oh, I do not doubt that my husband would," she agreed. "But every woman isn't fortunate to have men as we do."

Sheyna winked. "They're Beaumonts. That's what they do."

"I agree to that," Debra replied and then sobered. "Do you have any idea who it could be?"

"No. Not at all. And don't you dare tell my brothers."

She shook her head. "I won't."

Speak of the devil. She looked across the arena to see Darnell coming through the door, followed by her brother Scott and his wife, Zanaa. Everyone was coming out to see JJ play. Sheyna grinned. Her son had no idea how lucky he was to have a family as he had. At ten, going on eleven, as JJ often reminded her, he already had a fan base.

As they made their way up to where she was seated, JJ's hockey team, the Revels, skated in formation across the ice, and the fans cheered. JJ was wearing a helmet and gloves with a hockey stick in his hand. Proudly, Sheyna waved then watched the team warm-up. They were seated directly at the center of the ice so she wouldn't miss a thing.

"Hey, you two!" she shouted to her brother and Zanaa as they finally made their way up to their bleacher.

"Sheyna, I'm so excited to be at my first hockey game!" Zanna said excitedly and snatched the knit cap from her head.

"I'm glad you could make it."

The beautiful wedding planner playfully rolled her eyes. "Oh, please! Scott was not missing his nephew's first game." She brought a protective hand up and stroked her round belly. The couple was expecting their first child in April.

Sheyna smiled. The love and support of their families always warmed her heart.

Hearing activity at her left, she spotted her father and his wife Jennifer rushing through the double doors. His eyes were shifting frantically around the arena, and then he sighed with relief when they realized the boys were still warming up.

By the time the game began, most of their local family members had arrived, including Jace's parents, Roger and Jessica.

The Revels were young, but they were fast and took the game seriously. The puck was passed and then sent sailing across the ice so swiftly, Sheyna felt herself jump and was on edge with each shot. JJ was quick and had heart. His coach had been raving about his speed, but she had no idea how good her son was until she saw him chase down a puck and then send it flying at the net before the goalie saw it coming. Each shot had the family jumping up off the bleachers to cheer. Every time the opponents made a shot, one of the Beaumont men was screaming and yelling at the referees. The game was aggressive, and JJ moved so fast Sheyna refused to look away in fear of missing something. All the years of ice-skating lessons had indeed paid off because he was practically sprinting across the ice.

"Nephew's a beast!" Scott shouted.

The score was tied, and her eyes were glued to the ice. JJ snapped the puck to a teammate, who pushed it with his stick. As he reached the goalie, he snapped it back to JJ, who lifted his stick and slammed it hard into the net. The family went crazy, and Jace was standing and cheering along with Jaden and Jabarie. Sheyna saw her father-in-law patting Jace proudly on the shoulder.

After that, the teams were pumped, and the rest of the first half was even more exciting. Her heart was pounding heavily with excitement. Sheyna watched with pride as the ice exploded. With so much going on, her eyes were shifting in every direction as she tried to keep up. JJ zipped around the ice pushing the puck with expertise, and by the time he made the last shot, the buzzer sounded, ending the first half.

Leaning back, Sheyna expelled a sigh of relief.

"Goodness, that was intense!" Debra exclaimed.

"And it's only halftime." She pushed up from the bleacher. "I'm going to run to the ladies' room before they start the second half." Jace was talking with his father. While his back was turned, Sheyna hurried up to the top, exited the door, and down the long corridor. The concession stand was open, and several people had gathered in line for popcorn and candy. It also meant everyone was going to head to the restroom.

Not before I got there, she mumbled under her breath as she hurried along. The heels of her boots clicked against the shiny concrete floor as she made her way around the corner of the arena. Instead of moving toward the restrooms closer to the arena floor, Sheyna traveled to the far end with less crowd. She pushed open the ladies' room door just as a woman and a little girl were headed out.

Moving toward a stall, Sheyna glanced at her reflection in the mirror. She smoothed down the frizz, then hurried inside and slid the lock in place. Within seconds she was sighing with relief. *That's what you get for waiting so long.* She'd realized that as she got older, her bladder just wasn't what it used to be.

She was lifting blue jeans over her hips when she heard the door swing open, and then there were hard, slow footsteps.

Her breath lodged in her throat as she listened and noticed that the steps suddenly stopped, and everything grew quiet. A wave of uneasiness flowed through her chest. What in the world was she thinking coming down here all by herself? She felt a tinge of panic when she realized she'd left her cell phone on the side of her purse.

"Hello?" she said and then waited. Within moments, there was the sound of footsteps again. Her knees shook; her whole body quivered. She held her breath as the sound drew closer. And then he began humming the words to a song she knew all too well.

"Isn't she lovely... Isn't she wonderful... Isn't she precious..."

She felt a distinct chill. Her heart practically leaped from her chest when the footsteps stopped right outside her bathroom stall. Slowly, she leaned down and peered underneath and saw a pair of Air Jordans. Pulse racing, she placed a palm over her mouth to muffle her heavy breathing; whoever it was reached out and pushed the stall door, trying to get in.

Sheyna screamed. "Whoever you are, leave me the hell alone!" she spat and tried to look through the crack but was unable to see. Tension hung thick and heavy in the air.

"Carla?"

She drew back. *"Carla?* My name isn't Carla."

"Oh, my bad," he replied, followed by an obnoxious chuckle. "I thought you were my girlfriend. She asked me to meet her in here at halftime."

"Well, I'm not Carla. Now get out of here before I scream!" she cried. How dare he scare her that way? He hurried away, and Sheyna waited until she heard the door swing close before she opened the stall and peeked her head out. The moment she found that she was alone, she released a sigh of relief. She stood shakily by the sink, her legs feeling like rubber. She was afraid that at any moment, she was going to collapse in a heap on the hard, cold floor.

Coming in here alone had been a stupid move.

Sheyna washed her hands and barely dried them with a paper towel before she hurried across the room, anxious to get back to the game and their families before her husband noticed. The moment she swung the door open, her eyes flew wide open, and she screamed his name.

"Jace!"

"What the hell are you doing in here by yourself?" Jace asked. His question and his tone made her blood go cold.

"I needed to go to the restroom," she said with a soft, shaky laugh. He had no idea how happy she was to see him.

"Then you should have told me." He bit out the words between his teeth. "I would have gone with you."

"I'm a prisoner now?" she teased.

He leaned in closer, so close his breath skated across her face as he countered huskily. "No, you're my wife, and I need to know you're safe." She stilled, her heart fluttering. "Do you understand me?"

"I'm not a baby!" She tried to walk past him, but Jace swung her up into his arms. Laughing, she draped her arms and legs around him as he stalked out of the room. She instantly brought her lips to his and kissed him.

"I love you, precious. Do you know what I would do if anything happened to you?" His expression was both tender and savaged.

She blushed as she stared at the only man who took her breath away and watched his eyes roaming all over her face. "No, what would you do?" she asked, sliding her hands inside his jacket for warmth.

"I'd have to find me a new wife," he teased.

Sheyna quickly went upside his head with a playful pop.

Chuckling, Jace slowly lowered her to the floor, but he didn't release her; instead, he held her tightly against his rock-hard body. Even in high heel boots, Sheyna had to tilt her head to look up at him.

"Don't you even think about it," she whispered hoarsely.

"Never that," he murmured, sending shivers along her spine. Jace leaned down until his lips were mere inches from hers. "No one could ever replace you. I'm yours forever, which is why you've got to stop being so hardheaded. You understand me?"

She nodded her head obediently the way JJ did when he was in trouble. "Yes, daddy." She gave him a look of amusement.

Jace brought her into his arms and kissed her hard in a deep, provocative kiss that had her moaning. Tongues. Lips. Teeth. He made sure to put his mark on her so that there was no doubt in her mind he loved her.

Up ahead, there was loud screaming and applause in the arena that pulled them apart.

"Damn, we're missing the game."

Holding hands, they rushed back to join the others, smiling like two fools in love.

After the game, the family stopped for hot chocolate at a twenty-four-hour coffee shop on Main Street to celebrate before heading home.

"How does it feel to be a champ?" Jace asked, beaming with pride. The Revels had won, twenty-six to twenty.

"Great dad," JJ said and yawned as he stepped inside the house.

"He's worn out. Let me get him to bed," his wife insisted.

"Sheyna, he's ten years old. He can get himself to bed," Jace teased. Sheyna was determined to keep their son her baby boy. "You go ahead and get yourself together. You had a long day."

Sheyna hesitated, biting her bottom lip before she finally nodded in agreement. Tilting her head, she looked up and met his kiss halfway.

While Jace made sure JJ jumped into the shower, Sheyna had her own. By the time he'd made it upstairs, she was walking across the room in a see-through white nightie.

Her body was perfect, all curves and softness. There was her tiny waist and the flare of her hips. His eyes traced her round breasts with chocolate peaks and the dark triangle between her thighs. As he dragged the sweatshirt over his head, Jace closed the distance, anxious to feel her body against him, to hold her breasts in his palms. For years, he had fought relationships, had a three-week rule, not allowing a woman to get close, but Sheyna had been different. She had always been there, somewhere, on his mind, and eventually, she had captured his heart. Now his entire life revolved around keeping her safe and happy.

He felt her slender fingers slide across his chest then down along his erection, causing him to ache to join their bodies together.

Jace sucked in his breath and said, "Shey—"

"Shhh," she said, silencing him. "Let me make you feel good."

Sheyna unfastened his belt and lowered the blue jeans, followed by his boxers down over his waist. His penis sprung forth.

"What do we have here?" she purred, and his balls tightened at the sound of her voice. She took a seat on the edge of the bed, and he felt her fingers sliding down his length.

"Why don't you take a little taste and find out," Jace challenged, dick twitching in response.

Her voice was low and intimate. "I plan on doing a lot more than a taste." With a devious smile, Sheyna leaned forward and licked the head.

He drew in a long breath and slowly released it as her hand began stroking and maintaining a rhythm.

Fuck, she knows what I like.

"You okay?" Sheyna asked, taunting him. She was staring up at him innocently with those big eyes of her.

He nodded. "Hell yeah, but I'll feel even better if you'd put it in your mouth."

She licked her lips. "I'm not sure if I know how."

"Then let me teach you." With his hand gripping the back of her head, he gently pushed her down until warm lips brushed the head. His dick jolted and strained toward her mouth.

"Like this?" she breathed on the head, and every muscle tightened. She was torturing him. Sheyna had been married to him long enough to know what he loved, and nothing felt better than the feel of her wet lips wrapped around his dick. No. He stood to be corrected. Nothing came close to the feeling of being inside of her warm honey.

She looked up at him, eyes dark and filled with lust as she began to suck him slowly like a child trying to make a bomb pop last forever.

"That's it, baby, suck me as your life depends on it."

A soft giggle escaped her lips, but with his hand gripping her hair, she couldn't have eased back even if she'd wanted to. Thank God his wife was always so willing.

Her tongue ran up one side and down the other before she focused her attention on the head. Jace gritted his teeth as heat filled his belly. Sheyna was so attentive, so willing to please her man. She was always ready. Lust scorched through his veins. For the last twelve years, she'd belonged to him to do with as he pleased. How the hell did he get to be so lucky?

Moaning, Jace raised his other hand to her head, taking control. Lifting his hips, he rocked into her mouth, and he guided her up and down along the head. He looked down and watched as his penis disappeared between her lips before reappearing wet with warm saliva.

"Shit," he hissed under his breath. He couldn't seem to get enough of seeing that sight. "Take all of it," he instructed. "Put all that dick in your mouth." Not that it was possible, but he loved watching her try. His fingers tightened in her hair, and he gripped and raised his hips higher, fucking her mouth deeper. She swallowed him inch by torturous inch, taking him even further between her lips. "That's it, precious. You can handle it," Jace whispered.

She began rolling her tongue the way he liked, over the head and along the vein on the back side where he was super sensitive. Fire filled his loins, and his balls tightened; he was so close.

He felt her other hand sliding across his inner thigh then she reached down and cupped his balls. Squeezed. Released. Massaged. Released. He took every ounce to hold on. He was so close to coming in her mouth. He thought about squirting his warm seed, but he had never been a selfish man, and tonight he wanted to please her.

With a groan, Jace eased her back until she released him with a pop.

Sheyna rolled on the bed, wiping away at her mouth. That sweet, delectable mouth. "Why'd you stop?" she asked, although her eyes were dancing with mischief.

"You know why. I need to be inside you."

Laughing, Sheyna yanked the nightie up over her head and spread her legs. His eyes lowered, and he drew in a breath. She was beautiful and everything a man wanted in a wife.

And she belonged to him.

Images of someone attacking her burned before his eyes that Jace angrily pushed away. No one would ever touch Sheyna Carmichael Brown Beaumont but him.

She crawled across the bed, sending her heavy breasts jiggling. He rose and stood naked before her. Her eyes traveled heatedly down his chest and landed right at his cock that was painfully hard. Reaching down, Jace lifted her into his arms. She wrapped her legs around his waist; Jace carried her to the fireplace and lowered her gently to the rug. His fingers found her dampness and heat. He stared as he touched and caressed her body. With every stroke, fire danced in her eyes. They were slanted, smothering, and waiting. Jace nudged her legs wide and drove inside, filling her with every erect inch of him.

Sheyna cried out softly as he pounded in and out. Her arms came up to rest at his forearms, and then her legs were around his waist, pulling him in deeper. She was warm and wet. He thrust back and forth, loving how good it felt to be inside her. When she locked her ankles behind his ass, he pumped with short steady strokes. Soft moans escaped her lips. She moved with him, desperate for him. Lowering his mouth to her, he slid his tongue inside, stroking her at the same rate as his dick. He kissed her possessively. First her lips, then her neck and throat before returning to her mouth. She tasted delicious. When the whimpers slipped from her lips began to increase, Jace eased back, resting his weight on his arms as he gazed down at her. He lifted her legs high and watched the way his dick disappeared inside her sweet pussy. It was so accepting and closed around him, holding him in a slick grasp. Digging her fingers into his ass, Sheyna clamped down around his cock, tightening and releasing. She drew him in further and held him there. His entire body was fueled by the fire she was causing.

"Fuck!" he growled.

Gripping her hips, Jace parted her butt cheeks, drawing her even more profound. He began to pump at a hard, rough tempo, letting out his rage and overwhelmed with possession. She felt so good wrapped around his length. He knew it wouldn't be much longer with the heat of her body and the incredible scent of her arousal. Her breathing was coming out in short sputters that informed him she was also close.

Jace withdrew and rolled Sheyna over onto her stomach. With his hands at her hips, he drew her toward him until she was up on all four. In an instant, he filled her from behind. His cock stretched and pumped at a furious tempo while his eyes greedily took it all in. The sight of his dick sliding in and out beneath her round lush ass and his heavy balls brushing the back of her gorgeous thighs was so sexy; it made him hot and increasingly hard. Desire swarmed. Passion erupted. A fire roared through him. When Sheyna cried out in ecstasy, he didn't stop. He couldn't have if he wanted to. Her moans were so arousing, he drove even further, pulling her up onto the head of his dick and then back down again. His thrusts became deeper and faster, and he wanted more, and yet it still wasn't enough.

"Jace!" she gasped, and then she was crying out his name. Her muscles tightened, holding him in place. His orgasm roared closer, but he held on long enough to make sure she had reached her climax, and then he was pounding her so hard his balls tightened.

"Fuck!" he growled. Slamming inside, Jace gave her everything he had left. Her body tightened, milking him until they collapsed on the rug together.

CHAPTER 6

Sheyna yawned and stretched languorously in the king-sized bed as she woke to find she was alone. Slowly, she crawled from underneath the warm covers and peeked out the window. It had snowed during the night. Jace was out front, bundled up tight in a bomber jacket and boots, shoveling the driveway. JJ was at the far end of the yard, using the snow blower like a pro. She smiled at the sight. It reminded her of a picture on one of those Hallmark cards.

She slipped into a long red robe and tied the belt tightly around her slender waist. It had been a gift from Jace along with a matching sheer gown that had barely stayed on three minutes before he had stripped it from her body. Smiling to herself, she slid her feet into fluffy slippers and shuffled toward the rear staircase that took her directly down to a large kitchen. Last spring, she'd hired an interior designer who had helped to bring her vision to life with updated appliances, elegant cabinetry, and a timeless flair. A massive island with six barstools made the spacious Tuscan-style kitchen layout a hot spot for entertaining. Plentiful countertop space provided room to spread out when cooking. Exposed ceiling beams, antique kitchen lighting, and terra-cotta tiles lend the kitchen a graceful blush of age. The rugged brick Tuscan backsplash complemented the space. Stone exuded an aged look, especially with the distressed finishes she'd selected. Various shades of brown meld together for a warm, consistent vibe.

While placing a mug on her Keurig and popping in a K-cup

with her favorite Columbian blend, Sheyna stared out the backyard and noticed the snow was starting to come down quite steadily again. She loved fresh white snow and was so lost in the sight that she jumped when the timer chimed on the coffeemaker. She'd been daydreaming about the insatiable night before with Jace. As she reached for the sugar bowl, she grinned sheepishly, remembering they had finally dozed off shortly after two a.m.

Through the window, she spotted JJ racing across the yard as he and his father were in the middle of a snowball fight. She giggled as she watched JJ toss one right at his father's head, the way she and her father used to do.

Turning away from the window, Sheyna leaned back against the kitchen counter, holding the hot mug in two hands as fond memories flooded her brain.

Her father had always been her hero. His devotion to his children following the loss of her mother to a brain aneurysm warmed her heart. To this day, an old tire hung from a large tree trunk in her father's backyard. She used to spend hours swinging, hoping to soar high enough that she would be able to see her mother smiling down from heaven.

Feeling in the holiday mood, she padded into the living room long enough to turn on the stereo. The merry sounds of The Jackson-5 singing Christmas carols filled the house through the surround sound system. Humming softly, she shuffled back to the kitchen, took another sip from the mug, and moved over to the refrigerator. She had never been much of a cook, whereas her mother had been fantastic in the kitchen. Nevertheless, she'd fried bacon and warmed frozen waffles in hot margarine in a pan within minutes. By the time Sheyna heard her family coming through the rear door, she had turned off a pot of boiling water.

"Hey, Mom! Dad said, after breakfast, I can take my sled

over to Uncle London's." JJ came rushing into the kitchen breathing heavily, face wet and eyelashes sparkling with snow.

"That sounds like fun," she chimed in. Jace strolled into the room, and their eyes locked. She felt a zing while staring at rosy cheeks and the shadow of a beard along his jaw. He looked handsome, standing at six-two, wearing blue jeans, a Sixers cap, and a hooded sweatshirt. Her flesh heated at the memories of his strength pounding her from behind, doggy-style.

"Why don't you go get dry before you catch a cold," she suggested, and JJ quickly dashed into the mudroom.

"Jaden challenged the men to another battle on the hill," Jace explained in an amused voice. "He's determined to break the tie."

As he approached her, she wagged her head. "Oh really?" She knew all about the Beaumont brothers and their challenges. It meant they were going to be gone most of the day. Sheyna grinned inwardly. She could use the time to do housework and clean JJ's room while no one was watching. "That means I have a day all to myself."

He leaned down and kissed her lips. "You can always come with us."

She gave an exaggerated eye roll. "Nope. I think I'll pass."

Chuckling, Jace moved back into the mudroom to hang up his coat and removed his boots. While she poured hot water into two mugs, the two disappeared into the half bathroom to wash their hands before joining her at the table. She handed them both a cup of hot chocolate that was sure to warm their cold hands. They moved to the table and had breakfast as a family the way they did most weekends.

As soon as he finished eating, JJ hurried up to his room. Sheyna looked over the rim of her mug to find Jace staring. The hunger in his eyes made her stomach tighten.

"What?" Her nipples tingled when he leaned toward her.

"Do I need permission to look at you?"

Smiling, she dropped her eyes shyly to the table then back up at him. "Of course not."

Taking a sip of his cocoa, Jace murmured, "You're beautiful this morning. Almost glowing. I wonder why?" He had a speculative gleam in his eyes.

"Good loving will do that to a woman," she replied with a saucy grin.

His dark eyes glinted with amusement over the rim of his mug. "Is that what it is? Well, then, I need to make love to my wife more often."

Sheyna sighed dramatically. "If we make love any more than we already do, I'll never get any work done."

Jace chuckled. "Oh, so you're complaining?"

"Not at all, but I can see you're fishing for compliments this morning," she teased lovingly.

He shook his head. "No, not at all." Jace sobered and then asked, "How are you this morning?"

"I'm okay," she said.

"You sure?" He didn't sound convinced.

"Baby, yes. I'm sure." Deliberately clearing her throat, Sheyna rose and carried their plates to the sink. "I'm going to go shopping with Brenna later. She wants to pick up a few things for the party. If you don't mind, I'd like to drive the Armada today."

She still couldn't bring herself to drive the other two vehicles. Maybe she'd try in a few weeks or wait until her attacker was caught; either way, she wasn't driving her Volvo until it was over. Yesterday, she had even considered trading it in for something new.

Something he won't recognize.

Before she could turn, Jace had moved behind her. His arms came around to hold her close. "What's mine is yours," he told her in a voice that was so soft and seductive her eyelids fluttered close.

"Thank you," she breathed.

"Precious, it's okay to be afraid. But you have absolutely nothing to worry about." He brought his lips to her neck and dropped soft kisses. "I got you. Believe that."

"I do." She just hated being afraid. It made her feel vulnerable and so needy.

"I vowed to love and protect you, and I'm a man of my word. I have hired around-the-clock security for you."

She whirled toward him. "*Around the clock*? Does that mean someone will be following me?"

"Absolutely. Only you'll never know it."

Her eyes rolled up in her head as she huffed, "Now that you've told me, I'll know." It was going to feel creepy.

"Sorry, but it's either that or me."

She skewered him with a frown. "You...shopping with me...? I think I'd rather have security."

Jace laughed a deep, rumbling sound that made her chest flutter lovingly. "I figured you'd say that." he pulled her tightly in his arms and kissed her with so much passion her nipples hardened with desire.

"We could always drop JJ off with Jaden and spend the rest of the day in bed," he suggested in a voice so low and seductive she was almost tempted. It was hard to resist him when she said things like that.

The doorbell chimed.

"Saved by the bell." Giggling, she wiggled free of Jace's embrace and hurried into the foyer. Donny Hathaway was singing Christmas cheers, and she sang along as she moved to the front door. The moment she swung it open, she frowned.

"Good morning," Scott said, kissing her forehead.

Sheyna moved aside as he, followed by Darnell, stepped into the house. The looks on their faces set off warning bells in her head.

"What are you doing here?" she asked curiously.

"Why do you think?" Darnell barked. "How come you didn't tell us somebody attacked you?" he demanded. They both towered over her in the foyer and stared.

She swallowed dryly. "Who told you that?"

"Really?" Scott gave her a telling look. "You live in Sheraton Beach. Need I say more?"

She shook her head regretfully—one of the pitfalls of living in a small town.

"Wipe your feet off!" Sheyna snapped and didn't care if they knew she was irritated. They had come over to question her. Scott and Darnell still thought she was a child who needed their protection.

She twirled on the toes of her slippers and moved back toward the kitchen. She didn't bother to tell them to follow because her brothers did what they wanted to do anyway.

When she stepped into the kitchen, Jace looked up from his iPad with a raised eyebrow. Sheyna rolled her eyes and moved over to make herself another cup of coffee.

Unzipping their coats, they stepped into the kitchen with a similar lazy swagger.

"Hey, Jace," Scott said with a head nod.

"Scott...Darnell...what's up?"

"Came by to see what's going on with my sister." Scott moved over to the large island and took a seat on one of the stools, Darnell on another.

"As you can see, I'm just fine," she replied and shot him a surly glance.

"What do you have to eat?" Darnell asked as he pulled off

his gloves and hat.

She met his amber-colored eyes as his lips curled into an irresistible smile that had melted the heart of countless women before he had fallen in love with Liberty Roth. "Didn't your wife cook you breakfast?"

"Yes, but that was hours ago. She had to head in to teach an early morning aerobics class." Liberty was the owner of the hottest fitness club on the beach.

Sheyna mumbled "freeloaders" under her breath as she slid over a plate of bacon. "This is the best I can do."

Her brothers didn't seem to mind as they both grabbed a slice of bacon.

"Coffee would be good, too," Darnell gently suggested.

She pointed to the Keurig. "Make it yourself."

Jace was trying his best to keep a straight face. "What brings you over?" he asked as if he didn't already know.

Darnell headed over and reached for a coffee mug from the cabinet above the sink. He dressed in a black turtleneck that molded his broad shoulders and dark jeans that hung low on his hips. "I came to check on my sister. I heard there was a problem a few days ago."

"I heard it wasn't the first time," Scott added with a snort.

Nosy folks are all up in my business.

"So, tell me, what's going on?" Darnell insisted as he popped a K-cup in the machine and pressed the button.

Before Jace could respond, Sheyna blurted, "None of your business."

Jace held up his hands in surrender. "Sorry precious, but I draw the line when it comes to your brothers." He looked at them. "A few weeks ago, someone attacked Sheyna in the employee parking lot. That's why she was working from home. After the Christmas holiday, she went back to work and discovered someone had been in my car."

Darnell twirled away from the sink and barked, "And you didn't tell me!"

Sheyna brought a hand to her hip. "I have a husband, which means I don't have to tell you everything."

Darnell carried the cup over to the island and took a seat, his eyes trained on her face. "You're my sister, so, yes, you do."

Before she could snap back, Jace held up his hands.

"Relax, I got it under control," he told them.

"You got *what* under control? Who attacked my sister in the parking lot?" Darnell demanded.

Alarmed, Sheyna gasped. "Shhh! Please lower your voice. I don't want JJ to hear."

Over the rim of the mug, Darnell eyed her warily.

"Is my sister in danger?" Scott asked Jace.

Sheyna looked over at him.

"Not as long as she's married to me, she isn't," Jace replied with a deadly stare that made her heart flutter, knowing he meant every word.

She shook off the effect with a dismissive wave and muttered in exasperation, "Quit talking about me as if I'm not here! I'm fine. Someone is trying to scare me, that's all, and I refuse to be a victim."

Scott was studying her, a calculating frown in his golden eyes that made Sheyna squirm. "I don't want you to be stupid either."

"Who's being stupid?" she barked, neck rolling with attitude.

Darnell intervened. "What Scott means is don't be out here trying to be Billy Badass! If someone is trying to scare you, then act scared."

Jace cleared his throat. "I've already got that under control. I've hired around-the-clock security."

Darnell nodded. "Well, at least that's something."

"Listen, you two, I'm okay!" She gave a dismissive wave and glared at Darnell. "Shouldn't you be somewhere defending bad guys?"

Scott chuckled. The smile slipped from his lips when she shifted her frown in his direction.

"And *you* should be in Wilmington with your pregnant wife, not harassing me."

Scott scowled. "I'll *always* be focused on you. Be glad I didn't call Dad."

Her eyes widened. "You wouldn't?"

Scott stared at her for a long moment before he swallowed hard and replied, "We won't unless you give us a reason."

Jace stepped to her defense. "You don't have to do that. It's my job to keep my wife safe. But if anything changes, you'll be the first to know."

Darnell took a sip of his coffee, watching her.

Scott hesitated before he finally looked at his brother, then back at Jace, and nodded in agreement. "Okay."

Sheyna breathed a sigh of relief and slid down onto Jace's lap. Her husband draped an arm around her waist, pulling her into his protective embrace.

Darnell scratched his chin, wearing a sheepish grin. "I came over to borrow your snow blower. Patrick and Dax are dropping by this afternoon, and I'm planning to take advantage of their energy."

She laughed. He was referring to their cousins and partners at Darnell's law firm. They were both single, gorgeous, and rich, and what was worse, they knew it. "Who would've ever guessed my brother would be clearing driveways in front of his own home!"

"Yes, well, a good woman will do that for you," he replied.

She was happy for him. A confirmed bachelor who had fallen in love with the mother of a son he hadn't even known existed.

"Sure, no problem. It's out back." Jace pointed toward the backyard.

Darnell nodded. "Cool. I drove over with the trailer on my truck."

"Let me get my coat." Jace rose, lowering Sheyna softly to her feet, and signaled for Darnell to follow him to the mudroom, where he retrieved his boots and coat.

Sheyna took a seat at the island and gazed at her brother. Scott wore short locs that complemented a handsome, almond-colored face with deep, dimpled cheeks and a broad nose.

Scott looked over at her with his eyes dark with concern. "Sis, you sure you're okay?"

She rolled her eyes in annoyance.

"I'm serious." His focused gaze made her shiver. Her brother was persistent.

"I'm fine! Really. I think someone is messing with me. Maybe an employee we terminated, only I don't know who that could be." She shrugged. "It's no big deal." She dropped her eyes momentarily to the table so Scott couldn't tell she was lying.

"Hey."

She glanced up at him.

"You know I'm always here for you, right?" His gaze gentled, searching the depths of hers.

Sheyna inclined her head. "Yes, I know, I know. Big brother is always watching." Reaching across the island, she wrapped her arms around Scott and squeezed him tight.

After they loaded the snow blower onto the trailer, Sheyna

waved goodbye and sighed; they were gone. She went back into the kitchen to finish the dishes.

She heard the side door open and then closed.

"I didn't think they would ever leave!" she said over her shoulder.

Large hands slid around her waist, and solid thighs pinned her to the sink as Jace leaned in close against her back. "They love their sister. Nothing's wrong with that. It's the same way my brothers and I used to act with Bianca."

She arched into his embrace and groaned. "Don't remind me."

"I'm going to keep reminding you as long as there is air in my lungs how much we all love you." His breath against her neck was warm and penetrating.

"And I love you."

His open lips moved to the nape of her neck and then her cheek, leaving a heated trail. Her body came alive. Jace turned her slowly in front of him. He took her hand and laced her fingers with his.

"Your hands are cold."

"I hadn't noticed," he replied.

His gorgeous face stalled her thoughts, and all she could do was stare. A serious expression flickered across Jace's face, but he took her mouth in a delicious kiss before she had time to respond. His tongue explored the interior of her mouth in a kiss so explicit and intimate. She moaned in protest when he finally lifted his head.

"We should have sent JJ home with one of them."

She sighed when the hand holding hers began caressing her skin. She knew if JJ hadn't been in the house, Jace would have lifted her onto the counter and made love to her right then and there.

His lips trailed across her skin. "He's so busy playing Scott's video game he wouldn't notice anyway," he said, and his eyes locked with hers.

A smile creased the corners of Jace's dark eyes when Sheyna held out her hand. "Come with me, sexy," she purred. Jace's fingers curled around hers.

She led him up to their room, then quietly closed and locked the door behind them. As soon as she swung around, Jace moved closer, his head tipping to one side as he lowered the bathrobe from her body. "You're so sexy." He brushed his mouth over hers.

"Not as sexy as you, my love."

Settling over her, Jace drew Sheyna's lips into the heat of his mouth. The kiss was hot, sensual, and everything a kiss should be.

And she was lost.

She was lost because it was Jace. Her husband. The man she'd known for more than half her life, and she knew him better than he knew himself at times. Sheyna knew what pissed him off. She knew he loved his steak medium-well and his eggs scrambled with sharp cheddar cheese. And she knew when Jace loved; he loved with all his heart.

Their clothes melted away like the snowflakes on the window, and in a brief moment, they were completely naked, stretched out on the bed, staring into each other's eyes. Jace's hands were gentle and loving as he stroked the curves of her body. His lips licked her neck and shoulders before sliding to the juncture between her legs that throbbed with need. But as delicious as his mouth felt, Sheyna wanted to show him how much he meant to her. Gripping his shoulders, she tugged until his lips were against hers. Rolling Jace onto his back, she kissed her way down his body and barely slipped the head between her lips when he lifted her up and over him. He lowered her down onto his length and plunged upward. She gasped. The fit was perfect.

"Sheyna," Jace moaned as he thrust upward.

"Jace!" she whimpered and rode him.

It wasn't long before they were both crying out in pleasure.

CHAPTER 7

The party was in full swing. Music. Laughter. Lights. Dancing. And, of course, food. Table and tables of delicious food.

Sheyna weaved through the crowded house with excitement pulsing through her veins. Three more hours and the clock would strike twelve, ushering them into a new year. She couldn't think of any better way to celebrate than being surrounded by family and friends.

While moving through the house in search of Brenna, she spotted her father-in-law coming through the front door. The devastatingly handsome gentleman she both loved and admired. Roger Beaumont, the man behind the Beaumont Hotels, was a stern, no-nonsense kind of guy, but over the years, he had softened and now seemed to warm up to people without being pretentious, making it hard to believe the man was a millionaire.

He swung around and beamed when he saw her. "Sheyna. Happy New Year!"

"Happy New Year's to you, too!" Smiling, she planted an affectionate kiss on his neatly trimmed, bearded cheek. His salt-and-pepper hair was naturally wavy and cut low. The monarch of the Beaumont family had always been her favorite of Jace's parents. "I was wondering if you were going to make it."

"Oh, you know my wife... we had to stop by the country club

and see some of our friends first," He replied with a playful sable eye roll that caused her to giggle. It was hard to believe this was the same man who had once tried to break up Brenna and Jabarie because he didn't think she was good enough.

"Hello Sheyna, darling."

Speak of the devil…Sheyna turned to face her mother-in-law, who, as bougie, as she was, had softened over the years as well, especially when she started having grandbabies to spoil. Tall and beautifully stunning, Jessica Beaumont knew how to make an entrance with the generous sway of her hips in a hunter-green cashmere sweater dress that emphasized her mocha skin. A stylist had professionally styled her long, graying hair, so her curls hung loosely around her shoulders. Her slanted dark brown eyes were large and her cheekbones high. Jace's parents were indeed works of art and the complete opposite of her simple and humble father and his wife, Jennifer.

"Happy New Year's, Mother," she murmured, accepting her warm greeting and a kiss to both cheeks.

"The same to you, darling. Where is everyone?" Jessica asked in a high-pitched cultured voice.

"Everyone is in the great room."

Nodding, she slipped out of a full-length black coat and handed it to one of the attendants standing by, waiting to serve the guests. He gave Roger a ticket before he carried their coats away.

"How are you doing, dear?" Jessica asked, and as she stared, the woman's full lips curved into a frown. Sheyna was stunned at how concerned she looked.

"I'm doing better," she told her. The last thing she wanted to do was discuss her attacker.

She nodded, and they made plans to get together and talk about a women's coalition conference scheduled for early spring that Jessica wanted to attend.

As her in-laws left to join the others, Sheyna looked over her shoulder at a man standing in the corner and muttered obscenities under her breath. He'd been following her all night. She noticed him when they had first arrived several hours ago, again while she was sampling pastries at the dessert table and while Brenna was giving her a tour of the renovations at the rear of the house. The man was short, five-nine maybe, beefy with a stern look on his round face. He'd kept his distance, barely looking her way, although she felt the sizzle of his attention. She wasn't dumb. She knew he was watching her. She had felt so uncomfortable around him; she had gone into the kitchen and entered the great room. But he'd followed. And there he was again, watching. And now, it was getting creepy.

Dammit, Jace!

She plastered on a smile and headed down a long hallway. When she reached Jabarie's office, she peeked her head inside and glanced around the room until she found Jace standing beside his brothers. Her heart gave a voluntary thump. He looked fine as hell in dark slacks and a burgundy V-neck sweater. She had bought it for him for Christmas because it brought out his dark complexion. He looked relaxed and confident talking to the bunch. The moment he spotted her, Jace put down his drink and sauntered toward her. Sheyna discovered she was holding her breath. When he'd stopped before her, he leaned down and kissed her lips. Sheyna purred. He tasted of cognac and peppermint, both warm and delicious.

Dragging his mouth away, he asked, "Everything okay?" His attentive eyes searched her face for any concerns.

She moistened her lips. "Why do I have security following me around the house?"

A slow, lazy grin curved his mouth as he regarded her, and

she knew the answer immediately. "I told you I assigned security to keep you in their sights."

"Inside?" She was mildly alarmed as she inclined her head and continued impatiently. "How am I supposed to enjoy the party with someone watching me?"

His lips twitched. "Just pretend you don't see them."

Sheyna shook a finger at him. "How can I do that if they're everywhere?"

Jace gripped her hand and kissed it. "Just focus on the party and family. You'll forget he's even there."

"That's easy for you to say. You don't have security staring you down your throat!" she exclaimed and tried to ignore the annoyance.

He winked, enjoying the playful exchange. "Would you rather have me up under you twenty-four-seven?"

"Yes and no." Someone was always there; while shopping with Brenna at the office, even standing outside the ladies' room. She should have felt relieved by the extra security, but instead, she was highly annoyed and pissed off that keeping her safe resulted in such extreme measures. Jace worried too much about her. Ever since the incident, he'd been too focused on her, and she didn't like that. He had way too much to worry about at work for her to be steering his focus.

"Okay. I'll just pretend I don't see him," she resigned with a long sigh.

Jace's grin flashed white. "That's the spirit." He caught her face between his large hands and lowered his mouth over hers. Her belly flip-flopped on contact.

"Hey, didn't you two get the memo? No women or children are allowed in this room," came an amused drawl from across the room.

Grinning, Sheyna looked over at Jabarie and frowned. "Oh yeah? I wonder what Brenna would have to say about that?"

With a wife, five children, and one on the way, Brenna had once said Jabarie took every opportunity he could to have a moment alone. She couldn't even imagine how the two of them did it.

"Shey, we love you, but a man cave is supposed to be men only," Jaden added with an amused sidelong glance. He swung long dreadlocks away from his face and laughed when she gave a rude snort.

"All of you are too much," Sheyna said and laughed.

"And you love it," Jace murmured, his eyes drifting to her lips.

"Yes, I do," she said adoringly. She kissed him once more then sashayed back toward the party. Of course, her bodyguard was only a few feet away, pretending to focus on a bowl of peanuts.

Sheyna moved around the corner and heard a deep feminine voice calling her name. Her eyes widened at the sight of the long-legged beauty with the spiky red hair. "Sage! You made it!" Sheyna hurried over and wrapped her arms around Jace's cousin.

"I wasn't going to miss it. I borrowed one of the sprinters we had over at the Mercedes dealership and told everyone who wanted to come to hop in," she explained. "I brought Reese, Remy, and even Sedona's somewhere around here with Keith."

"Did Uncle Richard come?" she whispered.

Sage rolled her eyes and replied, "Yes and no."

Sheyna arched a dubious brow as she waited for her to continue.

"Yes, he's in Delaware, but he decided to stay at the hotel. Mom is with him."

At least he's here. That was a good sign.

Noticing the worried lines on Sage's forehead, Sheyna

decided to leave that subject alone for now and said, "So where is this guy I've heard so much about?"

Beaming, Sage swung around and pointed. Sheyna spied a tall, gorgeous man with a medium build and broad shoulders, standing in the foyer talking to her brother Remy. His stance screamed military issued. Sage's older brother Reese and his beautiful wife Dominique stood beside them. She had a protective hand over a noticeable baby bump.

There are a lot of babies being born to the Beaumont family, she thought with a grin.

Sage gestured with her hand for him to join them. Sheyna found the handsome man striding purposefully toward them with such swagger. He had a squared jaw and a smooth peanut-butter-brown complexion with deep dimples. A pair of pleated black slacks in no way hid his large, powerful thighs. Massive arms and broad shoulders showcased a crisp red sweater. Sheyna nodded in appreciation and whispered under her breath, "Where did you find him?"

Sage blushed, something Sheyna wasn't sure if she had ever seen her do before. "I think it's more like he'd found me." Her eyes twinkled dreamily, and Sheyna could tell there was a story behind that look.

As soon as he reached them, Sage brought a possessive hand to his forearm. "Cser, I would like you to meet my cousin's wife, Sheyna." She was grinning like a girl wearing a new pair of shoes.

"It's a pleasure," he said in a low, husky tone. His dark gaze roamed over Sheyna's face with an intensity that made her breath quicken. Goodness, it's no wonder Sage had fallen hard for him!

"So, you're Remy's best friend. I hear you're serving in the military?"

He arched one of those devilish brows. "Yes, ma'am. I'm

getting ready to head back in the morning to join my unit," he explained. "I delayed my departure to spend a few extra days with Sage."

Sheyna noticed the way he latched his stunning brown eyes onto the petite beauty's face. There was no denying the two were in love.

"Where are you headed?" Sheyna asked, drawing his attention.

Cser hesitated, then frowned almost apologetically. "Sorry, but that information is classified," he said softly, almost as if he was afraid someone might have overheard.

She nodded. "Understood. Well, you just make sure you get back here safe."

"That's the plan," he replied with an irresistible smirk.

Sheyna talked to the couple a while longer before she made her way toward the rear again. The merry sounds of Nat King Cole filled the home that smelled just like gingerbread cookies. She was sure the delicious scent was something the party planner had put in place. She headed toward the far left. Poinsettias were all over the place. A giant Christmas tree took up one corner of the great room and was lit up with lights and glass bulbs twinkling.

The waiters they had hired were moving around the space with trays of snacks and drinks. They had been given strict instructions not to serve any of the children. Sheyna was turning the corner when she caught her niece tipping an unsecured glass to her lips.

"What are you doing, young lady?" she said as she took the glass out of her hand.

Arianna gave her aunt a sheepish grin and didn't look at all spooked by getting caught. "A lot of my friends at school get to drink champagne on New Year's Eve, so I want to do the same."

"Then ask your mother." Sheyna ruffled her hair. A wild main of honey-brown curls hung to the center of her back. Arianna was beautiful with a caramel-colored complexion and mesmerizing hazel eyes. She had already learned how to bat her lashes to get her way. Not to mention, over the last year, Sheyna noticed how much her body had begun to develop. She shook her head. Brenna was right; her niece was ready for a bra. Jabarie was going to have his hands full.

Arianna scowled. "Does JJ get to drink champagne?"

Sheyna blinked. "Nope, he drinks sparkling cider. The same thing your mother will be drinking this year."

"That's because she's pregnant *again*," Arianna said with an annoyed huff.

"What, you're not excited about having another brother?" Sheyna tipped her head and studied her.

"No, I have enough brothers. Mom's going to be so preoccupied with the baby she's going to forget about me."

"I seriously doubt that." Sheyna squeezed her hand. "Your mother adores all of you, but if you ever feel you need some extra TLC, you know you can always come and stay with me and Uncle Jace."

Cupping her face, the adorable teenager beamed up at her. The last time she'd taken her niece on a shopping spree, just the two of them, she had been so happy to have the attention. Arianna was a teenager. Sheyna remembered when she was her age and being able to do grown-up things with Aunt Belle had made her feel special. After her mother had passed away, her father's oldest sister would come and get her for the weekend, and they'd go shopping and get pedicures. Those memories had stuck with her forever.

"I'd like that," Arianna replied. "Can we go to the cosmetic counter at Macy's and try on lipsticks?" There was a gleaming sparkle in her eyes again.

"That's if you behave. Now go play." She swatted the teenager playfully on the butt, and she obediently hurried away to join the other children.

Thank goodness I have a boy.

Sheyna walked through the kitchen, snagged another slice of pecan pie, and then followed the sounds of feminine laughter to an extensive library with years of reading pleasure. Brenna loved books. As she popped the last bite into her mouth, Sheyna stepped into the room. Lounge couches and floor-to-ceiling bookshelves filled the walls. A fire sparkled invitingly in the hearth. Freezing temperatures frosted the row of windows that overlooked the immaculately landscaped grounds of the house. The women were gathered around the room looking at sketches of Danica's designs for the upcoming New York fashion show.

"*Ooh, girl!* Can I get one of these?" Bianca said as Sheyna sank onto the arm of an oversized chair beside her.

"We can't afford anything she's showcasing. These clothes are for the rich and famous," Debra commented from across the room.

Danica tossed her head, hair bouncing around her face as she argued, "No, they aren't. And you can always get the family rate."

Debra raised one perfectly sculpted eyebrow as she leaned back on the sofa. "Even *that's* too much for my blood."

"Debbie, please! You're married to a professional ballplayer," Bianca countered.

"Yes, and his career isn't forever, so I want what we have to last."

Sheyna loved how level-headed and intelligent Debra was, especially when it came to money. More NBA players needed wives like her instead of them trying to be on reality TV shows.

As she listened to the rest of the women chime in, Sheyna

gazed at the fantastic designs. Danica had talent. For years, her swimsuits were made available exclusively at Nordstrom, but now that she'd added the plus-size line, she wanted to make her swimwear available to everyone. Danica had an appointment with a buyer scheduled after she returned from New York. The possibilities were endless.

"If Danica hasn't told you, she's trying to get these designs in either Kohl's or Target."

"Now *that's* what I'm talking about!" Debra cried. "You get *these* gorgeous designs into one of *those* stores, and *I'll* be the first big girl in line."

While swinging her leg, Brenna gave a rude snort. "Oh please, there isn't anything big about you."

"Other than that mouth," Bianca mumbled under her breath, but it was loud enough to get the women giggling. Debra was strong and opinionated, but that was why they loved her so much.

Smiling, Sheyna rose. "I'm going to the bathroom." She moved down the hall with her bodyguard right behind her. Sheyna groaned. For a few moments, she had thought he had left, but there he was following her. As she made her way through the crowded room, someone stopped him. The second he turned, Sheyna dipped out of sight and headed up the stairs. The one in Jabarie and Brenna's master bedroom was less likely to be occupied. She was pleased to discover she was right.

While washing her hands with eucalyptus-scented foaming hand soap, Sheyna inspected her image in the large vanity mirror. The wide brown eyes that stared back at her were accentuated by silver eyeshadow that matched the shimmery cashmere sweater she'd complimented with gray slacks and black, thigh-high wedge suede boots.

When she felt her cell phone vibrate in her hip pocket,

Sheyna dried her hands on a decorative Christmas towel, then reached down, unlocked the screen, and read the text message.

The pecan pie was good. But the sweet potato pie was better.

Frowning, she quickly replied, *who is this?*

Do you have to ask?

The blood drained from Sheyna's head.

I still have your purse.

Alarm gripped her, and bile rose in her throat as she tried to steady herself. It was him, and he was here in Jabarie's home! How else would he have known she'd had a slice of pecan pie? Quickly, Sheyna hurried over to the bathroom door, locked it, and then slid down onto the tiled floor with her back against the door.

Get a grip, she silently told herself. She could hear voices and laughter, but they sounded so far away. She fumbled with her iPhone, fingers shaking. Taking a slow, deep breath, she dialed Jace. He answered on the first ring.

"Hey. Where are you at?"

"Jace," she croaked.

"Precious, I can't hear you."

"Jace!" she screamed. "He's here!"

"Here? Where is here?"

She took several deep breaths.

"Shey, what are you talking about?"

"He's here."

That time, Jace must have heard the fear because the line grew quiet, and voices in the background faded.

"Sheyna, where the hell are you?"

"U-upstairs," she stuttered. Her lips were quivering so bad she could barely get the words out. "In Jabarie's bathroom."

"Hold on. I'm on my way. Don't you dare move!" he barked.

"Do you hear me, Sheyna?"

"Yes. I-I won't move," she said in a low, shaky breath.

In a matter of seconds, Sheyna heard Jace's voice on the other side of the door. "Precious, let me in!" She scrambled to her feet, unlocked the door, and yanked it open. Jace rushed in and drew her close into his arms.

"Are you okay?" he asked, drawing his head back slightly to stare at her.

She nodded but knew he wasn't going to believe that.

"Tell me what happened?" Jace gently brushed her hair with his fingers while she told him about the text messages. Taking her phone, he scrolled through the exchange while she swallowed the lump in her throat, threatening to choke her. The silence added to the tension in the bathroom.

"I'm getting you out of here."

Sheyna blinked and was sure she looked vulnerable. "No, I don't want everyone knowing and ruining the party."

"There is someone in this house who's after my wife. I'm not going to act like we don't know it's happening," he stated firmly, not caring if he sounded bossy.

He stabbed the phone with his finger and called the unknown number the text messages had come. When no one answered, Jace yelled, "Listen, you sick fuck! I'm going to find you."

Jace ended the call. Leaning forward, he brushed a kiss across her forehead. His warm lips were soothing.

"Let's go." Turning abruptly, he took Sheyna's hand and walked her across the bedroom. She tried to smile and look natural, but it was hard to do when he could be anywhere in the house. As soon as they'd stepped out, she spotted her bodyguard lurking in the hallway.

"Is everything okay, Mr. Beaumont?"

Jace stormed over and pointed a threatening finger in his

face. "No, it isn't. You're supposed to be watching her!" The guard took a cautious step backward. "Go get Troy and then get a team ready to meet me in front of the house!" he barked.

Retaking Sheyna's hand, he made his way down the hall and descended the stairs. Jabarie was standing in the great room, talking to London. They turned, looked up, and immediately sensed something was wrong, excused themselves, and headed over to meet them.

"Is everything okay?" London asked.

Sheyna tried to suppress a shudder, but London was one she couldn't fool. The military had trained to read people's behaviors.

Jace gave them a quick rundown. When he finished, Jabarie shook his head, frowning deeply.

"That bastard is in *my* house?"

"Yes, in this house," Jace managed between gritted teeth. "No one leaves. You hear me. No one!"

A silent look of comprehension passed between the men. As soon as London signaled for the others, Sheyna knew hell was about to break loose.

"I'm taking you home," Jace announced.

Sheyna's eyes widened with alarm. "No, you can't!"

"Why not?" His nostrils flared slightly.

She clapped a hand over her beating heart as she replied almost hysterically, "You promised me you'd find out who this is! How can you do that if you go home with me?"

The last several moments, she'd watched as if in a trance. The brothers alerted security. Together they tried to keep the incident from the rest of the guests. The last thing Sheyna wanted was to scare everyone, especially JJ. They had sent all of the children up to the playroom.

"I'll go home with her," Bianca offered. She had overheard London talking on the walkie-talkie to the security manager and quickly came over to provide comfort and support.

Jace looked at the two women before he finally nodded. "Then I'm sending security with you."

It was on the tip of Sheyna's tongue to protest, but she would have been wasting her time. In all honesty, she was glad she had a detail.

Troy moved over to join them. "I have my men surrounding the house. No one can leave before being questioned."

"I need you to take my wife home, *now.*"

Troy stared at him alertly. "Mr. Beaumont, with all due respect, Brad's been with her all evening. I can get him to take her home. Brad!" He signaled with his hand, and the large man hurried over.

"No! I want *you* to go home with her, not him." Heeding the lethal warning in Jace's narrowed dark eyes, Troy looked from Sheyna to Jace and finally nodded in reluctant agreement.

"Yes, sir," he paused. "Let me give my men some instructions, and then I'll be ready to leave."

Jace pulled Sheyna close to him. "I will be home just as soon as I can," He whispered.

Their gazes met and held. "Hurry home." She hugged him tightly and felt his heart pounding hard enough to drown out the sound of her own. He was afraid and angry. She knew her husband well enough to know the only way he would be able to focus was with her away from the scene.

"Jace, over here!"

They both looked to see Jaden signaling for him to join the other Beaumont men, who looked like they were ready to hurt someone.

"Precious, I'll be right back. Don't move!" he grounded out

in warning.

Swallowing, she nodded and stood beside Bianca, who draped a comforting arm around her waist.

"Are you okay?" she asked.

Sheyna looked to her sister-in-law, who, over the years, had become one of her closest friends. "Yes, I'm fine. Thanks for offering to come home with me."

"There's nothing I rather do than hang out with my sister. I'm sure London is going to be at this all night."

"Into the wee hours of the morning," Sheyna mumbled under her breath.

A chill swept across her flesh that had nothing to do with the dropping temperatures. She could feel the heat of Jace's gaze trained on her. He was worried. So was she. Pretending not to notice him, she lowered her head, tucking her chin inside her wool coat.

"You ladies ready?" Troy asked.

Not really, she thought with a stab of anguish. Her legs were shaking so badly she was afraid she would collapse, and yet she managed a nod. The two followed him to Bianca's Jetta.

Jace stormed across the snow out onto the circle driveway. "I thought I told you to wait!"

"I—"

He brought his lips down hard over hers. Moaning, Sheyna wrapped her arms around her husband's waist and leaned into the kiss, desperate to take the pain away. As she lifted on her tiptoes, Jace surged downwards. Reaching up, she grabbed hold of his coat, feeling the flexing of his muscles beneath her fingertips. Their tongues collided and danced almost frantically. She needed to calm his mind and hers because she had an uneasy feeling that their lives would change after tonight.

When Jace finally released her, they were both breathing heavily. "As soon as you get home, set the security alarm and call me," he ordered in a rush of warm air over her cold nose.

Their eyes locked, and she nodded.

As she and Bianca climbed inside, she watched Jace walk over to speak with Troy. He folded his arms across his broad chest, and from the stern look on her husband's face, she was sure he was giving Troy strict instructions.

"It's going to be okay," Bianca said as she started the car.

Sheyna appreciated Bianca trying to reassure her, but until whoever was doing this was behind bars, she wasn't going to be able to relax. She shoved her fingers through her hair as she dragged in a long breath. "I just keep trying to figure out who I pissed off so bad they'd want to terrorize me like this."

"I don't know. It could be someone you know or someone you don't. Anything is possible. All I know is if London and my brothers get their hands on him, he is going to wish he messed with someone else's wife."

Sheyna gave a small smile but said nothing. Despite the way she was feeling, Bianca was right. She felt sorry for whoever it was.

Troy climbed into the patrol car, then pulled behind the Jetta and flashed his lights. Bianca put the vehicle in Drive.

Reaching over, Sheyna pushed the button for the seat warmer and said, "I think I could have gone home alone."

"Sheyna, please. We're sisters, and there's no way I was letting that happen. Sierra is going home with her grandparents. If the men want to go off like some vigilantes, then let them, but we girls have to stick together."

"I appreciate it." Sheyna slid down lower on the seat as she harnessed a shiver that threatened to rattle her spine. She didn't understand it, but she was being.

"When we get to your house, I plan on raiding my brother's

bar. I'm sure he has something strong to take your mind off that psycho."

Despair filled her chest. "I really could use something stronger than holiday punch."

"Then scotch it is."

Sheyna turned up her nose. "I'm not feeling bad enough to drink that stuff."

Her father-in-law loved scotch, and his sons had each acquired the taste, but no matter how many times Roger Beaumont made Sheyna a drink, she still couldn't stomach the taste.

"Jace has vodka. I can drink that."

"Then vodka it is!" Bianca cried out and caused Sheyna to laugh.

The car fell quiet, and Sheyna caught herself worrying again. What if someone followed them? *No way,* she told herself. They were safe. They had security, and Jace knew where they were going.

Quit worrying so much.

Bianca waited until they were on the main road before she spoke again. "Collin called me yesterday."

"*What?*" Sheyna slid up on the seat, startled with alarm. "Collin? Are you serious?"

Bianca's eyes drifted back on the road but not before Sheyna saw the shadow of pain wash over her. "He called me right after lunch. I don't know how he got through my secretary."

"What does he want?"

Bianca swallowed, and Sheyna saw the quiver at her throat. "He wants to see his daughter." Sheyna could hear the dark resonance of the past echoing through her.

As she listened to her explain, anger simmered at her chest. How dare that two-timer to demand the right to see Sierra!

She still remembered Bianca being pregnant and scared of what her bougie parent would say when they found out their only daughter was not only pregnant, but the father of her unborn child already had a family of his own. What was even worst was that Bianca hadn't the slightest idea Collin was married because he'd been playing her, pretending he was part of a special operations team. He always had to go away for training. Jaden had grown suspicious and had asked London, a former investigator in the military, to check out Collin. He followed him to the airport, where Bianca dropped him off. London watched as Collin slipped out the back door and into a parked car, then drove home to a wife in Pennsylvania.

After giving Bianca the devastating news, London did the honorable thing and married her, not just to give her unborn child a name but because he was in love with her. Before Sierra was born, Collin came back to stake a claim on his child and threatened to expose the truth if Bianca didn't pay him off. London made him relinquish his parental rights and warned him never to come back, but it appeared he was determined to cause trouble again.

"What are you going to do?"

Worry lines appeared across Bianca's smooth walnut-colored face. "I don't know. I'm still pissed about the way he'd treated my daughter and me, but at the same time, he *is* her biological father."

Sheyna shook her head. "No, he isn't. He signed away his rights."

Bianca swallowed. "Yes, but what if Sierra grows up and starts asking questions, or even worse, he starts snooping around?"

They exchanged tensed wary glances.

"What does London have to say about this?"

She hesitated. "He doesn't know. I wanted to tell him, but I already know how he's going to react."

"With good reason," Sheyna pointed out quietly.

Bianca nodded, expression grim. "I understand that, but you—"

BAM!

Sheyna's body lunged sideways on impact and her gaze shifted. Before she could scream, someone swerved over from the passing lane again and slammed hard into the side of the driver's door, sending the car sliding off the road into a ditch.

CHAPTER 8

Sheyna opened her eyes and felt a sharp pain throbbing at her temple. *What just happened?* she wondered as she tried to move, but the glove box was practically in her lap, pinning her in. Turning her head, she saw Bianca slumped down on the seat. The airbag had exploded. The blood streaming from her nose made it obvious she had been struck in the face.

"Bianca? Are you alright? Bianca! Talk to me, please," she pleaded. Terror gripped her as she tried to get out of her seatbelt. She needed to check Bianca's pulse, but the crash pinned her arm, and she couldn't get the latch to release. Reaching down, she fumbled around, searching for her purse so she could get to her phone, but she couldn't reach that either. Head spinning, she took a deep breath, trying to remember what had happened. Frantically, Sheyna tried to clear her head, and then slowly, she remembered a car had slammed into them from the side. Where was it? Where were they? Everything was silent except for the sound of heavy breathing, *her* breathing. She heard nothing coming from Bianca.

"Bianca, please, talk to me!"

Please, let her be okay.

Sheyna jerked upright on the seat when she heard a car door closing. Looking through the side mirror, she saw a figure coming toward them. The headlights beamed in her face, so she had a hard time making out who it was until the passenger's door was yanked open.

"Mrs. Beaumont, are you okay?"

Sheyna looked up and sighed with relief. "Oh, thank goodness, Troy! I'm s-s-so glad you're here. Someone r-ran us off the road!"

"Let me help you," he said. Reaching down, he unsnapped her seatbelt effortlessly.

"Bianca's hurt. I don't k-know if she's breathing," she managed around a sob and chattering teeth as he helped her to slide out from beneath the glove box. "I n-need to call and get someone to help her."

"Let's worry about you first. Are you okay..., can you stand?"

"Yes, I mean, I guess." Troy waited until she was steady enough before he released her hand. "I c-can't find my purse."

"Don't worry about that right now. You can use my phone. It's in the car. Let me help Ms. Bianca while you go and call the police."

Jerkily, Sheyna nodded, then made her way around the Jetta on wobbly legs. She tried to hold it together, but the accident had her badly shaken. Worrying about Bianca wasn't going to help the situation at all.

Hold it together, she reminded herself. *Bianca needs you to be strong for her.*

While Troy walked around to the driver's side and called out Bianca's name, Sheyna rushed over to the passenger's side of the security vehicle and climbed inside. In a stand on the dashboard was his phone. She grabbed it and shut the car door while she dialed for emergency assistance. It was freezing outside. Troy had left the car running, and she was grateful because it was nice and warm inside. Shivering while she waited for someone to pick up on the other line, she reached down and cranked up the heat. The moment the warm air circulated the space, a faint smell ruffled her nose, sending a jolt rippling through her body.

No, no!

Someone else would have missed it, but with her keen sense of smell, especially a scent that had been in her dreams for weeks, there was no way she wouldn't have recognized the familiar nauseating cologne. Cheap. Woodsy. The smell churned her stomach every time she smelled it..., including now.

No, it can't be!

Sheyna drew in a breath, dragging the sickening smell into her lungs. Her eyes frantically darted left and right as she heard someone talking to her on the other end.

"Hello?" she said.

"You have reached the national payment center. For information about this phone, please dial one."

Sheyna froze. Fear pulsed through her veins.

She suddenly snapped out of it and brought the phone from her ear and redialed 9-1-1. Hearing the snow of crunching snow, she looked up and saw Troy walking toward the car. Her breath came out in shallow gasps—fear pulsed through her blood. *Please, let me be wrong.*

Troy pulled open the driver's door. As he climbed in, Sheyna heard him say, "You're wasting your time. It doesn't work."

"What?" she said, almost in a daze.

"That phone." He slammed the door shut. "It's prepaid. I ran out of minutes." Turning his head, he glared over at her and said, "That's what happens when you cheat your employees."

The fine hairs lifted at the back of her neck. "It was you."

"And you were too stupid even to notice." His dark lifeless eyes twinkled.

Instantly, Sheyna reached for the handle, but Troy quickly hit the door locks.

"What are you doing? Let me out!"

"Sorry, but I can't do that." With that, Troy put the car in Reverse and then pulled off.

"Where are you going? I can't leave Bianca there like that!"

"You can, and we will."

She looked at him, her eyes meeting his, and saw the fury there. Sheyna shivered. "Why? What is going on?" she asked, blinking in stunned disbelief. She had no idea if Bianca was even breathing. "Please let me call and get help."

Troy was silent as he put his foot down hard on the accelerator and drove past Bianca's Jetta.

"Let me out of this vehicle!" Sheyna cried.

He tore his eyes from the road and stared at her, anger rolling off of him. "You rich folks think you can talk to regular people any kinda way."

"*What?*"

"You heard me."

Nausea surged upward that Sheyna pushed back to say, "But why? How could you do this to Bianca and me?"

"You're both rich. Rich folks *always* live," Troy spat distastefully. "Tonight, all of you were flaunting your money and looking down at me as if I was nothing."

"That's not true! We treat all of our employees like family."

"Family?" He gave a sadistic laugh. "I hate to see how you treat your enemies."

Again, Sheyna tried the door handle, and panic set off in her lungs when that didn't work. In a desperate move, she reached over and tried to grab the steering wheel, sending the car swerving wildly on the road.

This might be the only chance I have.

Troy tried to push her hand away, but her fingers gripped tightly around the wheel. She was relentless and determined. Troy butted her hard in the mouth with his elbow when he couldn't get her to let go. She let out a scream as her head snapped back with a painful thud.

"You dumb bitch!" Troy screamed and brought the car to a screeching halt.

Before Sheyna could look up, he punched her hard in the face, and everything went dark.

CHAPTER 9

"This is ridiculous!" Jace barked. "How was he able to get in your house, and no one knows he was here?"

"I don't know," Jabarie countered mildly. He lifted his long wool coat collar and was extremely upset about what had transpired tonight at his home. "It has to be someone that works for us."

"Yes, but who, dammit? Who is stupid enough to mess with my wife?" Jace was going insane trying to figure out who was behind the attack and the harassment.

"I don't know, but hopefully, after tonight, we'll get some answers." Jabarie had always been the reasonable one.

"We need more than answers. I need a name!" Jaden chimed in.

The air was cold, but Jace had barely noticed. Hot fury burned through his veins. They were all standing out in front of Jabarie's home. Sheraton Beach police cars lined the circular drive. While they questioned the guests, he reached a gloved hand inside his pocket for his phone and called Sheyna. After several rings, the call went to voicemail. Frustrated, he tried her again, and when it was the same, he tried his sister. Bianca's phone also went to voicemail. He searched the crowd for London and moved toward him. London was talking to one of his twin younger sisters.

"London, have you talked to your wife since she left here?"

He excused himself and walked over with his brow bunched. "No. I was so busy telling the family what was going on; I hadn't had a chance. Why? What's up?"

"I can't reach Sheyna or Bianca."

London was already removing his phone and dialed his wife's number. "Dammit, Bianca, pick up...pick up the phone." He met Jace's eyes with a scowl. "You're right. I got her voicemail."

Fear twisted at his gut. What the hell was going on?

London snapped his fingers. "Call that security officer, Troy. Wasn't he supposed to trail the women to your house?"

He had been so busy trying to figure out who was responsible; he hadn't thought about that. Instantly, Jace dialed Troy's number. His foul temper exacerbated further when it switched over to a recorded message.

This phone is temporarily not in service.

"What the fuck!" he yelled.

His brothers hurried over.

"What's going on?" Jabarie asked.

"Something isn't right. I can't reach Sheyna or Bianca." Jace felt a muscle in his jaw spasm as he ground his teeth hard.

Jaden combed his locks away from his face. "Where the hell is Troy?"

"I can't reach him either."

"Anyone knows how to reach Troy?" Jace cried, and his voice sent a quiet hush across the front yard. "I tried calling him, but his phone isn't in service."

"It's probably a burner phone."

He whipped around to one of the young security officers. Jace knew who he was. Aaron Reagan. He had been working the night his wife was attacked.

"You, get over here," he said in an authoritative voice, and

Aaron knew he better not waste his time. "How do you know it's a burner phone?" he asked once the slender young man was standing in front of him.

His green eyes traveled to each of the Beaumont brothers, surrounding him before a crease lined his brow. "Troy keeps several in his locker. I saw them the night of Mrs. Beaumont's attack."

Jabarie cut in. "Wait a minute. I thought he wasn't working that night?"

"He didn't, but he... Ummm...stopped in to talk to me." Aaron shrugged. "He wanted to know if I was interested in making some extra money working security at a nightclub for him."

Jace blinked in stunned disbelief for a moment, not wanting to accept what he was hearing. Tightening his fist, he leaned in close until Aaron's eyebrows rose with uneasiness.

"That bastard is with my wife, so I'm going to ask you again...Did anything unusual happen that night? Anything that may have seemed odd?"

"Well..." he began and seemed almost frightened to say. "I had to go to the men's room. And since Troy was there, I asked if he minded watching the desk until I got back, and he agreed. By the time I returned, he was gone."

That would have given him plenty of time to turn off the camera at the corner of the lot. "Did he come back?" Jace asked in a steady voice.

Aaron nodded and folded his arms. "Yeah, after I found out Mrs. Beaumont was attacked, I called the cops, and Troy showed up."

Jace's pulse rocketed, and the front yard began to spin, making his breath slip past his lips in a sickening rush. "What the fuck?" No way was this happening. "That bastard!" He whipped out the phone and showed a number to Aaron. "Do you recognize this number?" When he hesitated, Jace added,

"I asked you a question!"

His nose scrunched up as he grimaced. "Yes, that's the phone he was using tonight."

He quickly dialed the number but once again got a recorded message. *This phone is temporarily not in service.*

Jace shook his head jerkily. No, he could not have heard him right. Not Troy. He had been working for them for almost a decade. He trusted him.

He has my wife.

Trembling inside, he swallowed the sudden tightness in his throat. "Do you know how I can reach him?"

Reluctantly, Aaron shook his head.

Shaking with outrage, Jace took off toward the end of the yard. He'd heard enough. London followed.

"We're going to get him, Jace."

His chest heaved. "It was him. All this time, it was Troy!" he growled under his breath and paced the yard angrily.

"We can give his information to the police," London said in a deceptively soft voice as he pulled a knitted black cap down over his ears.

Anger spiraled out of control. "How could I have been so stupid?" Jace swung a fist through the air. Guilt and fear were tearing through him in one relentless lash that wouldn't cease until Troy was behind bars and Sheyna was safely back in his arms.

Turning around, he found Aaron coming his way. The look on his face said there was more. Jace stormed over to him. "What? What aren't you telling me?"

Aaron swallowed nervously. "If he has Mrs. Beaumont, well... He's nuts. I've seen the way Troy treats women at the club. Choking, burning them with cigarettes. He has no respect."

"And you're just telling me this now!" he bit out impatiently.

Aaron jerked so hard he'd be surprised if he hadn't pissed his pants. "All these weeks, and you said nothing!"

His brothers rushed over and stepped between them.

"Relax, bro. We're going to find her," Jabarie assured him.

As he stood at the edge of the lawn furiously pounding a fist into his palm, his eyes shifted over to Aaron. Jace glared until the man timidly turned on his heels and hurried over to stand near the closest police car.

"I need to go find her now," Jace said icily, and his brothers nodded.

London regarded him in shrewd silence, showing no visible reaction as he said, "And my wife."

"Your wife is *our* sister," Jabarie reminded. "We're going to find both of them."

"Then what are we waiting on?" Growling, Jace turned away. Eager to escape the tension and do something other than wait, he started across the snow-covered lawn. "Jabarie, stay here with the family. I'm sure they'll have a lot of questions." Their cousins Remy and Reese were already suspicious that there was much more going on than he'd let on. "C'mon, London. Let's go."

CHAPTER 10

Sheyna pushed past the pain that was clouding her brain as she struggled to open her eyes. Her lids were heavy, so it took several attempts before she was able to pry them open. Her face felt stiff and throbbed with every beat of her heart. It was dark and cold. Wherever she was didn't have heat. She tried to move her arms but found she couldn't. They were practically numb. He tied her hands behind her back. Desperately, she attempted to yank her wrists free, but instead, the zip ties just pulled at her skin. She breathed heavily, wailing her legs, and felt the damp dirt floor beneath her. *Where the hell am I?*

Blinking her eyes, she tried to ease the burning pain while trying to focus. A glimmer of moonlight beamed through a small dingy window. It was a tiny house, she decided. *Whose house?* She had no idea.

It was a struggle, but she finally managed to roll her body over into a sitting position. Pain throbbed at her lips. Her head pounded. But at least she was alive. She indeed was on a damp floor; her slacks felt wet. Her back was resting against a cold wall.

"You're awake."

Frantically, her eyes snapped over to where she found Troy sitting on a chair in front of a small wooden table—legs parted and elbows resting on his knees.

"Where have you taken me?" Sheyna demanded.

"Don't you worry about that; we've got more important things to talk about."

She felt a thrill of terror at his words. "Talk about what? Tell me what it is you want from me!" she spat with a defiant tilt of the chin.

"Keep being smart at the mouth, and I'll give you another black eye," he warned as he pointed an accusatory finger at her.

That explained why she could barely see out the left one. Fear crept through her veins. She looked up at him through the veil of lashes, her eyes pleading. "Please, just tell me what it is you want, and I'll give it to you," she said firmly through her tears.

"Oh, course you will," he replied and then chuckled. The sound was so eerie it made her skin crawl.

Troy rose and came toward her, sending Sheyna's heart sprinting inside her chest. The boards of the floor creaked beneath his feet. He reached down and lifted her as if she weighed nothing. Once Sheyna was on her feet, he yanked her over toward the table.

"Sit," he ordered.

She hesitated too long, and he put a hand on her shoulder, applying pressure until she had no choice but to drop down onto the chair.

He reached for his, dragged it over, and took a seat directly in front of her. Even in the darkness, Sheyna could see the satisfied gleam in his eyes.

"Can you turn on the lights?"

He gave a rude snort. "There's no power here. This here old cabin belonged to my mother. After she died, I turned off the utilities. No point in wasting money."

A cabin. Troy had her somewhere deep in the woods. Her pulse raced. How would Jace find her?

Sheyna forced herself to meet his steely gaze again, even though panic welled up in her eyes. "Please, I just want to go home to my husband and son." She sounded so desperate.

"I just bet...to that big fancy house you have with all the Christmas lights twinkling merrily while some of us can barely pay the light bill!"

"You should have told me! The Beaumont Corporation has a financial assistance program! We've always been willing to help any of our employees who are in need," Sheyna mentioned in a rush of words.

"Ain't that a bitch!" he snapped. "If you were that concerned, then you wouldn't have stopped giving the Christmas bonuses you used to give us every year."

"Everyone knows we went through a reorganization a few years ago! We did everything we could to make sure that no one lost their jobs. We're still recovering."

"I just bet," he sneered with disgust.

"I'm serious. I haven't earned a full salary in five years."

He gave a rude snort. "Like that makes a difference."

He was right. It didn't make a difference to her, but it made a huge difference in keeping the corporation afloat. For the second year in a row, they were finally starting to see profits. Corporate shares had gone up, and the finance department had determined Christmas bonuses based on performance. Some had received them, and others had not. As the head of employee relations, she had hoped that giving their employees leave the day before and after Christmas, with pay, would have compensated for the smaller bonuses.

"Just tell me what you want and let me go!"

"I will when I am good and damn ready." The expression on his face was so demonic-looking, Sheyna reared back on the chair.

"I can give you anything you want. Just tell me what it is.

Please," she pleaded.

Troy reached out, and she flinched, afraid he was going to strike her again, but instead, he brushed her cheek with the back of his hand that felt rough and dry. "You're saying I can have anything I want?"

She flinched at the disgust in his voice. Troy had this sick smirk on his lips that suddenly made her stomach repulse.

"Money," she said, lip quivering. "I c-can give you money."

Greedy eyes stared straight at her. "Maybe I want more than money. Maybe I want to know what it feels like to be the boss. To be in control." His hand traveled slowly down across her neck and then to her shoulder. Her entire body recoiled with fear as his hand slid down to her sweater and rubbed across her breasts. "I have always thought you were a beautiful woman. Too beautiful for that pretty boy, Jace."

She tried to jerk away, not wanting to feel his touch. "Troy, y-you don't want to do this," she stammered. "Please just let me go, and I'll give you money."

"Liar!" He shouted and slapped her hard across the cheek, sending Sheyna's head rearing back. "If I let you go, I'll be in handcuffs before sunrise." Shaking his head, Troy added, "Nah. If I'm going to jail, I want it to be worth more than just money. I want to know what it's like to be with a beautiful woman like yourself, to make love to a Beaumont."

She sobbed and pleaded. Both, he ignored. Grinning sinisterly, he brought his hand up to test the weight of her breasts. Sheyna tried to wrench away, but her wrists were bound, and there was nowhere to run. When Troy slid his chair back, the sound was like nails on a chalkboard and caused her to shudder. Reaching down, he lifted her to a standing position. She tried to resist, shifting her weight to the balls of her feet.

Her breath left her lungs in a rush. "Troy, no. Please, you don't want to do this!"

"Yes, I do. It's time you learned that even a poor man is good in bed. Don't worry; I'll make sure it's enjoyable for the both of us," he added in a soothing voice that launched her heart into a skitter that made her breathless.

He reached for her arms. Again, Sheyna stilled and tried to resist the best she could, but she was powerless without her hands. She squirmed, writhed, and kicked as he attempted to drag her away.

"No, let me go!" she screamed.

Angrily, he gripped her hair and snapped her head back until she had no choice but to look at him. "Quit resisting!" he warned, and yet her boots dragged across the floor as Troy led her toward the closed door ahead. Vomit rose in her throat at the thought of a bed inside with a filthy mattress.

Her heel caught on a loose board, and Troy lost his grip, releasing her hair. He twirled around, and without wasting time, Sheyna connected the toe of her boot with his groin.

Whump!

Troy cried out like a wild animal as he leaned over, holding his crotch. Sheyna reared back and kicked him hard in the face. With an earth-shaking thud, he fell back and collapsed on the floor. Stacks of boxes crashed onto him. Sheyna heard the sound of broken glass.

"You bitch!" he screamed out in rage.

Quickly, she scrambled toward the door. Hands behind her back, it took several attempts before she managed to get the door open. But as soon as she was out onto the porch, Sheyna started sprinting across the snow-covered field as fast as she could manage. Without using her arms, she stumbled, yet she managed to make her way into the woods. It was dark and cold. She had no idea where she was going, but she didn't care. She had to get away. She had to get home to her husband and JJ. She had to make sure Bianca was okay.

Thorns and branches snagged at her coat, and yet she didn't stop.

Behind her, she heard Troy bellow in rage, "You can't run!"

Oh, she was running as fast as she could. She could barely see and was moving blindly, but that didn't stop her. Panic hummed through her veins. Sheyna ducked around a tree, stepped over a fallen trunk, but when she missed a step, she felt herself falling, and her chest hit the icy ground with an *Oomph!* Her face landed on a mound of fresh snow. As she struggled to catch her breath, cold air filled her lungs. Immediately she started to flail and quickly inch-wormed her body into thick bushes. She tried to lay as still as she possibly could, but the thumping of her heart was almost deafening.

Within seconds, she heard the crunching of snow and the sound of branches brushing against someone as he made his way in her direction. Nervously, she lay still clamping her lips tightly together, hoping and praying Troy didn't hear her. The wind was blowing, the snow was cold against her cheek, yet it soothed the bruising Troy caused to her face.

He drew closer until she spotted a pair of sneakers hitting the snow right beside the bush where she was hiding. Heart pounding so hard, she held her breath to still it and waited for what felt like an eternity before Troy turned and ran in the opposite direction.

Sheyna breathed a sigh of relief but continued to lay still in case he decided to come back. When she was sure she was alone, she slid over to a tree and used it to bring herself back to a standing position. Instantly, she started running away. Pain ripped at her lungs; she could barely catch her breath, and yet she refused to stop. Her life depended on it. Tree branches scratched at her face, but she had to get as far away as she could before he found her.

Sheyna wasn't sure how long she had been running before

she heard movement behind her, closing in fast. Panicking, she ran smack into a tree and cried out as she fell. Tears of frustration welled up in her eyes. She didn't have the strength, and yet she had never been a quitter. Quickly, she inched her body behind the trunk of a large tree and waited. Her breathing hitched in her lungs with every breath. When she heard footsteps approaching, she rolled further into the thick of the bushes. Somehow, she lost her footing, felt herself falling, and screamed.

CHAPTER 11

Londonondon drove down the road possessed by rage, weaving in and out of traffic with anger and fear leading him. They had used the GPS coordinates in Bianca's car to track down her location. Jace was on the passenger's side, frantically searching the ditches on the sides of the road to make sure they didn't miss his sister's Jetta. Jabarie had insisted on joining them. He and Jaden were on their way, in his car, a few miles behind them. The police had also been alerted.

Jace closed his eyes and swallowed thickly around the fear clotting his throat. They had to get to them in time.

"There's the car!" London shouted.

Jace's eyes snapped open, and he spotted rear brake lights over near a tree.

London eased off the road, slammed on his brakes, and had barely parked before he was racing across the snow. "Bianca!" Jace was right behind him, rushing over to the Jetta that had slammed into a tree. London peered inside, tapping hard on the glass. "Bianca!" he called out again. He pulled hard on the door handle, but it was useless. The driver's side had been hit and resembled a crushed, discarded beer can. Before Jace could look inside, London had rushed around to the passenger's side door and yanked it open.

"Bianca!" Jace shouted as his heart slammed against his ribcage. Her lifeless body was slumped down in the seat with the airbag in her lap.

London slipped inside and reached over to cradle her face. "Baby, it's me. Please, wake up! Please," he pleaded.

Bianca shifted and moaned just enough for Jace to release a sigh of relief. His sister was alive. *But where is my wife?* He thought as London pulled out his phone and dialed for help.

A few seconds later, there was a flood of lights. Footsteps hurrying across the snow behind him caused Jace to swirl around. It was his brothers.

Jaden looked over his shoulder. "Is she--"

"She's alive," Jace replied, cutting them off before he could verbalize that thought.

They hurried around the car. Jace followed. London was seated with Bianca's head draped over his lap while talking to an emergency dispatch operator.

"Where's Sheyna?" Jabarie asked and met his worried eyes.

"I don't know." Jace dragged a hand across his hair.

"He must have taken her somewhere," Jaden swore under his breath. "Just let me get my hands on that son-of-a-bitch."

"You're going to have to wait in line," Jace growled possessively. "In the meantime, I need to find my wife, and someone needs to get Bianca to the hospital."

"We'll take her," Jabarie offered.

"No, you won't! I'll take her," London shouted as he ended the call. "She's my wife."

"And she's my sister," Jaden countered.

London glared at them. "Jace needs you to help find Sheyna."

Bianca stirred in his arms and slowly opened her eyes. She appeared in shock. Disheveled. There was bruising around her face, and her nose looked crooked, almost broken. Both signs that the airbag had ejected.

"Hey, baby," London said soothingly.

"Troy did this," she said barely above a whisper.

A low growl rumbled in Jace's chest.

"Bianca, baby, we know." London kissed her forehead. "Don't you worry about him."

"Please, find him," she whispered. "Please."

Jace walked around, so he was standing in front of her as he asked, "Lil Bit, do you know where he's taken Sheyna?"

Her bottom lip quivered as she shook her head. Cold fury settled in his bones.

Jaden reached down. "London, let me help you with her."

His brother-in-law quickly pushed him away, staking his territory. "I'm not letting her out of my sight. You need to go help Jace find Sheyna." When no one budged, he roared, "Get the hell outta here! Your sister is my responsible."

With London by Bianca's side, Jace knew it was time to go. His throat tightened as he tried to swallow back the heavy emotion. From a distance, he could hear sirens. Help was on its way. "I'm going to go find my wife. You go to the hospital with London."

Jabarie shook his head. "No, you heard London. Lil' Bit is in good hands. If you're going to find Sheyna, then we're in this together."

Jaden nodded in agreement. "He's right. Besides, if we aren't with you, there's no telling what you'll do to that bastard when you find him."

Those weren't truer words. He would kill him; there was no question about that.

Police cars and an ambulance were coming fast up the road. Jabarie signaled for him to follow. "Come on, let's get out of here before the police detain us for questioning."

Quickly, they rushed over and climbed into his Mercedes G550. Jaden was behind the wheel. He put the SUV in Drive and accelerated down the road, sending the vehicle sliding around in the snow. This time Jace said nothing about the way anyone was driving. There was no time to waste.

"Where do you think he took her?" Jabarie asked from the back seat.

"I don't know. I don't fucking know." He was so frustrated.

His phone rang. Frantically, Jace reached inside his pocket, hoping it was Sheyna.

It was his secretary.

"I went back to the office and pulled Troy's file," she said.

"What did you find?"

"He lives with his wife and kids. I called his wife, and she says he was working tonight, and she hadn't seen him. "

"Send the police over there anyway. What else did you find?" he asked impatiently.

"I found an emergency contact name and address from when he first began employment with us. It's to his mother. She owns a farm on the outskirts of town. I tried the phone number, but it's disconnected. I'm not sure if it's still a good address, but worth checking out." He could hear the worry in her voice as she rattled off the address. "I'll text it to you."

"Thank you, Silvia. You did well."

"I pray it's enough to find her. I'll send the police out to both addresses and call you back if I find anything else."

"What did she say?" Jabarie said from the rear just as Jace ended the call.

Quickly, he relayed the information she'd provided. "She's sending me the address." His eyes were glued to the screen. As soon as he received her text, he pushed the navigation link. "Fuck! We're thirty minutes away." Even then, there was no guarantee Troy had taken her there. He just prayed they found her in time.

"Relax, bro, we're going to find her," Jaden said with an air of confidence.

His brothers engaged in a conversation, but his mind was with Sheyna. Time had never passed so slowly. Fear had never choked him like this. All he could think about was how afraid she might be. She was a strong woman, one of the strongest he'd ever met but deep down, Sheyna was vulnerable and would be frightened out of her mind. That ripped at his heart.

Hold on, Sheyna.

"We should be coming up on the house," Jaden said, snapping him from his thoughts.

Jace scanned through the thick of the trees, eyes searching, and then he spotted the security vehicle. "There!"

Nodding, Jaden turned the car up the long dirt driveway toward a small white house that hadn't seen any attention in a long time. The blue trim was chipping. Someone boarded up most of the windows, and the rest were broken. All that mattered was that they had tracked down Troy's vehicle.

Jaden barely shifted the SUV into Park before Jace was out running toward the decapitated house with no thought but to get to her. Jabarie was rushing to join him, but he just kept moving at full speed. Heart pounding heavily, Jace raced up the rotting wooden steps and burst through the door. Quickly, his eyes scanned the area. It was dark, cold, and empty. No one had lived there for years. Desperately, he used the flashlight app on his phone to bathe light as he scanned the space.

"Any sign of her?"

He whipped around at Jabarie. Jaden was coming up the steps. "No, but there's a six-pack of beer on the table with two empty cans, which means he's been here."

Jaden tilted his head toward the rear. "I hate to say this, but he might have taken her out in the woods."

He had thought the same thing after hoping Sheyna would

have been inside waiting for him. "Let's go," Jace said and stormed out the house, his brothers following. As soon as they rounded the house, he saw him.

Troy was coming out from the thick of the trees, walking toward the house. The sight of him made Jace's blood surge with rage, his skin prickled. The moment Troy's eyes shifted, and he saw them, he froze. Jace didn't hesitate. He raced across the snow toward him. Troy didn't move; he stood there with his arms folded and waited.

"Where the hell is my wife?"

"Wouldn't you like to know," he said and then started laughing hysterically.

Jace roared, lunged at him fast and hard, knocking him to the ground. He was on top of Troy. His fist landed on his face. "Tell me where she is!" he cried. Jace continued to hit him, landing punch after punch. "Tell me, dammit!" *My wife. My wife!*

Troy didn't even bother to try and defend himself; he just lay on the cold ground, hands shielding his face, laughing and taking the blows.

Jaden and Jabarie came rushing over and dragged Jace away. He wrestled, trying to remove their grasps, but his brothers were relentless. Once he was standing, he yanked free of their hold while Troy lay there, still laughing.

He heard police sirens in the background.

Jaden squeezed his shoulder. "Sheyna's here, somewhere. We're going to find her."

"Yeah, Jace, you're gonna find her," Troy mocked with a chuckle. "Probably after hyperthermia has already set in."

Jace drew his foot back and kicked Troy hard in the nose. As soon as his boot made contact, he heard a crack. Jaden instantly dragged him away.

"Yo, chill! You don't want to kill him. We might need this

bastard to help us find Sheyna," he told him, his gaze drilling into his.

As Jace breathed cold air into his lungs, he told himself, killing Troy didn't sound like such a bad idea. Nevertheless, his youngest brother was right. He needed to reel in his fury. As much as he hated the thought, they might need him.

Jabarie shoved him against the shoulder. "Come on. We know she's out there somewhere, so let's canvas the area and locate her." He pushed Jace again, drawing him away from Troy.

Jace's eyes stayed on him, watching him lying on his side, blood dripping from his nose, tainting the white snow.

Jabarie went over to his vehicle, opened the trunk, and retrieved two flashlights. He handed one to Jace. "Let's go!" he ordered in a stern voice. "Jaden, you stay with this son-of-a-bitch until the police arrive." He nodded, and they headed off into the thick of the trees.

Jace had no idea which direction to turn, but they spotted the footprints going away from the house. There were two sets. He took one, and Jabarie took the other as they set off into the woods.

"Sheyna!" Jace shouted every couple of feet then waited to see if he heard her voice. The cold wind was whipping at his face, and the muscles around his heart tightened at the thought of his wife being out in the cold night alone and frightened.

"Sheyna, precious, answer me!" he screamed until he was practically hoarse. The woods were dark, and even the moon wasn't allowing enough light to bathe his path. Thank goodness for the flashlight. He moved deeper into the woods, calling her name and yet still nothing. Silence blanketed the scene. His hands were practically numb; his feet felt like lead. His cheeks burned, but none of that bothered him. He had to find her.

Hearing the crunching of snow coming from behind, Jace swirled around to find light beaming in his face.

"You hear anything?" Jabarie asked.

Jace shook his head and dragged a frustrated hand across his cap.

Together they continued on the course.

He had made a vow to protect her with his life. How in the world could he tell her brothers he had not honored his promise? "Sheyna!" he cried again, and then he spotted a bush that had been trampled and crushed.

"Jabarie, over here!" He moved through the thick of it and followed the footsteps in the snow.

"Sheyna! Sheyna, where are you?" he shouted until his lungs hurt. "Sheyna!" And then there it was a faint voice calling out to him.

"Jace."

It was barely above a whisper but enough to stop him dead in his tracks. He grabbed his brother's arm. "Jabarie, wait!"

He called out again. He needed to make sure it wasn't the wind and that his ears weren't playing tricks on him. "Sheyna, is that you?" he shouted. Holding his breath, he waited.

"Jace."

It was her! He started racing in the direction of the sound of her voice when an arm yanked him back.

"Whoa! That's a drop-off. Look."

He beamed his flashlight, and ahead was a steep hill that someone with a sled would have found a thrill ride if it weren't for the dangers of landing hard against one of the many trees below.

"Jace."

There was her voice again.

"Keeping calling my name, precious! I'm coming. I just

need to know where you are!"

And then she was crying. The terrible haunting sound ripped at his chest. He and Jabarie frantically beamed their flashlights down the hill until he found something lying on the ground below.

"There she is!" he cried. Wasting no time, Jace lowered onto the ground and pushed off, sliding down the hill toward his wife.

Sheyna was cold. Her entire body was numb. She was trying her best to stay awake, but it wasn't easy. It was dark, damp, and windy. She was exhausted and dreaming. She realized it when she'd heard Jace's voice. Oh, how she wanted to believe he had found her.

"Jace," she called out again, praying to the Lord her husband could hear her.

As she lay there, unable to move, all she could think about was Jace and JJ. She couldn't leave them. Especially not JJ. When she was young, she remembered the pain and the emptiness in her life at her mother no longer being there to teach her things. To hug her and read her stories. To make her feel loved. She also remembered how devastated her father had been. Despite his three children, they were never able to fill the void of losing his wife, and it had taken years before he had given love another shot. She didn't want her family to have to endure that.

"I can't die," she whispered. "I just can't. Not yet."

"Sheyna!"

There was her husband's voice again just as she threatened to drift off to sleep. "Jace," she said softly. "Jace. I love you."

"Sheyna, precious, hold on!"

As her eyelids lowered, she heard the snapping of tree limbs and footsteps in the snow. The sound grew louder, and panic skipped through her chest. What if Troy had found her? She couldn't get away. Her arms were asleep from being bound behind her back. She no longer could feel her legs.

Suddenly, light bobbed before her eyes. Had someone found her? Or was it an angel who had come to take her to heaven with her mother?

"Sheyna!"

And then she felt her body being lifted off the ground and into an envelope of warmth.

"Oh, Sheyna."

Someone pressed their cheek against hers, and warm lips were at her neck.

Sheyna went utterly still, and then she pulled back slightly. "Jace?" she croaked.

She struggled to open her eyes, and with the aid of the flashlight, she saw him staring down at her. His gorgeous lips were quivering from either fear or cold, or maybe both. "Jace, is that you?" she whispered faintly. A sound escaped her, a whimper of pain.

He pressed his lips into the nape of her neck again—his teeth scraping gently along her skin. "Precious, it's me," his voice cracked. "I've come to take you home."

Tears flooded her already fuzzy vision.

Jace frantically worked at the ties at her wrists. She figured he used the pocket-knife he carried around. A gift JJ had given him for Christmas that he kept on his keychain. Who would have known it would have come in handy? And then she was free, arms falling limp beside her. He clutched her close, wrapping his arms around her. His heart was thumping hard against her breasts.

"I'm here, precious. I'm never letting you out of my sight again."

Sobs quivered at her chest. "You promise?"

A growl ripped from Jace's throat as he replied, "Damn right, I promise."

CHAPTER 12

Sheyna slowly opened her eyes to find sunlight beaming through the window shades. Her mind was a haze, and it took several seconds for her to remember. Instantly, she jerked.

"Whoa, relax."

Jace stretched out beside her, his arm draped over her waist and his breath at her nape.

"Jace," she said his name softly.

Sheyna relaxed her head on the pillow and took a breath. As she closed her eyes again, he whispered loving words to her.

"What happened?" she managed and moistened her lips. Her throat was raw, her voice harsh. Her ribs hurt.

"You're safe," Jace said in that authoritative voice of his, but for once, she didn't care that he overly guarded her. The sound was soothing.

She slowly opened her eyes again. Shifting onto her back, she looked around. She was in a hospital room. An IV drip was in her arm, and the hum of an oxygen machine was beside her. Oh, what a beautiful sound! Sheyna bit down hard on her lower lip, but it didn't help. Tears started falling, and once they did, she couldn't stop them.

"You're safe now."

Safe! Her heart fluttered. She didn't think that would have ever been possible again.

Jace slid off the bed and pulled a chair over. His eyes were tired, and worry lines surrounded his mouth. His five-o'clock shadow was overgrown. He never looked more handsome.

"How are you feeling?" he said softly.

"Like I've fallen off a cliff."

He chuckled softly. "I guess you could say that. Thank goodness for the snow." He reached for a small glass of water and brought it to her mouth. Sheyna drank just enough to wet her lips and throat. After returning the glass to the side table, Jace leaned over, his hand at her forehead, brushing back her hair.

"Hey," she said as she stared up at her husband.

"Hey." His lips formed a smile as he gazed down at his wife.

Her eyes widened as she remembered. "Bianca...is she okay?"

He nodded. "She's in the next room. A few injuries, but nothing life-threatening."

She was crying again, with tears coursing down her cheeks. Reaching up, Jace swiped her skin gently with the pad of his thumb. Sheyna blew out a shaky sigh. "Where's JJ?" she asked, voice trembling.

"With Darnell."

"Do they know?" She pulled her bottom lip between her teeth.

"Your family, yes. JJ no."

Sheyna gave him a grateful smile while tears of relief spilled onto the pillow.

Vulnerability like she'd never seen before flooded Jace's gaze. "It's over precious. Troy is behind bars and won't ever get near you again."

A shudder went through her body at the thought of Troy touching her. "I'm so sorry. This is all my fault. I had no idea our employees depended so much on those bonuses. I had hoped by giving them an extra day off during the holiday to spend with family that would compensate, but instead, they'd rather have the money."

Shaking his head, Jace spat, "There's no excuse for what he did." There was a warning in his tone.

Sheyna sighed. He was right.

Jace brought her hand to his lips, his fingers circled her wrist, and she saw red bruises where the restraints had been. He kissed her there, tenderly.

"You're alive. That's all that matters."

Jace leaned forward in his chair. His lips were so soft. His touch was so gentle, her breasts tingled. She moistened her lower lip and said, "How did you find me?"

His dark eyes drifted over her face while he recounted the chain of events. "It wasn't easy," he concluded. "I'm just glad we got there in time." His expression smothered as he bent to brush his mouth gently over hers again.

"Uncle Richard was here last night," he murmured against her lips.

Sheyna lifted her incredulous gaze to his. "He was?"

Jace nodded mischievously. "*And* my father."

"Your father?" Her eyes widened. "Did they talk?"

"No, they grumbled at each other, but it's the first communication they've had in years." He started laughing. She smiled and was so grateful to hear that throaty sound again.

"Maybe we might be able to get them both to the family reunion after all."

"I hope so, but right now, all I want is to take my wife home," he drawled, finally looking relaxed.

"I'd like that."

Their eyes met and held. "I love you, precious."

"I-I was afraid I would never hear those words from you again," she said, releasing the pent-up breath she hadn't realized she was holding.

"I wouldn't have stopped until I found you. Trust and believe that." He smoothed a hand along her cheek.

"I know," she said softly, smiled, and he kissed her again.

Jace stretched out on the bed beside her again. Sheyna brought one arm up and wrapped it tightly around his neck. "Happy New Year. I love you, Jace."

"I love you more," he said gently.

All I want...all she needed was right there beside her, and she was never letting him go.

THE BEAUMONT SERIES

The Second Time Around (Jabarie & Brenna)
The Playboy's Proposition (Jace & Sheyna)
The Player's Proposal (Jaden & Danica)
For You I Do (Bianca & London)
Before I Let You Go (Diamere & Kelly)
Every Second Counts (Jabarie & Brenna)
A Beau for Christmas (Reese & Dominique)
Do Me Baby (Rance & Debra)
Breathless (Sedona & Keith)
Stilettos & Mistletoes (Sage & Cser)
All I Want (Bianca & London)

The Sexy Simmons Series
In Her Neighbor's Bed (Scott & Zanaa)
Claiming What's Mine (Darnell & Liberty)

Other Books by Angie Daniels

Feinin' (*Big Spankable Asses Anthology*)

Tease

Seduced into Submission – Curious

Seduced into Submission - Serve

Seduced into Submission – Obey

Seduced into Submission – Surrender

Seduced into Submission – Bound

Talk a Good Game

Intimate Intentions

When It Rains

The Campbells - Love Uncovered

The Campbells - When I First Saw You

The Company - In the Company of My Sistahs

The Company - Trouble Loves Company

The Company - Careful of the Company You Keep

The Company - Misery and Company

Hart & Soul (Fire in My Soul)

Time is of the Essence

A Will to Love

Endless Enchantment

Destiny in Disguise

The Beaumonts - The Second Time Around

The Beaumonts - The Playboy's Proposition

The Beaumonts - The Player's Proposal

The Beaumonts - For You I Do

The Beaumonts - Before I Let You Go

The Beaumonts - Every Second Counts

The Beaumonts - A Beau for Christmas

The Beaumonts - Do Me Baby

The Beaumonts - Breathless

The Beaumonts - Stilettos & Mistletoes

The Beaumonts - All I Want

The Sexy Simmons - In Her Neighbor's Bed

The Sexy Simmons - Claiming What's Mine

Show Me

Any Man Will Do

Coming for My Baby

Diva Diaries- Strutting in Red Stilettos

Diva Diaries - Running to Love in Pink Stilettos

Decadent Delight - A Delight Before Christmas

Decadent Delight - Say My Name

Decadent Delight - Naughty Before Christmas

Decadent Delight - Put Your Name on It

Pleasure Series - Time for Pleasure

Pleasure Series- For Her Pleasure

Pleasure Series - Wicked Pleasure

Beg for It

Wilde Pack - Wilde About Her

Wilde Pack - Wilde and Wicked

Time for Desire

Command and Control

Other books by Angie (under a different name)

R.A. Daniels – Justin Case

Sasha Campbell – Confessions

Sasha Campbell - Scandals

Sasha Campbell - Suspicions

Sasha Campbell – Consequences

ABOUT THE AUTHOR

Angie Daniels is a free spirit who isn't afraid to say what's on her mind or, even better, write about it. Since the *USA Today* Best-Selling Author strutted onto the literary scene in five-inch heels, she's been capturing her audience's attention with her wild imagination and love for alpha men. The RT Reviewer's Choice Award winner has written fifty novels for imprints, including BET Arabesque, Harlequin/Kimani Romance, Kensington/ Dafina, and Kensington/Aphrodisia Books. For more information about upcoming releases and to connect with Angie on Facebook, where she is likely to say just about anything, please visit her website at www.AngieDaniels.com.

Printed in Great Britain
by Amazon

25248662R00148